EXTRAORDINARY PRAISE FOR SARA BLAEDEL AND THE LOUISE RICK SERIES

"Blaedel is one of the best I've come across."

—Michael Connelly

"Crime-writer superstar Sara Blaedel's great skill is in weaving a heartbreaking social history into an edge-of-your-chair thriller while at the same time creating a detective who's as emotionally rich and real as a close friend."

—Oprah.com

"She's a remarkable crime writer who time and again delivers a solid, engaging story that any reader in the world can enjoy."

—Karin Slaughter

"One can count on emotional engagement, spine-tingling suspense, and taut storytelling from Sara Blaedel. Her smart and sensitive character, investigator Louise Rick, will leave readers enthralled and entertained."

—Sandra Brown

"I loved spending time with the tough, smart, and all-too-human heroine Louise Rick—and I can't wait to see her again."

—Lisa Unger

"If you like crime fiction that is genuinely scary, then Sara Blaedel should be the next writer you read."

—Mark Billingham

"Sara Blaedel is at the top of her game. Louise Rick is a character who will have readers coming back for more."

—Camilla Läckberg

THE LOST WOMAN

"Leads to…that gray territory where compassion can become a crime and kindness can lead to coldblooded murder."

—*New York Times Book Review*

"Blaedel solidifies once more why her novels are as much finely drawn character studies as tightly plotted procedurals, always landing with a punch to the gut and the heart."

—*Library Journal* (starred review)

"Long-held secrets and surprising connections rock Inspector Louise Rick's world in Blaedel's latest crime thriller. Confused and hurt, Louise persists in investigating a complex murder despite the mounting personal ramifications. The limits of loyalty and trust, and the complexities of grief, are central to this taut thriller's resolution. A rich cast of supporting characters balances the bleakness of the crimes."

—*RT Book Reviews* (4 stars)

"Sara Blaedel is a literary force of nature…Blaedel strikes a fine and delicate balance between the personal and the professional in *The Lost Woman*, as she has done with the other books in this wonderful series…Those who can't get enough of finely tuned mysteries…will find this book and this author particularly riveting."

—Bookreporter.com

"Blaedel, Denmark's most popular author, is known for her dark mysteries, and she examines the controversial social issue at the heart of this novel, but ends on a surprisingly light note. Another winner from Blaedel."

—Booklist

"Engrossing."

—Toronto Star

THE KILLING FOREST

"Another suspenseful, skillfully wrought entry from Denmark's Queen of Crime."

—Booklist

"Engrossing...Blaedel nicely balances the twisted relationships of the cult members with the true friendships of Louise, Camilla, and their circle."

—Publishers Weekly

"Blaedel delivers another thrilling novel...Twists and turns will have readers on the edge of their seats waiting to see what happens next."

—RT Book Reviews

"Will push you to the edge of your seat [then] knock you right off...A smashing success."

—Bookreporter.com

"Blaedel excels at portraying the darkest side of Denmark."

—Library Journal

THE FORGOTTEN GIRLS

WINNER OF THE 2015 RT REVIEWER'S CHOICE AWARD

"Crackling with suspense, atmosphere, and drama, *The Forgotten Girls* is simply stellar crime fiction."

—Lisa Unger

"Chilling…[a] swiftly moving plot and engaging core characters."

—*Publishers Weekly*

"This is a standout book that will only solidify the author's well-respected standing in crime fiction. Blaedel drops clues that will leave readers guessing right up to the reveal. Each new lead opens an array of possibilities, and putting the book down became a feat this reviewer was unable to achieve. Based on the history of treating the disabled, the story is both horrifying and all-too-real. Even the villains have nuanced and sympathetic motives."

—*RT Times* Top Pick, Reviewer's Choice Award Winner

"Already an international bestseller, this outing by Denmark's Queen of Crime offers trademark Scandinavian crime fiction with a tough detective and a very grim mystery. Blaedel is incredibly talented at keeping one reading…Recommend to fans of Camilla Läckberg and Liza Marklund."

—*Library Journal*

"*The Forgotten Girls* has it all. At its heart, it is a puzzling, intricate mystery whose solution packs a horrific double-punch…Once you start, you will have no choice but to finish it."

—Bookreporter.com

ALSO BY SARA BLAEDEL

THE STOLEN ANGEL

SARA BLAEDEL

Translated by Martin Aitken

GRAND CENTRAL
PUBLISHING

New York Boston

Copyright © 2018 by Sara Blaedel
Translated by Martin Aitken, translation © 2017 by Sara Blaedel
Excerpt from *The Undertaker's Daughter* © 2017 by Sara Blaedel

Grand Central Publishing
Hachette Book Group
1290 Avenue of the Americas
New York, NY 10104
Hachettebookgroup.com

First American Edition: January 2018

Grand Central Publishing is a division of Hachette Book Group, Inc.
The Grand Central Publishing name and logo is a trademark of Hachette Book Group, Inc.

The Hachette Speakers Bureau provides a wide range of authors for speaking events. To find out more, go to www.hachettespeakersbureau.com or call (866) 376-6591.

The publisher is not responsible for websites (or their content) that are not owned by the publisher.

Library of Congress Cataloging-in-Publication Data

Names: Blaedel, Sara, author. I Aitken, Martin, translator. Title: The stolen angel / Sara Blaedel. Other titles: Dødsenglen. English Description: First Grand Central Publishing edition. I New York : Grand Central Publishing, 2018. Identifiers: LCCN 2017036654I ISBN 9781538759752 (softcover) I ISBN 9781478993933 (audio downloadable) I ISBN 9781538759776 (open ebook) Subjects: LCSH: Women detectives—Denmark—Fiction. I Kidnapping—Investigation—Fiction. I Policewomen—Fiction. I BISAC: FICTION / Suspense. I FICTION / Crime. I FICTION / Contemporary Women. I FICTION / Mystery & Detective / Police Procedural. I GSAFD: Suspense fiction. I Mystery fiction Classification: LCC PT8177.12.L33 D6413 2018 I DDC 839.813/8—dc23 LC record available at https://lccn.loc.gov/2017036654

Printed in the United States of America
LSC-C
10 9 8 7 6 5 4 3 2 1

For Kristen

THE STOLEN ANGEL

The smell of acetone was so pungent it tore at his nostrils, seeping out through the cracks of the door and bleeding into the dark cellar.

The space was lit only by the ceiling lamps. He had bricked up the windows so their empty frames were flush with the wall.

He stood there for a moment in the passageway, then put the mask in place over his mouth and nose before carefully wriggling his long, slender fingers into a pair of tight latex gloves.

As meticulous as ever.

Listening to the sound of his own breathing, he sensed the dampness that clung to the cellar walls. He found it odd that the ventilation system with its charcoal filters wasn't more efficient, but dismissed the thought from his mind as quickly as it had arisen. The system had been running twenty-four seven, but the muggy smell of the cellar lingered still. He was getting used to it by now. He pulled the three keys from the pocket of his lab coat.

He was pleased that there was no direct access from the ground floor. A person had to go outside into the garden in order to find the steps leading down. One of the first things he'd done after moving in was to have separate keys made for the cellar.

The yellow key opened the cold store where the freezer was; the blue one was for the room containing the two-meter-long shallow bath with the vacuum suction unit. The last key was red and gave access to the back room. The exhibition, as he called it, with its three rectangular glass display cases lined up in a row.

He had taken particular delight in arranging the lighting that illuminated the three women in their transparent open caskets. The lamps were positioned with all the fastidiousness of a portrait photographer, their light falling so softly that no shadow was too dark and no detail remained anything but crystal clear to the viewer. He had already begun to prepare the lighting for the next display case, which would soon be ready for the new woman, and had rearranged the space to make room.

Standing there now, he beheld the three naked women.

How beautiful they were, with their different shapes. It was all exactly as he had planned.

The first was thin. He considered the next one to be of normal build. And then came the pride of the collection, the one with the perfect womanly curves, the heavy, pendulous breasts and chunky thighs. Smoothing his hand over her hip, he felt the tingling rush of blood through his body as his erection swelled.

He always took such care to restore the original shapes. Before commencing work on a corpse, he'd photograph it in detail. From the front, back, and sides, noting the rise of the chest, the line of the waist.

His inspiration had been Gunther von Hagens's exhibition *Körperwelten* and the worldwide touring exhibition *Body Worlds*. He had become fascinated with the thought of being able to preserve the beauty of a woman for all time.

The blond girl was hardly a feast for the eyes. She lay there in the empty steel bath under the glare of the neon lighting, her naked body fallen in on itself. Over the last few months, the acetone had done its job, expelling all water from her body to the very last drop.

And yet a shiver ran down his spine. This was the final phase. The room was cold and sterile, the walls clad with white tiling, a stainless steel table installed at the rear for the chemicals and silicone. Next to the plastic tubs were the tubes and the wooden box.

He stepped closer but could not stop himself from glancing away. This was the least flattering stage of the process. The eye sockets were empty, the face collapsed. Muscle and bone were the only things left inside the sheath of skin. But although the outer covering lay loose around the skull, he thought he perceived the beauty he would now set about restoring. Her long hair was protected from the liquid by a tight-fitting cap. She would be so beautiful with her hair tresses about her perfect shoulders, he thought. Like an artist, he felt the love for his work well inside him with every step he took toward completion.

It had been most surprising to him the first time. He simply hadn't prepared himself mentally for the transformation into such a magnificent and wondrous specimen. He knew, of course, that the body consists of 70 percent water, and that the same amount plus an additional 10 to 15 percent would vanish in the acetone bath. Nevertheless, he had been astounded, and it had been some days before he again felt ready to return to the cellar and complete the work.

On the other hand, he could never in his wildest dreams have imagined the euphoria he'd feel when at last the silicone had hardened and he had finally returned her comely curves to her, perhaps even having exaggerated them slightly to accord with his taste.

Stunned, he had stood there feeling like the creator of the universe.

He stepped up to the stainless steel table and picked up the tubes. Lifting the heavy tubs of silicone onto the cart, he pushed it over to the shallow bath. Two tubes ran from each tub. He glanced up at the clock. It would take less than half an hour to fill the bath. When it was done, he would put the lid in place and switch on the suction unit. Then all that was required was for her to simply lie there as the silicone gradually seeped into her cells and filled her body.

With a small knife, he sliced away the protective caps and broke the seal, allowing the silicone to flow. Slowly and reluctantly to begin with, though he had made sure to warm the substance so as to quicken the process, but then it began to run, a fluid thicker than water gradually pouring into the bath, spreading itself to the four corners.

The whole operation required patience and the greatest of accuracy.

His women were small masterpieces. Perhaps even grand masterpieces. He closed the door now, ready to devote himself entirely to the blonde. He owed it to her.

1

"No, I'm afraid not, Fru Milling. As far as I'm aware, there's still no news about your daughter," Louise Rick said into the phone, with regret. She was sweating in her training gear and had just gotten back to Police HQ after six hours with the rest of the negotiation unit.

The exercise had been planned for some time; the theme was suicide. At seven in the morning, Louise had met the others out at the city's Zealand bridge, and although by now she was reasonably experienced, she was never exactly going to enjoy dangling from a bridge trying to talk a fictional suicide candidate into giving up their bid to depart the world. It had been a good day, nonetheless, and Thiesen, who was in charge of the unit, had heaped praise on her, telling her she was getting better all the time. Next up was the Storebæltsbroen, the monumental suspension bridge that spanned the Great Belt between the islands of Zealand and Fyn.

"I certainly do understand your concern. You haven't heard from her in months."

Louise sank back in her chair and unzipped her jacket. The office was boiling hot, the air stale and clammy. The radiator was on full blast to banish the winter's cold, and the grimy floor was streaked with slush from outside. She had only just walked through the door and was already on her way out again when fru Milling had called.

Hardly a week, certainly never two, passed without a phone call from Grete Milling. The retired woman's daughter had disappeared more than six months earlier while on a package vacation to the Costa del Sol, and since then there had been no trace of Jeanette Milling anywhere. Spanish police were dealing with the case on the ground, while the Search Department of the Danish National Police was handling the investigation. Nevertheless, the old lady continued to phone Police HQ to ask if there was any breakthrough.

Louise looked up at the clock. She had to pick up Jonas from school today for a dentist appointment.

"I'm sure the police in Spain are still out looking for Jeanette," she comforted the anxious mother, but of course she wasn't sure at all. The Spanish authorities were all too familiar with amorous women getting carried away with their vacation flings, so it was no wonder they didn't take such cases seriously—especially when the woman in question was over thirty, childless, and still single.

The only thing that could possibly point toward a crime in Jeanette Milling's case was the fact that her bank account hadn't been touched since the day she went missing.

As if Grete Milling somehow could sense through the phone that Louise wasn't paying full attention, she cleared her throat and repeated what she had just said:

"I tried to get in touch with that journalist again, the one who wrote about Jeanette at the time she disappeared."

She explained that it was to satisfy herself he hadn't dug anything up the police might have missed.

"But he wasn't employed there anymore, and the man I spoke to had never heard of Jeanette. It's as if everyone's forgotten about her."

⚭

Jeanette Milling had flown with Spies Travel from Billund to Málaga, where a guide had been waiting to receive the group of vacationers at the airport. The guide remembered the tall woman with the long, blond hair, but his only contact with her had been in pointing her to the bus that would drive the package guests to Fuengirola, where Jeanette was staying. He never saw her again.

The *Morgenavisen* newspaper had described how Jeanette had arrived at the hotel and been given a room with a partial sea view. It had been established beyond doubt that she had stayed at the hotel for four days, her name being crossed off the list each morning when she appeared for breakfast. But after the first four days she had not visited the restaurant at all.

She had bought provisions at a small supermarket adjoining the hotel. Police had ascertained as much by going through her bank statement. Several guests had seen her, at the pool and in the hotel restaurant. They described her as smiling and outgoing and remembered her having been chatty with almost everyone.

But then all of a sudden she was gone. From that moment on, there was no trace. The Jeanette Milling case had received massive media coverage in the days after her disappearance became known. After she was reported missing, *Morgenavisen* had dispatched a reporter and photographer team to the Costa del Sol to see if they could retrace the young woman's footsteps leading up to the time she had seemingly vanished off the face of the earth.

Interest in the story had long since gone the same way. No one cared anymore about Grete Milling's disappeared daughter.

❧

"We should also at least entertain the possibility that your daughter might not want to be found at all," Louise ventured cautiously.

There was a silence at the other end, and Louise lowered her gaze to the floor.

"No," came the reply after a moment, softly and yet with conviction. "She would never leave me on my own with that uncertainty."

Jeanette Milling had been living just outside Esbjerg, and after her disappearance her mother had kept up her rent so her daughter might still have her flat to come home to. For the six years prior to her disappearance she had been working as a secretary and receptionist for two physiotherapists, but apart from that Louise knew very little about the woman who had booked and gone on a package tour for a two-week vacation in the sun.

Nor was it a high-priority case, not anymore. Certainly not today, she thought with another glance at the clock above the door.

And yet she could hardly bring herself to ignore fru Milling's phone calls, since the woman invested so much hope in them.

"You're welcome to call again, of course," said Louise before saying good-bye and ending the call.

She sat for a second, struck abruptly by a sense of the woman's desolation at her daughter's disappearance. It was touching indeed, the way Grete Milling steadfastly held on to the belief that Jeanette would be found despite the months that had already passed. At the same time she could hardly bear to think of the day someone would have to extinguish that hope and tell her that the lease on her daughter's flat could now be terminated.

"Want a coffee?" Lars Jørgensen asked. Her work partner had gotten to his feet and was already on his way out the door.

Louise shook her head. "I've got to get Jonas to the dentist, so I'd better be off," she said, checking the text message that popped up with a ping as she spoke.

Got off early, her son wrote. *Pick me up at home.*

"See you in the morning," Louise said, smiling as Lars Jørgensen tunelessly mumbled the lyrics of some vaguely memorable song about a woman's work never being done.

2

I t wasn't there!" Carl Emil Sachs-Smith almost screeched as he
marched right past the receptionist. He barged into attorney
Miklos Wedersøe's office in Roskilde on Thursday morning, with
no regard for whatever he might be interrupting. "There was just
an empty space on the wall!"

Carl Emil could feel the perspiration trickle down his back underneath his high-necked sweater as he tossed his coat on the floor
and dumped himself heavily in the chair in front of the attorney.
The celebrated glass icon had hung there as long as he could remember. He sat for a moment with his eyes closed and felt that his
blood seemed to have difficulty reaching his head despite pumping
through the rest of his body so fast, it made him dizzy.

"I can't understand it," he added in a whisper, as if the notion were
incapable of sinking in. "It's always been there, above my father's desk."

It had been six months since he had confided the family secret about the Angel of Death, as they called it, to his attorney. One evening in late summer following a meeting of the Termo-Lux board of directors, he and Miklos Wedersøe had dined together at Roskilde's Prindsen restaurant. His sister had gone home early to be with her daughter, and as the two men sat enjoying a cognac after their meal, Carl Emil told him about how the fabled icon had fallen into the hands of their paternal grandfather.

As a young glazier in Roskilde, the grandfather had been commissioned to do some restoration work in the cathedral. The job had required some consignments of old church glass from Poland and there, among the great iron frames with their centuries-old stained glass covered in dust, he had found the Angel of Death.

At first his grandfather had been unaware that what he had discovered was a thousand-year-old treasure, but he had sensed right away that it was a very special piece of glass. Having pored his way through various religious history books he realized the icon had been part of the decoration in the Hagia Sophia, the principal basilica of the Byzantine Empire until Constantinople fell to Ottoman forces in 1453 and the sultan turned the Orthodox church into a mosque.

Carl Emil told him, too, that the myth of the unique icon made it a highly coveted piece for collectors all over the world. During the time it hung in the Hagia Sophia—whose name apparently translated from the Greek as "Holy Wisdom"—the Angel of Death had been part of a stained-glass window in the side aisle, above the poems carved into the curvatures of the half domes that to this day rose over the marble peacock tails. The clear blue colors of the icon were said to cast a ring of light down onto the church floor between two thick pillars inlaid with glass that stood flanking the window.

According to legend, a poor peasant went to the church one day to pray for forgiveness after accidentally having taken the life of a common thief. Under cover of night the thief had attempted to make off with the peasant's two cows. The peasant had caught him red-handed, and when the thief took to his heels the peasant had picked up a rock from the field and hurled it after him. To his misfortune, the rock struck the thief in the head and killed him on the spot.

And so it was that the peasant had stood in the church, in the ring of light, his eyes directed upward at the icon as he prayed for forgiveness. Afterward he told of how the light had grown brighter and still clearer, and the Angel of Death had spoken to him.

"Your sins shall be forgiven."

Relieved and more than a little shaken by the experience, the peasant journeyed home. The legend said he would never be prosecuted for the death he had caused.

The tale of the poor peasant and the thief spread quickly, prompting pilgrims in the thousands to flock to the Hagia Sophia in order to receive forgiveness for their sins.

✵

The attorney gathered together the documents that lay spread out over the desk in front of him. He put them away in a folder, then pushed it to one side before giving Carl Emil his full attention.

"Who else knew of its existence?" he asked gravely, wiping his shiny bald head with a handkerchief.

"No one, besides the family," Carl Emil replied, distraught. "There's been no shortage of art historians and antiques dealers trying to track it down over the years. My father was contacted on a number of occasions by a German art historian who believed he was on the scent. He claimed he'd been able to map the Angel's journey from Constantinople after 1453, up through Bulgaria, Romania, Hungary, and Slovakia, then on into Poland. He even had the particulars of where and when. But on each occasion my father managed to convince him he had reached a dead end. Various scholars and other experts have written articles and presented papers airing their theories about what might have become of the icon since it disappeared from the Hagia Sophia. As yet, however, none has succeeded in locating it. But maybe now someone has. We've given them the perfect opportunity, leaving the house empty for so long."

He ran his hands despairingly through his fair hair then buried his face in his palms, silently shaking his head.

After their dinner at the Prindsen restaurant, Wedersøe had offered to investigate how much the treasured Angel might be worth on today's market. They agreed that he would at first put out some feelers, to get an idea of what kind of sum they might be talking about if the right buyer came along.

Wedersøe's contact in New York had acted in the strictest confidence, inquiring within a few highly exclusive circles of fabulously wealthy, and in some cases rather eccentric collectors. These were the individuals who would have enough cash on hand to easily permit the illegal purchase of vanished artifacts and treasures categorized by the auction houses as priceless. Eventually, shortly after three o'clock the night before Carl Emil's sudden entrance into his attorney's office, Miklos Wedersøe had received a phone call from his American contact informing him that he now had a serious bid for the Angel of Death. A dizzying $175 million US, amounting to more than a billion Danish kroner.

This information had prompted Carl Emil to leap into his black

Range Rover, with the astronomical figure still buzzing in his ears, and drive out to his parents' large and magnificent property, a manor farm outside Roskilde, to fetch the icon.

The house had stood unoccupied for almost half a year since their father had vanished in the days following their mother's suicide. Most people guessed that after a lifelong marriage Walther Sachs-Smith had elected to follow his wife into death, but his body had yet to be found, so the manor by the fjord felt almost like an unvisited museum.

"What do we do?" Carl Emil burst out, immediately falling silent and staring feebly at his attorney, the man's bald pate, the expensive suit, the lip salve on the desk in front of him.

That evening at Prindsen, Miklos Wedersøe had responded to Carl Emil's confidence by telling him about his own upbringing as an only child. His mother was Russian, his father a Dane passing through the country when Communism was at its height. Miklos retained no recollection of his father at all, the man having abandoned his mother even before Miklos was two years old, leaving nothing behind but a photograph and his surname, which always sounded so out of place during roll call at school. His mother died when he was only fourteen, and after her death he decided to continue his education at a boarding school in Denmark.

Miklos's decision had very much been prompted by the thought of his father; Carl Emil understood that. But at the same time it was a decision made not with the purpose of finding him; more to demonstrate that he was able to look after himself and get by without his father's help. Carl Emil admired him for that. And he felt compelled to say that Miklos Wedersøe had turned out rather well, with his own established law firm and seats on the boards of a number of very good companies.

Right now, however, Carl Emil had difficulty comprehending how the attorney could remain so calm. In lieu of a fee, they had agreed that Miklos Wedersøe would receive a commission of 20 percent of the sale, since it was he who had incurred the rather considerable risk involved in alerting his American contact.

Wedersøe produced a plastic folder and nudged it across the desk for Carl Emil's perusal. On top was an illustration of the Angel of Death.

Carl Emil recognized it immediately, the angel with the lily in her hand, her great wings behind her. And though it was little more than a sketch, the colors were nevertheless bright and clear: silver, pale blue, and a deeper, darker navy. It was an exquisite representation of the icon his father had kept on display on the wall of his office.

"It says here that the archangel Gabriel is considered to be the Angel of Death. He is linked with magic and works by way of the human subconscious," Wedersøe explained. "This is from that German art historian who's been trying to track the icon down for quite some time."

He placed his hand on the folder and explained how the documents had turned up while he had been going through some older files in Carl Emil's father's archive.

"It was filed together with the correspondence they seem to have kept over the years."

He opened the file and removed the documents.

"Take a look at the dimensions noted here in the margin," Wedersøe instructed.

Carl Emil stared but failed to fathom what the attorney was getting at.

"How big was the icon your father kept on the wall?" Wedersøe asked.

"Certainly not sixty by eighty centimeters," said Carl Emil. "It was smaller, quite a bit smaller."

Miklos Wedersøe nodded. "But those are the dimensions of the real icon. Which makes more sense given the size of the basilica, if, as we believe, it took pride of place in the side aisle."

Carl Emil slumped back in the chair and folded his hands behind his neck, ruffling his hair at the nape. For a moment he closed his eyes and tried to fight the desperation that had engulfed him.

"You mean that what my grandfather found back then was a smaller copy?"

Miklos Wedersøe shook his head. "I think your father had a copy made of the real icon."

Carl Emil's eyes snapped open. He leaned forward attentively.

"This was attached to a receipt from an acknowledged glass artist. Unfortunately he's no longer alive, but the receipt is from 1986 and I'm convinced that was when your father had his copy produced."

Carl Emil straightened up. "So what you're saying is that what's missing from my father's office is just a reproduction?"

"Indeed," Wedersøe confirmed. "That would be my assessment. However, since the copy is gone it would appear that someone is trying to track down the real one. The question, of course, is who will find the original first."

All of a sudden Carl Emil could no longer think straight. The fact that they had no idea who was behind the theft made him feel extremely vulnerable.

"Who has had access to your parents' home?" Wedersøe asked.

"No one."

Carl Emil shook his head. As far as he knew, no one.

"The alarm's switched on and only my sister and I can get in.

We've changed the code, not knowing who my parents might have shared the old one with. They had a housekeeper and a cleaner who came in several times a week."

"Does that mean your father wouldn't be able to get into his own house if he happened to turn up again?" Wedersøe went on.

Carl Emil sighed and sank back again.

"He's not coming back. It's been too long now. I don't even think of it as a possibility anymore," he replied, feeling an immense sadness come over him. "We had the choice of either removing everything of value from the place, which would be most of the contents, and in any case we're not allowed, not before the estate has been divided. Or else we could safeguard the house with a new alarm code and a CCTV camera that registers every time the alarm is deactivated."

Wedersøe nodded. "Have you spoken to your sister?"

"She's on her way," Carl Emil said, nodding. He felt his chest tightening already.

3

"I can't go anywhere looking like this," Jonas grumbled when they got home from the dentist.

Louise smoothed a hand across his cheek.

Train tracks. She wasn't surprised that a twelve-year-old boy wouldn't think braces were cool. It had been ten days since they had fitted his lower teeth with a permanent retainer, and now he had this to contend with, too. A mouthful of metal.

"You'll get used to it, I promise," she said, trying to be comforting. She had the good sense to stop herself before uttering any more clichés. It wouldn't do the boy any good to be told he would appreciate it in the long run. "For now, it's only Camilla and Markus who are going to see you. They went to get some ice cream at Paradis, they'll be here in a minute."

"I don't want ice cream, and I don't want them coming here to stare at me."

At that moment, they were interrupted by a flurry of canine paws bounding across the living room floor, and a second later Dina came hurtling out into the hall, tail whirring like the rotor blade of a helicopter. The yellow Labrador was so overjoyed that they were home, she hardly knew what to do with herself. Although the puppy was deaf in both ears she could always sense when someone was there. Now she leaped about, jumping up at Louise's legs, until Jonas, beaming, sat down on the floor to play with her, baring the full array of armor in his mouth.

Louise's foster son would soon be thirteen and hardly a year had passed since she had become his closest kin under the most tragic of circumstances. Jonas had no one else. No family, no distant relatives. His mother had died of a blood disease when he was only four, but when Louise first met him it was clear to her that he had adjusted to the loss and was living a full and happy life together with his father. Then, only a few years later at the age of eleven, his world fell apart when his father was gunned down and killed in front of his eyes.

To Louise's great surprise, when the authorities were looking for a suitable foster family, it had been Jonas himself who had asked if he could come and live with her. They had met while she had been working on a case involving the church where his father had been a priest, so they hadn't known each other that well at the time. And yet they had made a bond, and in the time after the tragedy it was Louise to whom Jonas attached himself, still hospitalized and in therapy to help him cope with the trauma. Furthermore, he was in the same class at school as Camilla's son Markus, so while the most obvious step might have been to approach the families of his school friends, Louise had nonetheless been his first choice.

To begin with, Louise had seen it as a purely temporary solution, having been unable to find it within her to reject the boy. She had always made a point of keeping her independence and appreciated being in full control of her time. But suddenly all that had changed.

She knew how much happier she felt when Jonas was there. His new family comprised Louise, Melvin—their elderly neighbor downstairs—and Dina, the yellow Labrador pup Louise's ex-boyfriend Mik, much against her will, had lent the boy for as long as he wanted.

Now Jonas spoke about his past with diminishing frequency. Whereas to begin with they had talked a lot about the things he could remember, the good things from his early childhood, he seemed now to have settled into his new life. At least that was what Louise had thought until quite recently. Jonas, the happy, adorable boy who had seemed so grateful to be living with her, had suddenly become surly and introverted. Louise understood him only too well. So much had happened during the past year, and apart from losing his father he had also lost a good friend from school in a tragic accident that autumn. It was no wonder he would have some kind of emotional reaction at some point, Louise told herself.

But she was unused to him withdrawing, unused to his sudden irritability, the sullen behavior. Perhaps it was time for a follow-up session with Jakobsen, she thought, the therapist the Homicide Department used when necessary.

She went out into the kitchen. Her arms were aching after the day's training exercise, though given their infrequency it was only to be expected. She had been attached to the negotiation unit since

2006, and Willumsen, her team leader in Homicide, still seethed over the fact that their training took place during his hours, despite it having been his idea in the first place that she apply to go on the special training program after two FBI officers had been drafted in as instructors. The unit numbered thirteen in all, and although it had no direct bearing on her work in the Homicide Department, it was something she continually carried with her in her mind, not least because she never knew when they would be called out next, and she made sure to have her negotiation phone with her at all times. While she had been under no obligation and could easily have passed the opportunity on to one of the others on the team, she nevertheless had the good sense to realize that it would be beneficial to her to make herself available when Thiesen called, especially if she wanted to be involved in potentially rewarding negotiating jobs.

She needed to start running again, she told herself. It was a grind to drag herself out in the winter, but she could make a habit of taking Dina with her, even though Jonas against all expectations had been good at taking her for walks.

Ice cream, soup, and yogurt the first couple of days, the dentist had instructed, preparing Jonas for the fact that to begin with it could hurt a bit and his cheeks would be sore from chafing the edges of the metal braces. They had been given a tube of wax to rub on the braces so they wouldn't feel as abrasive against the tender skin inside his mouth.

Louise set the tube down on the kitchen table before putting the kettle on so the coffee would be ready when Camilla and Markus arrived with the ice cream.

Immediately the entry phone buzzed.

"Get that, will you?" she called out. But when there was no reply, she went out into the hall herself.

The door was wide open. Both boy and dog were gone, and the leash that hung on the wall wasn't there, either.

The entry phone buzzed again, and she pressed the button to let Camilla and Markus in.

"You didn't see Jonas on the stair by any chance?" Louise asked when they eventually appeared on the fourth floor.

They shook their heads.

"I wonder where he's gone," she said, mostly to Markus. "He can't be far. You make yourself at home in his room until he gets back, Markus. The TV's on, I think."

MTV around the clock, almost. Not loud, just all the time.

Louise went back into the kitchen. She picked up the cozy for the coffeepot and asked Camilla to grab some bowls for the ice cream, then they took everything into the living room.

"I met with Nymand today," Camilla said once they sat down.

"Really," Louise replied, increasingly annoyed at Jonas for disappearing like that. Granted, he would soon be a teenager with all the self-centeredness that entailed, but he couldn't swan off without a word just because he'd gotten braces on his teeth. "How did it go?"

"It went fine. Thanks for all your help."

Camilla had known the chief superintendent for a number of years, from the time she worked as a journalist on the *Roskilde Dagblad*, but had felt the connection to be too flimsy for what she wanted to discuss with him now. Her inquiry needed more weight behind it if he was going to take it seriously. Which was why she had asked Louise to call him.

"He probably thinks I've gone crazy, but I'm sure it meant something, you putting a good word in."

"Can't blame him if he does. Maybe you have," Louise replied with a smile.

"Perhaps," Camilla acknowledged, picking up her mug. "Not in this case, though. I really do think Inger Sachs-Smith was murdered and that someone is very close to getting away with it."

Louise shook her head. "How can you be so sure?" she asked, though she was already aware that during her two-month sabbatical, Camilla had run into Walther Sachs-Smith, supposedly vanished without a trace, at a beach house in Hawaii that she and Markus had borrowed. But she still failed to understand how her friend could be so convinced by the elderly man's claim that his wife's death had not been suicide, or indeed why she seemingly harbored no suspicions that he himself could have been involved.

"That's because you don't know the story," Camilla insisted when Louise reiterated her doubts.

"True," Louise conceded. "But how can I when you won't tell me what else he said and what grounds he gave for his suspicion?"

Camilla spooned up the last of her ice cream before lifting her coffee mug and putting her feet up on the table. "I'm not ready for you to pass it on," she said, like a teenager with a secret.

Louise shook her head. As things stood she had no idea what, if anything, she might be able to share with others. All she knew was that Camilla had fallen in love with Walther Sachs-Smith's eldest son, Frederik, whom she had met while traveling down the West Coast of the United States, and that she must have gleaned some information in Hawaii seeing as how she was now prepared to involve the chief superintendent of the Mid and West Zealand Police.

"My lips are sealed," Louise promised, and sensed a niggling unease begin to displace her annoyance at Jonas still not having come home.

4

M y wife did not take her own life. She was murdered."

Walther Sachs-Smith had fixed his unblinking gaze on Camilla's to emphasize his assertion.

She could still picture him and almost feel the wind blowing in from the ocean as they sat on the deck in front of the beach house on the island of Kauai. The Pacific had been anything but, and the waves had been increasing in strength like the gusts that battered the tops of the palm trees. Camilla had felt the same when the aging man leaned toward her with a furrowed brow and sadness in his eyes.

"The killing was camouflaged as a suicide," he explained. "But I could tell they'd been inside the house. They killed Inger, but they didn't get what they came for."

For a moment he sat there pensively while Camilla studied him.

At the time she met Walther Sachs-Smith he had been missing without a trace since his wife's funeral some two months previously, and Camilla knew only what she had read in the papers: His wife had committed suicide and had been found in her bedroom with a pair of empty pill bottles on her bedside table. Like the rest of the country, Camilla had been gripped by the story when the widower disappeared only days after the funeral without leaving any kind of message for his three grown-up children, his son and daughter in Denmark, and his eldest son Frederik, who had settled in Santa Barbara, California.

"Before the snarling pack gets hold of me, I intend to go to the police and make them understand my wife was the victim of a crime. Which is why I need your help."

There was a determination behind his words, and he lit up a cigarette as he spoke.

The man in front of her was somewhere in his late sixties, but she knew little else about him apart from the fact that he was one of Denmark's most well-known businessmen. He looked fit and tanned. His shirt hung loose and his hair was still dark, though increasingly streaked with gray. Beneath his left eye was a characteristic scar that in photographs made his laugh lines stand out even more.

"How can you be so sure it was murder when there were empty pill bottles beside her bed?" Camilla probed, reaching out quickly to save her glass when a particularly harsh gust of wind nearly caused the tablecloth to fly up like a kite.

"Because," he began, putting his hand down on the table to keep the cloth in place, his chunky wedding ring conspicuous on his finger. "Because Inger would never take her own life. It sounds so banal, I know, but Isabella, our little granddaughter, meant so much to her. After my daughter's divorce my wife spent a great deal of time with our grandchild, several times a week in fact. She couldn't be without her, not for anything in the world. And in all humility I like to think she valued our own time together too highly as well. She would never just give up on life because of a few ripples on the pond."

Ripples on the pond. That was one way of putting it, Camilla thought.

Walther Sachs-Smith and his window-making company, Termo-Lux, were among the wealthiest in the country, and the concise version had it that while preparing to hand off power in the company he was ousted by his board and the executive leadership comprising his two youngest children, Carl Emil and Rebekka, who had conspired against him together with the company's new attorney. The despicable coup had shocked business desks throughout the media. As soon as it became known that Sachs-Smith had been overthrown by his own offspring, news hounds quickly linked Inger Sachs-Smith's suicide with the family scandal.

"Besides, she would never have had the courage," he said, interrupting Camilla's thoughts. "But none of that is the real reason I can say beyond a doubt that her death was foul play."

She looked at him, curious, and asked him to continue.

"The day my wife died, the Angel of Death was taken from my office," he said after a pause during which he gazed quietly out at the surf.

"I realize it may be necessary to inform the police that we two have spoken if you are to convince them to reexamine Inger's death, but apart from that I suggest it would be wisest not to mention our meeting to anyone else," he said, adding with a wry smile:

"That would include my eldest son, even if he did lend you the house here. I need time before I go home and pick up the gauntlet."

Camilla felt herself blush for a moment before setting all thought of Frederik Sachs-Smith aside and concentrating on his father instead. Something about him had changed compared with the pictures she knew from the newspapers and magazines. He had shrunk. Not physically, but somehow he seemed to be diminished. It wasn't hard to see the grief in the darkness of his gaze. Most likely the change had already occurred when his wife had been found. Or it could have come gradually, during the time he had kept himself hidden.

"The Angel of Death?" she ventured.

"A long story," he replied. "I won't tire you with it."

"I've got plenty of time," she replied quickly, at the same moment catching a glimpse of Markus inside the house where he had retreated from the weather. The air was still warm, but the wind had begun to stir up eddies of sand and they had withdrawn under the bamboo roof that covered the deck. She wanted to continue their conversation, feeling a need for distraction and sensing to her great pleasure that her reporter instinct seemed to be fully intact.

At the time she and Markus had taken off on their West Coast adventure, she had, to put it mildly, been in doubt as to whether she would ever return to journalism. She had quit her job as a reporter on *Morgenavisen*'s crime desk after a story had brought her to the brink of nervous collapse, and although she hesitated to admit it, she realized that her trip to the United States with her son was an escape designed to stave off her descent into a deep depression.

The trip hadn't worked out as Camilla had imagined. She had

hoped to find peace and the answers to some questions, but had instead found herself stricken with grief when the news from home came that Signe Fasting-Thomsen from Markus's class at school had been killed in a tragic car accident. Conversely, she had harbored no expectation at all that during the trip she would fall in love, and right now she was keenly aware of how impractical it was to have taken a fancy to a fabulously wealthy unmarried Dane who had settled in the United States.

She picked up the stack of colorful Hawaii postcards she and Markus had bought to tease family and friends back home in the darkness of the Danish winter, turning them over and using them as a convenient notepad.

"Very well," said Walther Sachs-Smith. "We have made an agreement, after all."

Camilla nodded. They had indeed. Camilla had promised to do everything she could to encourage the police to investigate his wife's death as a murder case. He for his part had granted her exclusive rights to the story.

"Most religious scholars believe that the Angel of Death was lost when the Byzantine Empire was conquered by the Ottoman Turks. But in art history circles the belief is that the icon was saved and brought to safety before the Hagia Sophia's conversion into a mosque. If it hadn't been, they say, it would have turned up when the church was restored by two Swiss architects in the late nineteenth century."

"So it was, then?" Camilla interrupted, looking up at him inquiringly. "Saved, I mean?"

Walther Sachs-Smith nodded deliberately, his heavy gaze turned inward. "Yes, it was," he confirmed.

They sat for a moment in silence.

"When my father was twenty years old," he eventually went on, "he established a glazier's business in a basement shop in Roskilde. He had just married my mother, who was from Poland, where her father was employed by the church at Wroclaw, southwest of Warsaw. A couple of years later my father was commissioned to restore some stained-glass windows in Roskilde Cathedral. Through my maternal grandfather he purchased a lot consisting of some very beautiful old church windows still in their frames that had been lying about for centuries in the attic of the church."

He paused and looked up at Camilla.

"It's never the same, you see, if you put new glass in," he explained. Along with his father he had built up a life's work in the field of double glazing, and Camilla sensed his expertise. "It's like with old houses, always best to retain the old panes no matter how imperfect. The light they cast possesses so much more beauty, it's as simple as that."

Camilla nodded. She'd had the same discussion with the chairman of her housing cooperative after they decided to renovate the windows in her building. They ended up reusing the old glass for that very reason.

"My father traveled to Poland himself and fetched the windows. They were big and heavy, and in order to avoid the marvelous glass being broken during transport he left the panes in their iron frames. Some of the glass had been painted over at some later stage and needed stripping, while some merely had to be dusted down," Sachs-Smith continued, adding that it was while his father had been at work washing the layers of filth from the panes of a double-winged window that the Angel of Death had emerged before him. There was something so special about it he became curious and eventually found out that the glass icon had once embellished the Hagia Sophia. After the Ottoman conquest many icons and mosaics featuring Christian motifs were painted over or else removed completely.

"But in—" Camilla began, only to stop herself when he raised his hand.

"Let me just finish this, if I may," he said. "Subsequently, my Polish grandfather was accused of theft from the church. As a result, he suffered serious vilification at the hands of the parish council, the whole sorry state of affairs ending in 1935 with his being forced to give up his position, banished to a small house outside the city, his reputation tarnished beyond repair, a common thief in people's eyes. According to my father, this came as a very severe blow to the family insofar as his father-in-law had done nothing at all improper. Before allowing my father to purchase the glass he had secured permission from the priest to make the sale and thereby earn funds for the church. Yet when the parish council brought the matter to the bishop, the priest had conveniently forgotten the agreement entirely."

He shook his head and sat quietly for a moment with eyes closed.

Something had clearly departed him, Camilla realized. The strength in his voice, the charisma that had previously been his hallmark in TV interviews. Sitting opposite her now he seemed old and vulnerable.

The sun had finally disappeared behind the blanket of cloud that had threatened all morning. Camilla wondered whether they should go inside, but then he opened his eyes again.

"You can imagine the consequences for my grandparents if it had become known that the celebrated icon had been hidden away among the glass my grandfather had found in the church and sold to his son-in-law."

⁃ Camilla nodded. She had run out of postcards on which to make notes, but it didn't matter. She would remember this part of the story without them.

"My father never really spoke of it. Yet for all this time it has been such a part of the family history, the fact that he discovered something so precious in that consignment of glass he took home from Poland. But not once did he ever mention the Angel of Death."

Walther Sachs-Smith became pensive again before continuing.

"He ought to have handed it in at the time," he said. "But he didn't want to cause any more problems for his parents-in-law. They were old by then, and the rumors had started, claiming they had sold a valuable cultural treasure and hidden the money away for themselves. They were never able to shed that suspicion, and it clung to my mother's sisters, too, who had grown up amid all the accusations and who are still alive today. When my father died, the family secret was passed on to me, and with it the responsibility of shielding the Polish side of the family from any more trouble."

"The Angel of Death," Camilla mused, her eyes absently scanning the ocean with its whitecapped waves. How easy the most experienced surfers made it look, riding the waves that crashed against the shore. "The merciful angel who comes for people's souls when they pass on?"

The elderly man's eyes glazed over and Camilla glanced away, allowing him a moment of privacy for his grief.

"I believe so, yes," he nodded, his voice choking up.

At once he collected himself and leaned toward her.

"Many years ago I had a copy made of the icon, which I hung up in my office at home. A kind of alarm, you might say. It didn't look like much on its own, but if it were ever to disappear I would know that someone was on the trail of the real Angel."

"And that copy vanished the day your wife died?"

He nodded again, his gaze tinged with sadness. "My secret has been discovered."

"By whom?" Camilla asked in near-breathless anticipation, following him with her eyes as he rose to remove the cloth from the table.

"If only I knew," he replied. "All I do know is that they'll be back as soon as they figure out that what they made off with was a copy."

5

Louise had fetched the rest of the ice cream and reached now for Camilla's bowl. She could hardly say she blamed Nymand for calling her at Police HQ to hear what she made of Camilla's claim that Inger Sachs-Smith's death, far from being a suicide, was in fact murder, and her insistence that the police in Roskilde should reopen the case immediately. He had also asked for her take on Camilla's theory that the perpetrator had camouflaged the killing to make it look like suicide. All the forensic results from the scene, including analyses of the empty pill bottles on Inger Sachs-Smith's bedside table, pointed toward suicide as the most likely cause.

"Personally I don't think you've anything to lose by taking Camilla's inquiry seriously," Louise had told him, suggesting furthermore that the chief superintendent at least let the forensic chemists screen the samples taken during Inger Sachs-Smith's autopsy one more time to make sure.

The Sachs-Smiths were well-known and highly respected people in Roskilde, and Walther Sachs-Smith was beyond doubt the city's most valuable taxpayer. For that reason alone, whether one liked it or not, his influence was enormous. Louise herself would under no circumstances fail to act on even the slightest suspicion the billionaire's wife had been unlawfully killed—especially since Sachs-Smith himself had gone into hiding, fearful of his life, as Camilla had argued.

"I suppose some things aren't always immediately apparent in the ordinary analyses," Nymand had eventually conceded. "Even if they do screen pretty much across the board these days."

"Nymand said they got the results back from the Department of Forensic Medicine," said Camilla, putting her ice cream down.

Louise nodded noncommittally. She couldn't quite fathom Camilla's motives for involving herself so fiercely in a case that in all probability wasn't a case at all.

The most obvious reason was that she had been served Walther Sachs-Smith on a silver platter while everyone else thought he had vanished off the face of the earth, and as was typical for Camilla she had secured the exclusive rights to his story. Clearly, that might be enough reason on its own for her to be so eager about it, Louise thought, studying her friend closely.

"What makes you so certain Sachs-Smith is right?" she asked, wincing at the skepticism in her voice.

"It's not me who's certain," Camilla retorted with ill-concealed annoyance. "It's him."

"Yes, I know that," Louise protested. "But you believe him."

"Because he *is* right," Camilla said, going on to tell her how the forensic chemists in Copenhagen had sent a blood sample from

Inger Sachs-Smith's autopsy to a lab in Germany. "The Germans have discovered a method to pinpoint instances of insulin overdose. In large amounts, diabetes medicine is lethal."

"Insulin?" Louise raised an eyebrow.

"Inger Sachs-Smith's youngest son has suffered from diabetes ever since he was a child. They've always kept insulin in the house."

They sat quietly for a moment and looked at each other.

"Could she have taken it by mistake?" Louise ventured after a while.

Her friend shook her head. "It was injected into a muscle, and we're talking about a dosage big enough to kill several people at once. That kind of thing doesn't happen by mistake."

Louise shook her head and conceded she was right. "What about her son?"

Camilla gave a shrug. "He's certainly got access to insulin."

Louise nodded.

"The police already know from the first examinations that she ingested sleeping pills," Camilla went on. "That much is obvious, since they were found in her stomach. Nymand has a theory the perpetrator took advantage of the drowsiness they induced. Most likely he dissolved a couple more in water and forced her to drink. After that he could comfortably inject the insulin into a muscle. The hypodermic is so thin the pathologist just failed to see any mark to begin with. The empty pill bottles were designed to lead the police up the garden path, and they went right along."

"Good God!" Louise exclaimed, her thoughts suddenly racing. It was plausible indeed. An almost perfect crime.

"Nymand is reopening the case," said Camilla, drawing a rug over her legs. "This time, the death of Inger Sachs-Smith is being investigated as a murder."

6

There was a knock on the door, and Rebekka Sachs-Smith
stepped into Miklos Wedersøe's office. Her long, fawn-colored
coat was draped over her arm; she had her dark hair gathered in a
loose ponytail and her Chanel sunglasses pushed up on her forehead.

"Already started, I see," she said somewhat contemptuously,
hanging her coat on a hanger inside the door. "I'm rather curious
to know what it is that's so important you think I can just drop everything and come running."

With a look of annoyance she crossed the room and air-kissed
Carl Emil in her usual cloud of perfume. She was an elegant
woman in the classical sense. Soft cashmere cardigan and splashy
silk scarf around her neck. And she was tall, slim, and quite
as dark as her father, unlike Carl Emil, who was fair like their
mother.

"Thank you both for coming at such short notice." Wedersøe courteously drew out a chair for her. "Coffee?" he asked, already opening the door into reception to relay the request to his secretary.

They both nodded.

Carl Emil sank back in his chair and gazed out the window.

Through it there was a fine view of Roskilde Cathedral, the winter sun so bright it made the sky look pale. From the other window the city sloped down toward the fjord and the Viking Ship Museum. The office was exquisitely furnished. Brass door handles and lamps. Cabinets, desk, and chairs of mahogany, offset perfectly by the high white paneling.

His thoughts miles away, Carl Emil heard Miklos inform his sister about the offer they had received for the Angel of Death and about the reproduction that had gone missing from their father's property, but he felt barely able to distinguish the attorney's words.

One hundred seventy-five million dollars. He had not been intending to involve his sister at all, but the sum was so huge he could hardly afford not to ask for her help if they were to have any hope of finding the original and completing the deal.

"Certainly not," his sister burst out emphatically once the attorney's secretary had served coffee and closed the door behind her again. "The Angel of Death has never been and will never be for sale, no matter how ridiculous the money."

She turned angrily toward Carl Emil.

"Is this because you've run out of cash and Daddy's no longer here to sort out your finances for you?" she inquired scornfully. "If it is, then sell the apartment or the car. Just keep your hands off what doesn't belong to you."

Carl Emil was the middle child, two years older than her, and the only one of the three never to have completed an education. His and Rebekka's relationship had already taken a downturn when it was discovered he suffered from diabetes. As a child he became the object of his mother's devotion, his sister turning toward her father, forever demanding his attention and recognition.

"But I can't sell the icon, can I?" he said, sinking back in his chair and battling not to lose his temper. "I don't know where it is. Was it you who removed the copy from his office?"

His sister stared at him as if he had thrown a rotten tomato at her.

"Of course it wasn't me," she answered directly. "I haven't removed a thing from that house. And none of us would have any right, either. Including you!"

She turned to Wedersøe. "When did you receive this offer?"

"I got the call at three o'clock this morning. My contact in New York had just received confirmation of the bid himself."

She looked across at her brother. "Does that mean you've known how much the icon was worth since this morning?"

Carl Emil nodded grudgingly.

"So you two bastards were thinking of selling it without my knowledge," she concluded matter-of-factly, glaring at them both in turn. "Only now you're stuck and don't know what to do."

"Of course not. We wouldn't dream of doing anything without your full acceptance," Wedersøe protested. "That has never been our intention at any time."

She stopped him in his tracks with an abrupt gesture of her hand. "You must think I'm stupid. If that was the case you would have called me, too, but I didn't even know you were looking for a buyer."

She shook her head, her lips tightened in anger.

"Oh, come on," Carl Emil interrupted. "We'll be cashing in more than a billion kroner, less the twenty percent Miklos and his contact in New York will be getting in commission."

"My view is that we should consider it very seriously indeed," Wedersøe added, looking her straight in the eye.

For the first time, Rebekka's gaze flickered briefly. A second later her brown eyes glared back at him.

"Nothing's ever enough for you two, is it?" she spat. "We made a nice little packet selling off Termo-Lux, all three of us. When are you ever satisfied?"

Carl Emil could no longer control himself. He leaped to his feet and bore down on her threateningly. "Who are you to play holier-than-thou? You were the one who talked us into forcing Dad out in case he found out the Brits were waiting in the wings. You put the pressure on so Miklos could join the board, making sure we had enough votes on our side that Dad had no choice other than to pull out. None of that was my idea."

Rebekka rose to her feet, shoving him away in the process.

"Oh, please, don't give me that," she said coldly. "You signed all the documents, each and every one, so it's a bit late in the day to be playing innocent, don't you think? Besides, you were perfectly aware of what was going on and couldn't get your hands on the money quickly enough."

Her words hit him like a punch in the diaphragm. He had indeed been stupid enough to put his signature on everything having to do with the takeover.

She turned to Wedersøe. "How much did you get out of it? Are you prepared to do anything at all if it means money flooding into your account?"

"That's enough!" Carl Emil burst out, grabbing her by the arm.

"No one here's even half as power-crazed as you, as well you know."

Whereas he had wasted his college years, she had been a model student. Since graduating she had supplemented her education with as many executive leadership programs as she could find, passing them all with flying colors. He was no match for her in that department, and yet he couldn't stop himself.

"All respect to Frederik for pulling out. The difference between you two is that he was able to make a career for himself, while you simply sat yourself down in Dad's chair," he added, relishing how much it clearly hurt her.

Their elder brother had been living in the United States for the last fifteen years working as a scriptwriter in the movie industry. He was the outsider who had turned his back on the family dynasty in order to pursue his dream. At the age of twenty-seven, he had gained admission to a reputable film school in New York, and during the last few years he'd been involved in several major Hollywood movies. Having no need of the money, however, Frederik had little interest in blockbusters. Alongside his movie work he had made a mark for himself as a financier and garnered a fortune on the property markets. He didn't need to earn any more than he already had and had long since pulled out of the family firm. Neither Carl Emil nor his sister had heard from him since the Termo-Lux takeover.

"Do you know where the icon is?" Carl Emil probed, taking advantage of his sister temporarily having lost her footing.

"No, I don't," she replied, her mouth narrowed to a slit by seething rage. "But if I did, you can both be damn sure I wouldn't be telling you."

"Listen," Wedersøe cut in, still seated with his hands folded in front of him on the desk. "Perhaps it would make more sense to talk about who might have removed the icon from your father's office. If someone's out there trying to get their hands on it, there's a reasonable chance they'll be back once they realize what they stole was a copy."

He fixed his eyes on Rebekka.

"Then it would be up to the two of you whether to find the real icon ourselves or sit on our hands and wait until someone else beats us to it."

"Let me put it this way," Rebekka began in a slow, measured voice. "Even if you do find the Angel of Death, I will never agree to it being sold. All our other plans have succeeded. None of us is in need of the money. We've all gotten what we want."

"You have, you mean," Carl Emil muttered to himself heatedly, decoding the look in her eye that told him he had lost. She was fully aware that the moment he gained true financial freedom he would be off, leaving her on her own, and the thought was obviously an unpleasant one for her to entertain.

"The Angel of Death is staying in the family. It's a part of our history," she underlined. "I won't sanction a sale, not even for that kind of money."

Carl Emil sighed heavily. She begrudged him, it was as simple as that.

"And if you ever do sell behind my back, then I shall go to the papers and tell them all about how our greed and avarice killed our parents."

"While you're at it, why not tell them about how our grandfather got his hands on it in the first place and kept one of the most fabled cultural treasures of all time for himself, hidden away so no one else could find it?" Carl Emil retorted sarcastically.

41

"Absolutely not. That story remains within the family. But I will tell them how Dad and Frederik were tricked into selling the major part of their A-shares in Termo-Lux shortly before their value went up a hundred thirty percent."

"That story will boomerang back and hit you square in the neck," Carl Emil pointed out, shaking his head in disbelief.

"That may be so," she said. "But the pen was in your hand."

She rose and bent over him. "If you start looking for the Angel of Death, I'm going to the media," she whispered in his ear before straightening up and striding over to take her coat from the hanger.

When the door slammed behind her, Carl Emil sank back in his chair and wiped his brow while he tried to assemble his thoughts.

"So, who's on the trail of the icon?" he asked after a moment, suddenly fatigued despite the increasing sense of unease now niggling beneath his skin.

Miklos Wedersøe looked at him and shrugged. "If only I knew," he replied. "But it would have been nice if Rebekka had agreed to help us locate the original before someone else finds it first."

"She'll come around," Carl Emil said without conviction, letting his hands drop to his lap. "She needs time, that's all."

"Do you think she could find it?" Wedersøe asked.

"If anyone can, she'd be the one. I don't think she knew the one in my father's office was a copy, though."

"What a mess," Wedersøe exclaimed, his voice revealing for the first time how much was at stake for him personally if the deal collapsed. "We've got the buyer there now. But if she's not going to sell—"

"We're selling, of course we're selling. What's the point of having a billion kroner's worth of stained glass stashed away someplace where no one can get any pleasure out of it? I'll sort her out, don't worry," Carl Emil broke in angrily. "And if all else fails, we'll sell without her."

"I think it's safe to say she didn't sound keen," Wedersøe maintained.

"Screw Rebekka," Carl Emil reiterated emphatically, his mind made up. "But find out where we stand if she goes public with that takeover story."

Wedersøe nodded and sat for a moment before responding. "I don't think it would be a problem. We should be able to refute her claims rather easily, and I would continue to maintain that in good faith, I advised your father and brother to sell."

Damn right you would, Carl Emil thought. He downed the rest of his coffee, the exorbitant fee he and Rebekka had paid the attorney for completing the deal flashing through his mind.

It had been a race against time because they had needed to close the agreement before the public got wind that they were negotiating with the company's British competitor without their father's knowledge. In view of the commission Miklos had received for sealing the Brits' takeover, he was anticipating no further problems on that account.

He also failed to see what leverage his sister might have when everything boiled down. They had covered their backs, not least in preparation for the eventuality that the facts would leak and the public would find out they had been fully aware that selling the company would hike up the share value considerably. And it had been she herself who had suggested they make the most of that up-ward trend, with their father and brother on their way out.

"Anyway, the deadline for complaint passed months ago," Wedersøe added. "It's a dead end."

Carl Emil nodded pensively, then got to his feet and picked up his coat from the chair.

7

Grete Milling wept when Louise got through to her on the phone.

She had just come into the office after Friday's morning conference. Lars Jørgensen had brought the coffee and put two clean mugs out on the desk. Her work partner was on reduced hours after his wife had left him on his own with their nine-year-old Bolivian twins. The children were with his mother this weekend, so he wouldn't have to get home so early. He was planning to make use of the extra hours to tidy up all the files that had accumulated on top of the low shelving unit.

He had just handed Louise a mug when her phone rang.

"The lease on Jeanette's flat has been terminated."

The words came out unevenly. The elderly woman sobbed heartrendingly.

"And now they're saying they'll be sending the bailiffs in if I don't come and clear the place out this weekend so they can paint and make it ready for the new tenants. They've already taken the money out of the maintenance account."

Louise put her mug down and drew her chair closer to the desk. "Is there any particular reason why this is happening now?" she asked. "Have they given you any prior notice?"

"No, none at all," fru Milling sniffed. "I've been paying her rent every month. I've got all the receipts here."

Louise heard a rustle of paper at the other end.

"They claim they sent a letter. But my daughter's mail gets redirected to me and I haven't received anything from the rental agent at all. They said the bailiffs will come and clear the place and that everything will be sent into storage if I can't take care of the matter myself."

Again her voice cracked into sobs. Louise let her cry.

"Isn't there anything you can do to stop them putting my daughter out?" the woman inquired once she had collected herself again. "What about all her things? And what's she going to do when she comes home?"

Louise hadn't the heart to say how unlikely it was that Jeanette Milling would be coming home again.

"She can always stay with me, of course," the woman added as an afterthought, pausing to blow her nose before going on:

"The lady who rang said it was the agent's policy to terminate the lease automatically if a flat was left vacant for more than three months, though always with prior written notice. She said they'd already been more than obliging in Jeanette's case."

There was nothing Louise felt she could say. Instead she listened.

"If only there were some news I could pass on to the agent, then perhaps they would give us an extension. But when I called the Search Department to speak to Ragner Rønholt they told me the chief superintendent was in a meeting. Now I'll have to go over and make sure Jeanette's things don't go missing," fru Milling went on.

The weeping took over again, and Louise cast a glance at her schedule. Not that she considered herself to be any more compassionate than her colleagues, but Grete Milling had somehow gotten under her skin. What she could do was call the Search Department and ask if there was somebody there who could deal with the woman, take some care of her. Otherwise the police in Esbjerg would have to get someone to clear the flat and make sure Jeanette Milling's possessions were sent over so her mother could get them into storage.

"Fru Milling, if you could just give me your number again," Louise said, pulling a notepad out from under a pile, "I'll try and get hold of Chief Superintendent Rønholt on your behalf and see if we can sort this out for you."

She jotted the number down with the pen Lars Jørgensen shoved across the desk.

"Let me call you back once I've had a word with them," she said and concluded the call.

Louise turned to her computer, accessed missing persons, and clicked on the menu for nationwide.

Jeanette Milling was number three on the list. There were two photos of her: a full-face portrait and another of her standing on a beach wearing an airy summer dress, her long hair lifting on the breeze, the sun in her eyes.

The brief text was the same as the one that had been sent out to the various police districts when she was reported missing:

47

Missing: Jeanette Milling, 30 yrs, resident Esbjerg. Last seen 26 July 2009, Fuengirola, Costa del Sol, Spain. Approx. 09:30 in hotel breakfast room.

Beneath the two photos it went on:

Information as to Jeanette Milling's whereabouts after said time and date may be given to South Jutland Police or Copenhagen Police, Search Dept.

The text was followed by a duty desk phone number.

No further information had been received. Louise called her colleagues in the Search Department at National Police and was put through to Hanne Munk.

Rønholt's secretary had worked in the Homicide Department back when Louise first joined. She was a bubbly woman with a shock of curly hair and a preference for ethnic Indian clothes and joss sticks. She had almost driven Willumsen out of his mind, and Louise had no doubt whatsoever that the superintendent's less-than-charming demeanor was why Hanne had jumped when the opportunity came to move to another department. Now she was with Ragner Rønholt, and her spiritual tendencies were a much better match for his passions for orchids and silent movies.

"He's in a meeting," Hanne informed her when she asked if she could speak to her boss.

"Who's got the Jeanette Milling case?"

"Just a mo, I'll look," Hanne replied. "I'm not sure there's anyone specifically assigned to that one. It's been there awhile and quite a few have come in since, so it's probably with Ragner himself. He gets the files on his desk once they've gone cold."

The former missing person department of the Danish National Police had been discontinued a few years before, its various functions being farmed out to the local police districts. Now the department comprised Rønholt, two constables allocated as part of the recent police reform, and Hanne. No wonder they never made any headway, Louise thought. The statistics showed sixteen hundred missing persons a year. There was no way they could investigate even a fraction.

"What does his schedule look like after that?" Louise asked, glancing at Lars Jørgensen to make sure there were no objections to her heading off.

Jørgensen gave her a nod. He had rolled his chair over to the shelving and was busy rummaging through a stack of folders that needed filing.

"Let's have a look here," Hanne replied, and Louise heard the clatter of her typing at the other end.

"He's due off at one o'clock. He's flying to Paris with Didder this afternoon," the secretary informed her with particular effervescence.

Louise stifled a laugh.

Ragner Rønholt was renowned for his way with women. Never married and just past sixty, he had never sought to conceal the fact that he loved all his girlfriends.

"If you get over here now, you might just catch him before he goes. He's got no more meetings after this one."

"Can I get you to put it in his diary that I'm on my way, so he doesn't take off before I get there?" Louise asked. "I promise to make it short, only I've just had Jeanette's mother on the phone and she's in a terrible state. Someone'll have to tell the poor woman soon that her daughter probably won't be coming home again, and if that someone happens to be me I need to read the report before I do."

"You just pop over, I'll make sure he makes time for you. But like I said, he'll be out of the door at one. His suitcase is all packed and ready here."

"All right, see you in a bit," said Louise and concluded the call. She had only just gotten to her feet when her cell phone thrummed on the desk.

"What absence?" she exclaimed, completely taken aback when Jonas's class teacher asked if there was any particular reason for his absence these past couple of weeks.

"I was just wondering if it had to do with him going into therapy again," the teacher explained. "In which case it would have been good to have been informed."

"Yes," Louise answered swiftly, her thoughts churning.

"Today he left after the ten o'clock break and yesterday he wasn't here at all."

Louise dismissed the idea of pretending it was something she knew about.

"I don't understand at all," she said instead.

He was always there when she came home from work, or else he was over in Frederiksberg Park with the dog, but then his lessons ended at two anyway.

"Very often he goes home at lunchtime."

"Why haven't you mentioned this to me?" Louise asked.

"I'm mentioning it now," the teacher came back at her. "But you don't know anything about it, you say?"

"No," Louise acknowledged. "No, I don't. Has anything happened at school that might make him want to stay away?"

The teacher hesitated. "He's not an easy child to get along with," she ventured after a moment.

Not easy? Jonas was the sweetest, easiest boy in all the world, Louise protested silently, sensing the anger well up inside her.

"I don't agree with you on that," she said curtly. "He's never neglected his homework or school before."

"I'm just ringing to tell you there's a problem," the teacher cut in. "And problems don't go away just because parents, or foster parents, choose not to acknowledge them."

"No, of course not."

Louise capitulated, not wishing to start an argument with the boy's teacher and unwilling to defend him after he had gone down to Melvin's when Camilla and Markus came. He didn't come back until they had gone, and Dina had been so hungry she wolfed down her food faster than ever before.

Thinking about it, Louise conceded she'd had an idea there might be something wrong, but she had put his sulks down to puberty problems. But what did she know about that? She had never lived with a teenager, had never even had a child in the house before him. Nevertheless, she'd had no idea he was skipping school.

"I'll speak to him about it," she promised and thanked the teacher for calling.

She felt weighed down as she drove out to the Search Department.

⚜

There was a vase full of red tulips on the reception desk. Behind it, Hanne was chattering away on the phone with a big smile on her face, acknowledging Louise with a lift of her eyebrows when she knocked on the counter.

The door of the chief super's office was open. Louise signaled to Hanne to carry on with her conversation, she would see herself in.

The head of the Danish National Police Search Department,

Ragner Rønholt, got to his feet and spread out his arms for a hug as she stepped toward him.

"Nice to see you, Rick," he beamed. "How are things over with your lot?"

"Fine." She smiled back. "Willumsen's been off on vacation all week. He's back on Monday, though, so there'll be no more slacking then." There was no need to mention that Michael Stig had been acting head in Willumsen's absence and had been driving them even further up the wall.

Police Superintendent Willumsen's loud and boastful manner was known by most in the Copenhagen Police, but while on occasion she found him insufferable to work with, Louise nonetheless rather liked him in a way. In his own words, he was either yes, no, or fuck off. There was nothing in between, a fact she found quite refreshing, and at least you knew where you stood. Michael Stig on the other hand was a detective constable like the rest of them, but ever since he had taken a management course he never missed an opportunity to boss his colleagues about.

"What an awful thing with Willumsen's wife. Cancer of the uterus, so I believe?"

"Yes," Louise said. "They removed a rather large tumor, but it seems they're not sure whether they got the whole thing."

"Just goes to show. Enjoy life while it's there, I say."

Rønholt indicated the small suitcase behind the door before changing the subject.

"I understand from Hanne that you've spoken to Grete Milling."

Louise nodded. "Regularly, in fact," she replied. "I think maybe the reason she phones me is to make sure her daughter's disappearance hasn't been passed on to Homicide. The thing is, I don't really know what to say to her anymore, not having been involved in the case. The lease has been terminated on Jeanette's flat now and the rental agency has apparently forgotten to give notice to her mother."

"Bailiffs now, then, is it?" Rønholt inquired, offering her a peppermint.

Louise accepted with a nod. "The Esbjerg flat's being cleared out this weekend and she called me to try and get the agent to give her some more time. She still thinks her daughter's coming home. What do I tell her when she calls?"

Rønholt picked out the thirty-year-old woman's file and opened the folder.

"Normally it's me she calls," he responded after a moment. "There's not a lot to say, so it tends to be rather brief. After the last time, I called the Spanish police for an update, but as far as they're concerned the case is cold, no developments whatsoever."

He took out the summary and skimmed it quickly.

"From the moment she disappeared from the hotel there's nothing to go on. She seems to have just vanished after leaving the breakfast room. Local police found her cell phone in her room along with her wallet."

He smoothed his neat beard.

"Have you been through her flat in Esbjerg?" Louise asked.

Rønholt nodded. "Top to bottom."

He listed all they knew, raising a finger for each point:

"Farewell note: none found. Emails: nothing untoward on her computer. Money: bank account untouched, no withdrawals apart from the currency she took out for her vacation. We've checked she was on the flight out, and witnesses confirm she arrived safely at the hotel."

He shook his head.

"We've got nothing," he reiterated. "And to be honest, Jeanette Milling's disappearance is one of the more frustrating I've come across. We've been in full contact with the Spanish police throughout. We've even had some of our own people down there, but the fact of the matter is we've made no headway. Either she planned her own disappearance so meticulously she can't be traced, or else she fell victim to a crime. In either case, her trail stops at the hotel. Who knows what happened. The case stays open, at least until a body turns up."

"Under the circumstances, I don't really see how you can defend not telling her mother how unlikely it is her daughter's going to come back," Louise said. "It's almost unbearable letting her cling to a hope none of us here shares."

Rønholt nodded pensively. "Perhaps, though I'd say she comes across as quite rational. But you're right, she doesn't seem to be entertaining the possibility that her daughter might be dead. I'll send Thune out to have a word with her on Monday, dampen her expectations, explain the sad realities. Hopefully, she'll realize."

"Monday?" Louise exclaimed. "But that'll be too late. The flat's being cleared this weekend and she's intending to go over there."

She threw out her hands despairingly.

"It'll be too much for her to cope with on her own. It's all her daughter's things. The case is still open, it'd be irresponsible just to leave her to it. Someone needs to be there for her. I don't think she has anyone besides her daughter."

Rønholt glanced up at the clock on the wall. "I can't send anyone over there today, not now," he said. "And I'm pretty sure Esbjerg won't have the personnel for that sort of thing on a weekend."

"There must be something you can do," Louise persisted. "What if she breaks down?"

He nodded and conceded she was right. She could see him weighing up the possibilities.

"You're used to talking to people in crisis situations," he said after a second. "How about you assisting us and taking fru Milling over there with you? I'll square it with Willumsen and make sure you get the proper overtime."

Louise dropped her hands to her sides again. It wasn't the extra money—it wasn't that much anyway, not even for being called out on a weekend—it was more something about working on missing person cases that had always appealed to her. It was like watching a movie backward: She knew the ending but needed to work her way back to the beginning in order to understand the plot.

"Okay," she said, immediately reaching for the case folder on Rønholt's desk. "But I need to go and talk to her first."

"Thanks," said Rønholt. "She lives out in Dragør."

"Right, then."

Louise got to her feet while he wrote down the woman's address for her. She asked him, too, for the number of the detective constable attached to the case over in Esbjerg so that she might get in touch with him if they needed to get hold of a crisis counselor.

8

Carl Emil buried his face in his hands and asked the female detective to repeat what she had just said.

He had not been properly awake when the Mid and West Zealand Police had phoned just after nine that morning. At first he had asked them to call back later, only to be instructed to present himself at Roskilde Police Station at eleven in the company of his sister instead.

"We are no longer certain your mother's death was a suicide," the policewoman said again, looking at him firmly across the round conference table in the chief superintendent's brightly appointed office. "New information has come to light that would seem to indicate murder."

"What do you mean?" Rebekka immediately cut in, swiveling toward the more senior officer.

Nymand had sat down at his own desk to allow the female officer to conduct the proceedings. He was the one who had phoned and summoned the two siblings for a meeting, with no further explanation of what that might entail. Nymand had prepared his investigator for the fact that Rebekka and Carl Emil Sachs-Smith would in all probability be expecting it to concern their father's disappearance. Perhaps they might even be hoping his body had been found so that they might finally go ahead with dividing up their parents' estate.

"Some results have come in from the most recent analyses conducted in the case," the detective explained.

"Case?" Carl Emil exclaimed in surprise. "You mean our mother's death is a case? I hadn't realized."

The air inside the office felt warm and clammy, and although it was painted white and light streamed in from the big windows, the room seemed cramped. The chief superintendent had plastered the walls with framed Scandinavian art that had the effect of making the space contract toward the middle.

Carl Emil perspired, his clear blue eyes fixed on the female officer in front of him.

"It is now, yes," the woman officer replied, glancing over at Nymand, who nodded affirmatively. "Our assumption until now has been suicide, as you know. However, new tests carried out by the Department of Forensic Chemistry have revealed that besides the very potent sleeping medicine found in her stomach, there was also a rather considerable amount of insulin present in your mother's blood. Since your mother was not diabetic and had never been prescribed any medicine to combat that disease, we have reason to believe that we are now dealing with a crime."

"That can't be true," Rebekka burst out, her angry gaze shifting from the detective to the chief superintendent. "There were two empty bottles of tablets on her bedside table."

Nymand nodded. "The autopsy indeed showed high concentrations of sleeping medicine," he replied. "But with these new analyses, I'm afraid there is no doubt whatsoever that your mother was killed by means of insulin."

Carl Emil pulled off his sweater and dumped it over the back of the chair next to him before bypassing the blond detective and looking Nymand straight in the eye. "So what you're claiming is that someone gained access to our parents' house, killed our mother, and then left again without taking anything with them?" he said, a tad more sarcastic than intended. "Our mother owned some rather precious jewelry. And what wasn't locked away she kept in the box on the bedroom dresser."

"We're not claiming anything," Nymand rejoined calmly. "We are, however, informing you of a new development in the case, and that henceforth we shall be investigating your mother's death as a murder."

"The jewelry was all still there when we found her," Rebekka added, folding her hands together under her chin and thereby causing her Rolex watch to slide down her arm. "There was no sign of any break-in. The police said so themselves."

Carl Emil sensed her looking at him and kept his eyes on the female detective. He thought about the Angel of Death but said nothing.

"For God's sake," he exclaimed instead, throwing up his arms. "The house was full of valuables—the silverware was there for the taking and the walls are covered in very costly art. If anyone broke in they'd have made off with at least some of it, surely?"

Nymand agreed. "Indeed. Your mother clearly must have let

the perpetrator into the house herself," he said. "Therefore, a team of forensic officers has been dispatched to the property and is already at work on the house's exterior."

The chief superintendent rose to his feet and approached them, placing a search warrant on the conference table for their perusal.

Rebekka paled and fidgeted nervously with her finger rings. Carl Emil, still aware of her piercing eyes watching him, nodded slowly.

Nymand went back to his desk, sitting down heavily again in his chair.

"We know this comes as a shock," the woman detective said, picking up the thread again. "But as you have suggested yourselves, there seems to be no indication of any intent toward robbery or theft. Your father didn't report anything missing, either, so I think we can safely rule out profit as a motive."

She spoke slowly, enunciating every word, her blue eyes calmly considering them both in turn.

"Therefore," she went on unhurriedly, "I need to ask if you know of any reason at all why anyone would wish to kill your mother."

Carl Emil shook his head mechanically. His thoughts were swimming, sweat trickling from the pores under his shirt.

"Might she have been having an affair?" the detective ventured, adding: "An affair your father may have discovered?"

The ensuing silence was so pronounced, Carl Emil heard his sister gasp. Slowly, she rose to her feet and turned to face the chief superintendent. Her dark eyes were almost black.

"Now, you listen to me," she began. "Are you trying to insinuate that our mother had a lover?"

She stood for a moment as she regained control over her quivering voice.

"And furthermore, that our father killed her?"

Without realizing, she had stepped toward Nymand and was already in his face.

"We're not insinuating anything," the chief superintendent said dismissively. "But we have to investigate the possibility in view of your father disappearing after the funeral. Perhaps he had a mistress? Perhaps they made off together? We don't know."

Carl Emil glanced at his sister, who had remained standing, and shook his head.

"I have never had any reason whatsoever to suspect either my mother or my father of having an affair," he said, fixing his eyes on the detective in front of him. "They were together all the time. If they went away on trips, it was always together. If they went out, they went together. They were together in life, that's how they lived."

The detective jotted down some notes. Carl Emil had yet to comprehend how what had started out as a routine meeting to inform them of a new development now seemed to have taken a turn toward interrogation.

He straightened his shirt, which now clung to his back.

Their mother had been devoted to Isabella, her only grandchild, and when Rebekka's ex-husband moved out of their big house on Frederiksborgvej, their mother had started picking up the girl from school a couple of times a week. It had surprised him somewhat, the mood in the family at that time being best described as icy after their father's exit from Termo-Lux, but their mother had apparently decided her grandchild should be shielded from the family strife.

Their father had disappeared, leaving no letter. Nor had he drawn his business matters to any kind of close. He had said nothing in the days leading up to his disappearance that had indicated what might be about to happen. Everything had been focused on their mother's funeral. Then all of a sudden he was gone, and after they started to get worried Rebekka discovered that his cell phone and wallet were still on the desk in his office.

They had been placed neatly next to each other, a fact she had taken as a sign that his actions had been deliberate. No one knew exactly when he had vanished. Following the takeover they no longer maintained any kind of day-to-day contact. It was mainly his sister who believed it to be a positive signal to the nearly one thousand employees of the company that the new leadership was making a clean break and reshaping company values for a new day and age.

She was probably right in assessing that it would have been difficult for their father to remold what he had built up by his own hand in very different times.

Carl Emil missed his father, yet he could not say he regretted going behind his back. The only thing he regretted was having trusted his sister.

"We need to speak to people who were close to your parents," the detective went on, jolting Carl Emil back to the reality of the chief superintendent's office.

He sat for a moment and stared blankly at her without answering, feeling the need to bring his emotions under control.

"Our father did not kill our mother," he stated with studied composure. "They loved each other, they spent their whole lives together. He has an alibi, he was at a board meeting on Fyn. As everyone else who was there will corroborate, if you bother to check. This just isn't good enough. Find another line of inquiry!"

"That may be so," said Nymand from his place over by the window. "But in principle he could have administered the injection before he left. In most murder cases we find the victim and perpetrator to be closely related. Your mother was certainly not killed in some heated exchange. All indications are that whoever did this sought to carefully camouflage his actions."

"We need a motive," the woman detective added, listing some examples: "Jealousy, revenge, lust, profit…"

"Who might your mother have let into the house?" Nymand cut in.

"It could have been anyone," Rebekka replied, now seated again. "Normally it was the housekeeper who went to the door. If she was off, my mother would go."

"And the housekeeper didn't arrive for work until after your mother was dead," the detective continued. "The report states it was she who called the ambulance after finding your mother in the bedroom."

Carl Emil nodded. The day their mother died she had been alone on the property. Their father had driven off to Fyn early in the morning for the board meeting.

"Whoever killed her, it wasn't anyone she knew," said Rebekka. "She was very well liked by everyone."

She paused for a second before skewering Nymand with a glare.

"But then you wouldn't know, because you didn't know her."

The chief superintendent shifted uneasily in his chair.

"I did know your mother, as it happens," he said unassumingly. "She was a very great asset to the community."

Carl Emil managed to control himself despite the rage he immediately felt rise inside him. An asset to the community! His parents had generously donated to the chamber of commerce every time they were out looking for sponsors for their summer events on the square or their Christmas lights in the high street. The taxes they paid kept half of Roskilde running. Damn right his parents were an asset. But apparently not so much that they couldn't be dragged through the mud the minute they were no longer there to protest.

He took a deep breath and tried to dismiss his anger.

"What do you need from us?" he asked, restlessly getting to his feet and going over to the window.

"A list of names, whoever was close to your parents. And we need access to the house," Nymand replied.

"In that case, I need to speak to my attorney first," Carl Emil said abruptly, precipitating a nod from the chief superintendent.

"Of course."

Carl Emil waited with impatience while the attorney's phone rang, but didn't have time to say anything when eventually it was answered.

"Listen, you've caught me at a bad time. Let me call you back," Wedersøe stated curtly.

"No, you listen to me," Carl Emil rejoined. "I'm at Roskilde Police Station. The police say they can prove our mother was murdered. They suspect our father."

He heard Wedersøe excuse himself to whoever he was with, then the sound of a door being closed.

"What do you mean?" the attorney asked, now fully attentive.

"They found a large amount of insulin in the tests they took when she died. Now they want to know all about our parents' relationship, who their friends were, everything."

"Let them have all they need, nothing to worry about there," Wedersøe said.

"They're asking for access to the house. What do I do, go with them or just give them the code for the alarm?"

"Give them the code, save yourself the inconvenience," Wedersøe replied. "I'm in conference the rest of the day, but don't worry, I'll make time to get in touch with Nymand myself. He needs to tell us what grounds he's got for suspecting your father. Technically, at least, I'm still your father's attorney."

Carl Emil stepped up to Nymand's desk and wrote the six-digit code down on a sheet of paper before calling his parents' estate manager and instructing him to furnish the police with a set of keys.

He had just picked up his sweater from the back of the chair when Nymand stood up.

"I must ask you both to accompany me next door. I need you to account for your movements on the morning of your mother's death. And before you go we'll need to take your fingerprints, too, I'm afraid. I do hope you understand," he added, showing Carl Emil the way.

"I gather you have access to insulin, is that right?"

9

Driving home from the police station, Rebekka talked non-stop. That morning, when Carl Emil had collected her outside Termo-Lux's main entrance on his way to the police station, she had hardly bothered to look at him. It was obvious she was giving him the cold shoulder after their meeting in Wedersøe's office, but now she was indignant, animated by the accusations the police had leveled against their father.

"At least he'll never know," he offered. "He might never have recovered if he'd known they suspected him."

She turned to look at him and shook her head.

"Is he the only one you can think about?" she burst out angrily. "What about how all this is going to fall back on me? How do you think people are going to react when it gets out? People may be sympathetic about a suicide in a family, but a murder accusation's a different thing altogether. There'll be gossip, and the papers are going to have a field day."

Speechless, Carl Emil took his foot off the accelerator, glanced quickly in the side mirror, and pulled the big Range Rover up on the other side of the cycle lane.

"So what's important here is how it all rubs off on you, is it?" he spat, barely able to contain his disgust. "Doesn't it make just a tiny impression on you that the police actually suspect our father of having killed our mother?"

"I won't be treated like this," his sister snarled back. "If the police want anything else you can deal with them. I've got a business to run."

Carl Emil stared out of the windshield without comment, staggered by what she'd said. He flicked the signal light and turned the car back onto Fredriksborgvej. No wonder Jeffrey had walked out on her. Their marriage had lasted barely four years before the Englishman had had enough and moved into an apartment on Kongens Nytorv in the center of the city.

He hadn't exactly enjoyed it himself, the bombardment of questions surrounding his comings and goings on the day their mother was found dead. And then there was the matter of the insulin. He could hardly deny he always carried some with him: He had diabetes. What's more, he kept a stock at the house, too, so in principle his father could easily have made use of it. Throughout the interview he had tried as best he could to remain composed, but he couldn't help becoming rattled at the accusations, and above all utterly confused.

The only thing he could remember with any certainty from that day was that he had been lying in a young woman's bed amid a near-suffocating aroma of roses when they called and told him his mother was dead. Fortunately he remembered where the woman lived and was able to furnish the police with not only her address but her name, too.

He pulled up at a red light and recalled exact nuances of the physical well-being that had rippled through his body before he had answered the call on his cell, and then the sense of sheer desolation when he was informed of his mother's suicide. It was as if his whole being had been gripped by an immense cold that left him paralyzed and helpless. It was there still, in the marrow of his bones.

"Dad didn't kill her," he said without looking at his sister.

"Insulin," Rebekka hissed after a moment. "What's your response to that?"

He declined to answer and concentrated on his driving instead.

"So the Angel of Death is just coincidence, is it?"

Murder made out to look like suicide, the police had said. He had difficulty taking it in. Right now, Carl Emil was wholly incapable of fathoming the consequences of this new turn of events. He stared at the road ahead, unable to look at his sister but sensing her eyes glaring at him.

"Grandfather and Dad could keep a secret. Why doesn't it surprise me you're the one to break it? Why couldn't you just keep your mouth shut! It's so typical of you! Enough is never enough, is it?"

Behind her dark sunglasses and with the garish scarf around her neck she looked pale and fragile, but the anger in her voice made his blood run cold. He had to acknowledge he found it hard to grasp the events of the last few hours. The accusation against his father. The suspicion he himself was now under. It wasn't until he was ushered into the detective's office next door to Nymand's own that it had occurred to him he was actually being interviewed in a murder investigation and that the whole family was now involved in the case.

They drove on for a while in silence until she took a deep breath as if collecting herself to say something to him.

"How many people have you let in on the secret of the Angel of Death?"

He sighed and signaled left, waiting for a gap in the oncoming traffic before turning into the driveway of his sister's mansion on the shores of Roskilde Fjord. The gravel crunched under the Range Rover's chunky tires as he slowly pulled up next to her smart little Mini Cooper convertible. Her big Audi was still parked in her dedicated space in the company parking lot.

"No one besides Miklos," he replied with a shrug. "But I can't guarantee the rumor didn't get out while he was investigating the market."

"You big idiot," she spat.

He nodded, surveying the fjord. He had no way of knowing how many inquiries had been initiated. He had written two emails himself to auction houses inquiring as to their expertise regarding an artifact such as the icon, and both had replied that if it really did concern such a treasure they would have to decline to be of assistance and could only urge that it be returned to Istanbul, to the museum of the Hagia Sophia basilica.

As he speculated, the door of the big white house opened and his eight-year-old niece came running toward the car in her pink Crocs. He jumped out and gave her a big hug before Rebekka intervened. He held the child tightly before yielding and planting a quick peck on each cheek.

"Hi, my little princess!" he said. "How's the dancing coming along?"

"Fine," she said, beaming proudly. "I'm going to be dancing first in the spring show, and I've sewn the dress myself. Do you want to come in and see?"

Carl Emil shook his head. "I'm afraid I don't have time today. But next time I come I'd very much like to. Then you can show me your dance, too."

The girl nodded eagerly.

Rebekka stepped between them and gave her daughter a kiss. Her arm was around her as they turned and started toward the front door. Carl Emil put his hand on his sister's shoulder and held her back.

"Bekka, for crying out loud. That icon's not giving us any pleasure, is it? And it looks like we haven't even seen the original, so we're hardly going to miss it, either. Help us find it."

He heard the pleading in his voice and hated himself for it. But she had no right to decide on her own what was to become of their parents' property.

She shrugged him off and without looking at him replied:

"The Angel of Death belongs to our family's history. We're not selling."

And with that she walked up the steps to the door, holding her daughter by the hand.

10

I'll take fru Milling to Esbjerg for you," Melvin offered when Louise came home to pick up the car after her meeting with Rønholt. She had explained to him rather hastily why she had to be leaving again in such a hurry.

Jonas and their downstairs neighbor were sitting in the kitchen engrossed in one of their thousand-piece jigsaw puzzles. Happily, they had started doing them on a big wooden board they could pick up and move somewhere else if the need arose.

NINE MAGNIFICENT LIGHTHOUSES OF BRITTANY said the lid they had leaned on its edge up against the wall. They had also sorted all the pieces according to color. Louise thought they obviously had too much time on their hands if such mind-numbing trivialities were all they could occupy themselves with, but they seemed to be enjoying it and that was the main thing. The schoolboy and the pensioner. The project had already been under way for a couple of days by the looks of it; Jonas was doing the edges while Melvin had the lighthouses and the sea spray.

Dina was lying on the floor with her head resting on Jonas's feet.

"She'll have to get a moving company to pack everything up and send it into storage," said Louise. "She won't be able to manage herself, I'm sure."

"Let me go with you, then," Melvin repeated. "If everything's going into storage, I'm sure there are some of her daughter's things she'd like to bring home with her."

Louise nodded. It seemed reasonable. She had grabbed a few minutes on her own in the living room to skim through the case file. There was nothing in Jeanette's emails or her phone's call history to suggest contact with anyone at all in Spain before she left. The missing woman had not, so it seemed, contrived to take off with anyone local.

Louise had gone through the reports, too. The Esbjerg police had spoken to Jeanette Milling's co-workers and people she knew. None of them offered anything of interest—there was no suggestion of a Spanish lover, nor had she ever obviously been particularly depressed. No one who knew her had the slightest reason to believe she could have taken her own life.

"It'd be such a shame if all her stuff got packed away without her mother having a chance to go through it first," Melvin maintained. "I can go with her, let her see if there's anything she'd like to put aside."

Melvin Pehrsson had lost his wife some years previously. She had spent her last many years in a coma in a residential care home, and having her things around him while she was artificially being kept alive had clearly meant a lot to him.

"But, Melvin," Louise said with a smile. "You don't even know the woman!"

"There'll be plenty of time for us to get to know each other on the train on the way over," he rejoined.

"Can I go?" Jonas chipped in.

"The only place you're going, young man, is school. And you can make sure you stay there, too, until the bell's rung after the last lesson," Louise snapped back, regretting her words immediately.

They hadn't had a chance to talk about it yet. She had been reluctant to bring the matter up over the phone, and seeing him having such a nice time with Melvin when she got home had relegated it to the back of her mind.

The reaction came promptly. A shadow came over the boy, his eyes disappearing from view behind his floppy bangs as he lowered his head and looked down at the table in front of him.

Melvin was just about to say something, but Louise shook her head at him discreetly and stood for a moment not knowing quite what to say next.

She had no idea what was going on with him. Right now he was as sweet as ever, with not the slightest hint of the brooding defiance she had seen when Camilla and Markus had been there. A good thing it was the weekend; it would give him a chance to get used to the braces before school again on Monday, she thought to herself.

"So my job's turning into a family outing all of a sudden, is it?" she said, with a smile designed to get the mood back on track.

Her original idea had been to drive Grete Milling over to her daughter's flat so they could be there before the moving men got started. That would also give her the chance to see how Jeanette had been living, as well as how she had left the place before going off to Spain. Louise was convinced that if Jeanette had had any intention of not returning home again then something in the flat was bound to give her away.

She shook her head at the two of them.

"I've spoken to the moving company and they say they can be there Saturday afternoon to start packing and then drive the whole lot back over to Zealand on Sunday morning. All they need is an address for the storage. To be honest, though, I don't even know if fru Milling will want to go when it comes down to it."

"Of course she will," Jonas asserted, prompting Louise to fall silent.

The boy had been there himself when the rectory had been cleared and packed away after his father's death. Mostly he had kept things from his own room, but he had taken some of his father's items, too. The rest had been packed away in boxes and sent into storage until he was old enough to move into a place of his own and select what he wanted to have around him in his own home.

"I can offer our assistance and see what she says," Louise decided, taking the car keys from the hook in the hall. "See you later. Not sure what time I'll be back. Depends on how she reacts."

❧

The house in Dragør was painted yellow with a small cobbled area out front enclosed by a low green fence. The lights were on in the windows and Grete Milling opened the door before Louise managed to put her finger to the doorbell. She must have seen her come in through the gate.

"How kind of you to come all this way," the woman said, smiling meekly. "I've been wondering when someone might have the time to see me."

She handed Louise a hanger for her coat. She was a small, gray-haired woman with kind hazel eyes and a chunky silver ornament around her neck. She showed the way into the low-ceilinged living room and gestured for Louise to sit down on the deep-red sofa.

A moment later she came back from the kitchen carrying a tray in front of her. Her hands trembled slightly as she stooped to put it down on the table. Louise reached out to help.

"I thought you might like some coffee," the woman said, sitting down opposite. "I've cleared out the guest room as best I could. I thought Jeanette's things might go in there, some of them anyway."

She poured the coffee and offered Louise a cookie from the plate.

Louise took a deep breath and folded her hands together in her lap.

"Fru Milling," she began. "I'm awfully sorry to have to say this, but I'm afraid you really must start coming to terms with the possibility that your daughter won't be coming home again. We don't know if she fell victim to a crime, whether she took her own life, or if she simply decided to start a whole new life for herself. But we do think it's time now to accept that the life your daughter lived in Esbjerg has come to an end one way or another and should be wrapped up accordingly."

The woman put her coffee cup down gently on the table.

"You don't think she's coming home, then?" she said, and began wringing her hands.

Louise shook her head in sympathy.

"No," she replied. "I'm afraid she isn't. The police in Spain have done all they can, but no one has seen Jeanette since she went missing. There just isn't a trace after the last time she was seen at the hotel."

"My daughter did not take her own life," the woman said, breaking the ensuing silence. "Nor would she just disappear of her own accord. We only had each other, she would have said good-bye. There's always been a mutual respect and understanding between us. We've often talked about there being a time when one of us might not want to be here any longer—mostly with a view to my own age, you understand. We both agreed that if that were ever the case, then we would always let the other one go."

Louise nodded and felt a knot tighten in her chest. But this was not her grief, and she needed to keep it at bay.

"But if one of us did make that decision then we were going to say good-bye in a proper manner so there wouldn't be any loose ends, things you wanted to say but never did. That was what we agreed. I would have respected if Jeanette had wanted to try something different. Start a new life, as you say. But she would never have walked out on everything and left me to sort things out on my own like this. She knew there was no one else to tidy up after her."

Louise cleared her throat.

"What do you think could be the reason your daughter hasn't come home?" she asked, giving her time to wipe away the tears that had begun to trickle down her cheeks.

"Because she's dead," the woman sobbed, lowering her chin to her breast and closing her eyes tightly. "I think she must be dead. But as long as no one's said so, and the police have still been out looking for her, there's always been hope. It's made it easier to push the thought from my mind. But deep down I've known all along."

Potted plants lined the windowsills, standard lamps stood in each corner of the room, and fine carpets covered the floors. But there must have been a man here once, Louise thought, noting the heavy mahogany desk with its inlaid desk pad and sturdy lamp.

"Nothing's ever certain, though, not before there's a body," she pointed out once the woman had collected herself again.

Grete Milling nodded silently, her eyes glazed, her hands clasped tightly in her lap as though they were the only thing she had left to hold on to. For a moment she seemed to be far away.

Louise poured herself some coffee, offering a top-up to fru Milling whose own cup, however, had barely been touched.

"I've spoken to a moving company in Esbjerg. They say they can clear Jeanette's flat and pack everything away in boxes and drive the whole lot over here this weekend."

Grete Milling looked up at her in surprise and suddenly clapped her hands together as if snapping out of her anguish.

"Yes, that's what we'll do," she said with resolve. "I must do as they say and empty that flat. I don't want my daughter to be seen in a bad light. If I make an early start I might be able to catch a train and be there before it all gets packed away."

She rose to her feet.

"I think I might even have a timetable somewhere. I'm sure there'll be an early train, even if it is the weekend."

She came back with the DSB timetable and sat down in her chair, reaching for her glasses on the coffee table.

"Let me see, there's a bus to the main station," she mumbled to herself, studying the schedule. "And then when I get to Esbjerg there'll be a bus from the station there. She lived in Hjerting, you see."

"Actually, I was thinking I might drive you there myself,"

Louise interrupted, immediately suspending the woman's planning. "If I pick you up here at ten o'clock that'll leave us plenty of time to get there before they start packing everything away."

"But, dear, you mustn't let me take your day off."

Louise smiled and said her downstairs neighbor and her twelve-year-old foster son had offered to lend a hand, too, and were already looking forward to the trip.

"I must say, that's very kind of you, but I could never accept. I wouldn't dream of putting you and your family out like that."

"But we'd like to very much," Louise insisted, not mentioning that it was the thought of the woman's emotional well-being that had initially prompted the suggestion. "We could do with a day out, and I'd like to see your daughter's flat before anything gets disturbed."

Grete Milling wrung her hands again.

"Then let me at least cover the expense," she said finally.

"Agreed," said Louise.

"In that case, thank you very much indeed. It's very thoughtful of you. I haven't owned a car since my husband died, shortly after Jeanette was confirmed. To be honest, I've hardly ever driven at all, even if I did get my license a few years after we got married."

"No problem. I'll gladly drive," Louise said. "And it's no trouble, really. Both Melvin and Jonas know what it's like to lose a loved one, so they know when help's needed, too."

Grete Milling smiled, nodding in response when Louise asked if ten o'clock the next morning would be okay.

"I'll make sure I'm ready. I've got the key to Jeanette's flat."

She showed Louise to the door and clasped her hands in hers.

"Thank you so much for coming to see me," she said before opening the door.

"No trouble at all," Louise smiled. "See you tomorrow."

11

Flesh, muscle, and bone were the only things left on her body; everything else had been replaced by silicone. Every cell was infused, thereby maintaining its original structure, and soon impervious to the body's natural processes of decomposition. In other words, she was now preserved, imperishable for all time.

The only thing spoiling the impression as yet were the empty eye sockets. The orbs of her eyes had been damaged in the acetone bath and could not be saved. As before, he would have to replace them with a pair from the wooden box, a process he had already made into a ceremony: the choice of color. Three pairs had already been selected for his other exhibits, and the green ones were being saved for the redhead that would complete his collection.

Green was no good for this one anyway. He had known from the beginning that this woman's eyes had to be blue, though whether they should be bright and sparkling or a deeper, subtler shade was something he would know only when she was ready to be placed in her display case.

A warm feeling passed through him.

He felt he knew her now, and though he had never seen her alive the fact did not prevent him from harboring strong feelings for her as she lay there before him. It had been exactly the same with the first three women—and indeed still was. They were part of his life now, just as he had hoped when he had ordered the first.

Perfect, he thought as he studied the fair-haired woman.

He had now removed the plastic tubing and the liquid silicone, moved the cart aside, and tidied the room so everything was orderly before he went to get the heat lamps.

Three large heat lamps of the kind he believed were used on poultry farms. The ceiling hooks were already in place. He drew the small stepladder toward him and hung the first lamp on its hook. The hooks were positioned fifty centimeters apart, ensuring the heat would reach over the entire length of the body, taking into account that length would vary from corpse to corpse.

He almost felt the urge to crack open a bottle of champagne. Until now he had reserved the pleasure of raising a celebratory glass until after each woman had been positioned in her display case, but somehow he already felt himself in the grip of a rising sense of euphoria. The woman in the shallow bath was almost ready. The silicone just needed to harden before he inserted the eyes, the jewel in the crown of his immaculate work.

As yet, the cap still sheathed her hair, but now that the bath had been emptied and she was ready to be transferred onto the gurney it could just as well be removed, its purpose fulfilled.

He wheeled the gurney from the first of the cellar's rooms, maneuvering it through the door and positioning it next to the bath before stepping over to the cupboard and taking out the white toweling sheet. The French lavender fabric conditioner made it smell so nice and fresh. He spread the sheet out over the gurney's stainless steel and smoothed it with his hand, adjusting it so it draped evenly on all sides.

Now he would do her proud. After six months of hard work on her corpse he could devote himself to the pleasure of pampering and coddling. Now, finally, they had reached the point where her dignity would be returned, and unlike all other women, who aged and declined, her beauty would be preserved forever.

Her body was slight and delicate, and he had no difficulty making the transfer from bath to gurney. He took a small towel and dabbed her dry.

Her breasts were small and firm, perfectly rounded like two droplets in shape. He adjusted her arms slightly, turning her palms downward and smoothing her fingers. The silicone appeared to be somewhat unevenly distributed in her legs; here and there it seemed to have collected, the smallest bulges under her skin, though nothing that could not be rectified before she was placed under the heat lamps. It was only when the substance was completely hardened that such imperfections were difficult to correct.

Now the artist inside him was awakened. Now, before the heat lamps were switched on, he would model and shape, lingering on the finer subtleties, the tiny details that made the female body so perfect.

He had already turned on the bright ceiling light; now he drew a work lamp over to her face. After rubbing his hands together to warm his fingers, he began to cautiously smooth her cheeks.

Her skin was white like mother-of-pearl, and quite as fine. She had been suntanned when she arrived, with hideous white bikini marks; now she was evenly bleached by the acetone.

Eventually, feeling confident the shaping was accomplished to his standards, he stepped back in admiration of his work and felt a rush of pride. He had done it again. There was no doubt, even though the work was not quite complete. Even now he could see the result would be perfect.

He smiled to himself and went into the next room to get the wooden box containing the glass eyes. They were easiest to insert while the silicone was still pliable. He had decided on deep blue, and when finally he put them in place she seemed almost to gleam at him.

His work was good. In fact, it was more than good: It was fabulous, he thought with delight, rolling the gurney underneath the heat lamps. He was still smiling as he packed away the wooden box and the microfiber cleaning cloth and flicked the switch to turn on the lamps.

❧

The first woman he had received remained his most stirring experience. So ravishing she had been. Young and pale, with long, dark hair. Their looks were by no means insignificant. They needed to complement each other if the exhibition was to be as consummate as he wished.

He did not want to know anything about their backgrounds. He placed his order, expressing his wishes as to their desired appearance with exactness. The delivered item was to correspond fully to his expectations. Nothing else would do.

One million Danish kroner was the price he paid for a corpse delivered to a rest area somewhere on Zealand. The exact location varied, the money paid only on delivery. It was a matter of mutual trust.

They never spoke when the body changed hands, and he asked no questions, noting merely whether the delivery was in accordance with what he had ordered.

Until now that had certainly been the case, and he was thrilled at having found a thoroughly professional supplier. It was no coincidence, either, that the Costa de Sol had been selected as a most suitable source. The region boasted a plethora of hotels to which single women flocked, so there was no shortage of potential subjects. Moreover, the open borders inside the EU meant they could be transported back to Denmark by road with an absolute minimum of difficulty.

Earlier that same day he had placed another order. He already felt excitement at the prospect of receiving what for now would be the final exhibit in his collection.

12

It was Saturday morning when film director Naja Holten's flight touched down in Málaga. She had been up since before the birds to make the 6 a.m. check-in at Copenhagen's Kastrup Airport, and she was grateful Jesper had given her a lift and saved her having to take the train.

It was stupid, but she missed him already. And not only Jesper, but the dog, the cat, and their house, too. They had only just moved in and the place was in disarray, they were still in the middle of doing up the living room, the builders were in and out, and there were forever decisions to be made about one thing or another. All of a sudden Naja had had enough.

In a premature attack of first-night nerves she had bought herself a cheap flight and booked into a rather more expensive hotel. Jesper had said nothing, had merely kissed her when she told him she had given herself a week's vacation in the sun in order to recharge her batteries and regain some measure of composure before her new movie was due to premiere. Next Tuesday, she thought, sensing once again the butterflies flutter in her stomach.

She pulled her shoulder bag down from the overhead locker and joined the flow of travelers heading toward the conveyor belts of the baggage claim.

Inside the airport building itself she failed to notice the man in the yellow hi-vis who stood surveying the female passengers who had just come in from Denmark. She did not see him when like a shadow he slid closer and concealed himself behind the arrivals board; nor was she aware of the way he swiftly identified the women who appeared to be traveling alone. Instead, her attention was distracted by three men waiting for their suitcases and already well into their duty-free Gammel Dansk.

"Tits out for the lads!" one of them bellowed, raising his little disposable glass in the air and throwing its contents down his throat.

She had not noticed them at all on the flight. Just as well, she thought, unable nevertheless to take her eyes off them. She could hardly avoid gleaning the fact that the three of them worked together in Frederikssund, a master baker and his two assistants off on a cheap and boisterous winter break together, totally without filter. They were having what they undoubtedly would call fun, looking forward to a week in the sun, and well on their way to getting plastered.

Many of the other passengers had already collected their baggage and were on their way through customs. Gradually the throng thinned out. One of the merry bakers missed his suitcase as it glided past. The two others had managed to retrieve theirs and raised their glasses in her direction. One of them lifted the bottle, too, and waved it inquiringly in the air. A little pick-me-up while she waited?

"No, thanks." She smiled, shaking her head and sensing a rising annoyance at her suitcase as usual being one of the last.

The conveyor came to a shuddering halt, prompting the guy with the bottle to loudly exclaim, "That's it. Tools down. Siesta!"

"Oh, for God's sake," she muttered to herself. The last thing she needed was to be stuck in an airport with a suitcase that had gone AWOL.

She swiveled around quickly when a man in a yellow vest cleared his throat behind her, and smiled when she realized he was standing with her suitcase. She glanced at the label to make sure. NAJA HOLTEN, sure enough. She tipped him two euros for his help and guessed the suitcase had fallen off the trailer on the way from the plane.

Swiftly she made her way toward customs and the exit. Once outside the airport building she stood for a moment and let the warmth seep into her body before following the signs for the car rental. She was unaware that the man in the yellow vest had followed her out, and thought nothing of it when she saw him get into a white Toyota parked a bit farther along the curb.

※

The hotel was situated directly facing the sea and when she pulled up in front of the archway of its entrance, a Spanish flag fluttering on each side, a young man came up and opened the car door for her. Having made sure of her reservation, he took her suitcase from the small trunk and put his hand out for the key. In return he gave her a receipt with a number on it before climbing in behind the wheel.

Naja Holten watched as the car turned toward the hotel parking area followed by a white Toyota. Then she went inside to reception, where she was received by a good-looking Spanish girl who in fluent English bid her welcome and asked for her passport.

As she checked her in, the receptionist explained that besides the breakfast room the hotel had two restaurants. There was also a wellness center with a steam room and a gym. She placed a brochure on the counter, turning its pages with a practiced air to show Naja the facilities on offer.

"You'll find the gym in the basement next to the spa facility," she explained, pointing outside toward the garden area where two large swimming pools were separated by a fountain in the middle.

Naja smiled and picked the brochure up, ready to step aside and make room for the man in line behind her.

"Just follow the path past the far pool and you'll find the stairs leading down. There's a sign saying WELLNESS," the receptionist told her, "so you should have no trouble finding it."

"Sounds good," Naja replied by way of thanks, glancing toward the first of the two pools where most of the sun beds were already occupied. The temperature may have been a modest sixty-eight degrees Fahrenheit, but the sun was shining from a cloudless sky and it wouldn't be long before she was out there, too.

"Oh, and if there are any phone messages or emails, could you pass them on to me right away, please?" she added, explaining briefly that she was trying to stay offline with her cell phone switched off for the duration of her break, but it was important the film company's PR department was able to get hold of her in an emergency.

"Of course," the receptionist twittered, indicating a board where each room was allocated its own little pigeonhole. As if to make sure Naja understood, she stepped across and patted her hand in the one marked 211.

"Two-one-one," she said with a smile, handing her the key card and directing her to follow the curve of the corridor to her superior room facing the beach.

When Naja Holten turned away with her suitcase, the man behind her had gone.

13

Carl Emil woke on Saturday morning with a thumping hang-over. It had been a late night. He had drunk far too much good wine and some very large gin and tonics at Umami, where he and a couple of good friends had run up a tab. He turned over on his side and felt his stomach turn with him.

Since coming home from his interview with the Roskilde police he had found it hard to shake off the experience. It kept flooding back in waves.

Had his mother really been murdered? Who could have done such a thing?

The chief superintendent had said so, and the finger of blame had been pointed squarely at his father.

Even now in his post-alcohol haze he found it to be a wholly ridiculous idea. Unlike the case of his mother, Carl Emil had rather quickly adapted to the notion that his father had decided to take his own life. It made sense for him not to want to be left on his own. However, not for a second had the thought occurred to him that their father might be implicated in his wife's death.

It was another reason why he hadn't been able to bear staying in the night before, along with all the other thoughts preying on his mind. The icon and the money. The insulin. Speculations that churned away as soon as he found a quiet moment.

The mood in the family had been, as might be expected, rather tense ever since he and Rebekka had ousted their father from Termo-Lux. Their mother had been furious when the change had become a reality, and the day their father formally stepped down from his position as chairman of the board she had appeared unannounced at Carl Emil's apartment a couple of hours after the meeting at a time when she could be reasonably certain to find him at home. He had never seen her so angry. She lectured him sternly about the virtues of decency and loyalty as they sat facing each other in his living room, before concluding her visit by raking him over the coals and reiterating the inviolable nature of family ties.

It was clear to him then that their mother had been far more affected by what had occurred inside the company than their father himself seemed to be. But then, he was a businessman and had always kept business life and family life separate.

Carl Emil buried himself deeper into his duvet.

Ungrateful, she had called him when she left the apartment that day, and after that he had hardly seen her again.

Fatigued, he reached over to the bedside table and found his watch. He had booked a Spinning session at the gym, and it started in half an hour.

Reluctantly, he pulled back the duvet, forcing himself to get up. Besides everything else, he was looking at almost half a billion kroner disappearing out of his hands if he did nothing but lie in bed nursing a hangover. If the Angel of Death was still on his parents' property, it had to be retrieved so Miklos could close the deal. But he realized there was a very real risk that it wasn't just the copy that had been taken.

So much money, and so close. He took a deep breath and told himself he needed to pull himself together and keep a cool head. *Just keep calm*, he coached himself, padding bleary-eyed to the bathroom and finding the aspirin in the medicine cabinet, his mouth dry as sandpaper. But his sister was right and he wasn't calm at all. Before long the media were bound to cotton on to the police suspecting their father of their mother's murder, and when they did all hell would break loose.

He showered quickly, went back into the bedroom and put on some workout clothes, stuffed a pair of jeans and a shirt into a bag, and found his keys.

❧

A floral display meant for a coffin had been left on the mat outside.

A wreath with a spray of white and blue flowers whose powerful aroma greeted his nostrils as soon as he opened the door. A flourish of curly gold lettering on the accompanying silk sash said REST IN PEACE, and a card had been inserted between the stalks.

He hesitated for a second before bending down and plucking the small envelope from the meticulously worked display. He held his breath as he opened it and removed the card inside.

THE ANGEL OF DEATH, it said.

Carl Emil dropped the card immediately and leaped back inside the apartment as if his legs had suddenly been licked by flames.

He stood collecting himself for a moment in the hall, but then when another door opened somewhere on the stairway he stepped quickly forward again, picked up the wreath, and took it inside. His heart thumped in his chest. He wondered fleetingly if it might be some kind of coarse practical joke and whether his friends at that very moment might be gathered at Café Jorden Rundt enjoying a good laugh at his expense. But they knew nothing about the Angel of Death, unless he had been indiscreet at some point during the night's proceedings.

He hoped he hadn't.

Once, they had sent a stripper out to another of his friends when they knew he was entertaining important business associates at home, and only a couple of months ago Carl Emil himself had bought plane tickets for the whole crew and surprised them all with a weekend trip to Nice. Having made sure they all met up at Café Victor on Friday afternoon, he sent them all home again to pick up their passports and nothing else before they all piled into a couple of taxis and headed off to the airport. But that had all been good, wholesome fun, nothing that could possibly cause offense.

No, none of them would ever dream of sending a funeral wreath.

He slumped down on one of his tall Starck chairs and stared out over the harbor of Tuborg Havn. His thoughts felt like porridge, a vague and inseparable mass. The only thing that seemed clear to him was the fact that someone had left a death threat outside his door while he had been asleep.

Fear gripped him like a sudden onslaught of winter, and all of a sudden he was freezing cold, his teeth chattering.

❦

"We've got to find the Angel," Carl Emil began when Miklos Wedersøe picked up the phone.

He told him about the funeral wreath and the white card.

"They want it. And they're going to kill me to get it."

The words rattled breathlessly out of his mouth despite his trying to remain calm. The shock of what had happened had leaked into his blood and was now an agitated unrest racing through his veins.

His mother's murder had very nearly gone undiscovered. If the same people were now after him, they had already demonstrated with all conceivable clarity just what they were capable of.

"What makes them think I've got it?" he asked, as if begging for an answer.

He took a series of deep breaths, struggling not to lose it completely in a bout of panic. His heart pounded.

"We've got to find that icon."

"Take it easy," Wedersøe replied calmly. "Why would they want to kill you?"

"Because they've killed before!" Carl Emil almost screeched. "Maybe they killed my father, too. We don't know!"

"Let's not discuss it on the phone. Come down here instead and we'll talk in person. I've got a meeting with the cathedral parish council at twelve, but after that I'm available. How does two o'clock sound?"

"Fine, yes," Carl Emil snapped back, annoyed by his attorney's priorities. "I'll try and find the icon while I'm waiting, shall I?"

He rummaged around for a big garbage bag under the sink, pressing the wreath and the card down into it before hurrying out to the elevator. He scurried to his car, dumping the bag in one of the green trash containers at the side of the building on his way.

He tried to appear relaxed as he climbed inside the Range Rover. As usual, the private parking lot was deserted, yet his eyes scanned the area twice before he reversed out. At the first red light he thumped the steering wheel impatiently with the flat of his hand, then tore off along Tuborgvej toward the highway the moment it changed to green.

※

"It's possible you're right," Miklos Wedersøe conceded when Carl Emil repeated his assertion that whoever was trying to get their hands on the Angel of Death had also left the funeral wreath outside his door.

Before his meeting with the attorney, Carl Emil had stopped off at Termo-Lux and had actually spent almost an hour searching possible hiding places for the Angel of Death. To begin with he had gone through the vast new storage facility, where consignments of window frames and panes were stored in meticulous order. Then he had searched the rooms under the roof and those in the basement. Finally, he had rummaged through his father's private cupboards.

Having no luck, he had then gone over to the old storage building a short distance from the main premises, where regular non-thermal glass was kept stockpiled, some of it dating back to his grandfather's day. He hoped until the very last that the icon would emerge before him, hidden away among the oldest and most forgotten items, but eventually he gave up without having found so much as a trace of its precious stained glass.

"We don't know who removed the reproduction from your father's office, so it would be rather difficult to state for certain that they have now come back," Wedersøe said, opening a small plastic bag and handing a paper napkin across the desk.

Carl Emil nodded, admitting that this at least was true. He had no idea when the Angel of Death had disappeared. It had been some time since he had last set foot inside his father's home office. He had simply no business there after all the trouble started with the takeover. Most likely Rebekka hadn't, either, he thought, unless it was she who had taken the icon.

"But we have to take this seriously," Carl Emil reiterated, reaching out for the sandwich his attorney handed him.

Wedersøe looked across the desk at his client.

"I can assure you I'm taking it very seriously indeed," he replied. "But if we're to discuss the matter properly you're going to have to calm down. As things stand, the police seem to have your father marked down as prime suspect in the case of your mother's murder, but I'm afraid we must accept that you, too, are of some interest to them in that respect."

Carl Emil closed his eyes.

"I spoke to Nymand late yesterday afternoon. He told me their forensics team found no signs of unlawful entry to your parents' property. What they did find, however, was that the digital surveillance device at the front door had been deactivated, and from that they secured what they think might be a number of leads that have been sent off for analysis. Nothing would seem to indicate that anyone forced their way into the house. Which means either your mother let her killer in herself or else that person was already inside. The police are leaning toward the latter and suspecting her family."

Carl Emil opened his eyes and nodded. "But they don't know about the Angel," he said quietly.

Wedersøe agreed. "And for good reason. Nevertheless, it might be expedient for us to explain to them how things might be connected. Then we can let them go through the property and confiscate the real icon if it should come to light."

Carl Emil hesitated before objecting:

"But that would mean forfeiting any sale."

Wedersøe folded his hands behind his head and tipped his chair back.

"That would be a consequence, yes," he concurred. "But wouldn't money be secondary if someone really is out to kill you?"

Carl Emil screwed his eyes up against the sun that slanted brightly in through the window. He felt the acute need for more aspirin.

"I wouldn't put it like that," he replied, popping two pills from the blister package in his pocket. "The question is more whether to put up with being threatened."

He swallowed the pills with a mouthful of the coffee Wedersøe had poured into his cup.

"I intend not to," he went on. "But I need to get hold of that icon. If someone is trying to get to me, it's because they haven't found it, either."

"So you want me to keep the police out of it?" Wedersøe ventured.

Carl Emil nodded firmly. "Let them proceed from their theory my father did it. What do you think their next move is likely to be?"

The attorney wiped some crumbs from the desk pad and looked thoughtful.

"I imagine they'll put a missing person notice out for your father through Interpol. Domestically, they'll intensify the search and go public in the media. I don't think you can avoid being put through the mill again."

Carl Emil supposed he was right.

"I'm going out to the estate now to turn the place upside down," he announced and got to his feet. "If I can't find it I'll have to get Rebekka to help me."

"If you can't find it, she's not likely to, either," Wedersøe added rationally.

Carl Emil smiled.

"If it's there, she can find it. If it's not on the estate, then it must be somewhere on the company premises. No one knows the place even remotely as well as she does. I'd have to get her involved, there'd be no two ways about it."

"Even if you talk her into helping you search for the icon, and even if you manage to find it, your sister made it very clear that she would not be party to a sale," Wedersøe pointed out. "And if her mind really is made up, nothing you could say would ever convince her."

"On the contrary," said Carl Emil. "I think I know something that might."

14

Grete Milling had brought a thermos of coffee and proper mugs with her for the journey. She and Melvin sat in the back, chatting quietly all the way there. In the front, Jonas slept, his legs drawn up underneath him, leaving room for Dina on the floor in front of his seat. He didn't wake up until Louise pulled into the parking lot in Hjerting where Jeanette had lived. She switched off the engine in front of the complex of two-story red-bricks with their little gardens facing the road.

"There it is, over there," said Grete, pointing in the direction of number 12. "My daughter's flat's on the ground floor."

The buildings were arranged in a chain of five on one side of a paved footpath, with three more on the other side that seemed to be a bit bigger. Beyond them, Louise saw a large lawn area with benches and tables dotted about, but here in February, the overall impression was bleak and dismal.

Melvin reached out and helped Grete Milling out of the car. She had already taken the keys from her bag and handed them to Louise.

"You go in first, I'll come in a bit," she said and remained standing with Melvin while Louise and Jonas went up to the building.

Next to the entrance door they found the mailbox with Jeanette's name on it. It didn't look like there was room for any more junk mail or free newspapers: they spilled, wet and pulpy, from the slot, a telltale indication that it had been some time since anyone had been there to empty it.

The hall was rather small. Against the wall, a small white dresser was placed under a tall, wood-framed mirror with some finely carved edging. Very feminine, Louise noted, stepping forward and opening the only door that led off.

The living room, too, was neat and prim. The walls were painted white and the room had an airy feel about it, Louise thought, glancing at the dining table with its four wicker chairs. Against the wall at the other end was a comfortable white sofa on which big Indian-inspired cushions with shiny spangles in the middle were arranged, while on the wall itself some generic floral prints hung in frames. The few books on the shelf next to the sofa were ordered according to color. There was a vase in the window with some withered flowers in it.

The room that presumably formed a centerpiece of Jeanette Milling's life contained not a single indication of anything even remotely masculine. The only thing Louise thought stuck out in all the neatness were some dirty marks from someone's shoes on the light-colored rag rugs.

The police probably hadn't bothered to wipe their feet when they came to investigate the place, she thought, returning to the front door and doing so herself once more for good measure.

Jonas lingered in the hall. "Wipe your feet properly," she instructed him. "And keep your coat on, it's freezing in here."

He nodded and went back to the mat.

"You think she's dead, don't you?" he said as Louise stepped toward the living room again.

For a moment she considered lying, but she decided not to. "I'm afraid it's likely, yes."

"It's like she just went out to work," her foster son commented as he followed her into the living room.

He was right. Apart from the dust and the dirty marks on the rugs, anyone might think Jeanette Milling had just gone out. There was a newspaper folded on the coffee table and on the kitchen counter a teapot in its cozy. She might just as easily have been at work like Jonas said.

Louise went over to the coffee table and picked up the newspaper. It was dated July 21, the day Jeanette had gone away. She put it down again and went into the bedroom. The bed was made, covered by a floral-patterned throw with small cushions arranged casually at the head. Jeanette had obviously had plenty of time before leaving. Louise stepped up and opened the wardrobe. Tops and blouses lay in neat piles on the shelves. Dresses, skirts, and cardigans hung from the rack.

"She wasn't short of things to wear," Louise mused. Some of the items looked expensive. Wouldn't she have taken some of them with her if she had disappeared to start a new life somewhere?

Louise opened the little cupboard under the bedside table. On the top shelf was a small, leather-bound jewelry box containing an assortment of rings, earrings, and necklaces. Some of them looked like heirlooms. She put it down on the bed so Grete Milling could look through it, before bending down to see what was on the lower shelf. Behind a tube of hand lotion and a lip salve there was a dildo in its case and an opened packet of condoms, so it seemed Jeanette had not been entirely virginal.

She heard Melvin and Grete come in through the front door and closed the cupboard again.

"I've brought a moving box and some IKEA bags with us," Louise said as Grete emerged into the living room. "I'll just go and get them."

They had about an hour before the moving men would be there to pack everything away.

"I've left your daughter's jewelry box on the bed," she added on her way out.

"I'll come with you," said Jonas. "I'll take Dina for a walk."

Louise smoothed her hand across his hair. He had grown pale, and she could tell the reality of the situation had gotten to him. The trauma of vacating the rectory was still there. They'd spent almost a week clearing the place out, and every night after they got home Jonas had cried himself to sleep.

She shouldn't have let him come. He could easily have gone to see Camilla and Markus instead. Louise had suggested just that, but he had declined. She wondered if he and Markus had fallen out with each other, and whether that had been the reason he had gone off that day when they came over, but she didn't want to ask and he had been as sweet as ever on the way over in the car. She just couldn't see what his teacher had been talking about.

Her eyes followed him as he went and opened the car door with Dina's lead in his hand. The yellow Labrador leaped out, wagging not just her tail but her entire hindquarters before straining the lead in the direction of the lawns where she obviously needed to pee.

Louise called out to Jonas to say the dog's water bowl was in the back of the car. Then she took the moving box out and went back to the flat.

Inside, Grete Milling had already put a few items on the dining table, among them the jewelry box. She had placed a chunky gold ring on top of it, which she indicated to Louise when she came back in.

"That was her father's wedding ring. She talked about having a goldsmith turn it into a ring she could use herself. Obviously, she never did, so I'd like to have it back."

Louise nodded.

Grete Milling smiled. "Jeanette had so many plans, but it wasn't always she found time to carry them through."

"I think we all know that problem," Louise replied affably, giving Melvin a hand assembling the box. "What about her clothes?" she added, stepping into the little kitchen where Grete had opened a cupboard and was carefully stacking some Royal Copenhagen china on the counter.

"All to be packed. If she doesn't come home I'll give them to the charity shop," she answered, concentrating on the china.

"She's been collecting this series ever since it first came out," she said with a smile. "Blue Fluted Mega. Every Christmas and every birthday she'd get something new to add to it."

The kitchen was orderly in the way of someone older, Louise thought, turning her attention to the fridge with its reminders and recipes, and a couple of party invitations stuck up with big magnets, a work outing in August and someone's thirtieth birthday in September, dates long since passed.

Her thoughts wandered as the china mounted up on the counter.

What sort of person collected dinner sets? She felt she was a long way off anything quite as grown-up herself, despite her fortieth birthday now looming. She managed perfectly well with the anonymous white plates and dishes she had bought on the cheap when Peter walked out on her and took the Italian set with him.

"I've got enough of my own at home, but still."

Louise nodded. She well understood. The expensive items had probably been gifts from Grete herself.

She went back into the bedroom, where a door led out into the bathroom. A small washing machine took up space in the corner. The shelves by the sink were crammed with all manner of lotions, scents, and hair products. Jeanette Milling had a marked preference for the more exclusive brands. There were several bags of cosmetics, too. Louise wondered if she had even taken anything with her on vacation. She herself had only a single little purse for her makeup. But Jeanette must have packed some toilet articles, since there was no toothbrush or toothpaste on the shelf under the mirror where she might be expected to have kept them. Nor was there any shampoo or soap in the shower cabinet.

Louise heard a rustle and tearing of paper from the kitchen, where Melvin and Grete Milling had obviously started packing the china. She returned to the bedroom and stood for a moment, taking in what she saw.

She looked out the window and noticed that Jonas had let Dina off the lead. He had found a stick he could throw, and the dog kept leaping into the air to catch it before it landed.

There wasn't much life in the area for a Saturday afternoon, she thought, her gaze passing over the unlit windows and empty gardens. It had started to drizzle, so maybe it was no wonder people were staying indoors.

"Is there anything from the bathroom you'd like to keep?" she asked as she walked back into the living room.

Grete Milling shook her head. "I've found a couple of things in the living room here, and then there's Jeanette's photo album. I think it's on the shelf over there."

She nodded to indicate a tall glass-paneled cabinet behind the dining table.

"At the bottom."

Louise went over and opened the front. At the bottom was a row of ring binders and a padded photo album. She crouched and pulled out a couple of the binders. The police would already have checked them out, but she flicked quickly through nevertheless.

Birth certificate, insurance papers, receipts for the rent. Exactly the kind of documents everyone kept. The next binder contained various papers from the bank, statements from her account, and an overview of her pension plan. She had some savings, almost two hundred thousand kroner, money deposited regularly over the last six or seven years.

"That's a tidy little sum your daughter's got saved up here," Louise blurted out in surprise and looked up at Jeanette's mother.

Grete Milling nodded and smiled. "She's good with her money. Always putting aside every month. She's been working at the physiotherapy clinic for quite a few years now, so it all mounts up. She was saving for a car to begin with, I think, but she still hasn't taken her test, so I imagine she was just being sensible," she said. "It's always nice to have something for a rainy day."

Louise nodded and could only agree, though it wasn't what she practiced herself. She kept a little emergency fund so she wouldn't have to borrow if the washing machine broke down, but that was it. Nothing at all that could be called savings.

She put the ring binders back and placed the photo album on the table with the other things that were being packed. Melvin helped carry the moving box out to the car. The Blue Fluted Mega was heavy. They took the IKEA bags back in with them.

In the living room Grete Milling was having a last look around. Louise didn't really know what she had been expecting, perhaps that the elderly woman would sit down and cry, but the way she was going about the place it seemed more like she was bidding her daughter a quiet farewell. There was something very touching about the way she smoothed her hand over the back of one of the wicker chairs, the armrest of the sofa. Silently she walked around the flat saying good-bye, and was quite serene when shortly afterward she came over to Louise and told her it was time to lock up and leave.

Louise stood for a moment and surveyed the room. Not for one second did she believe that Jeanette Milling had planned her disappearance. Nothing of what she had seen here gave her the slightest reason to suspect that the flat's occupier had not been intending to return.

She locked the door behind her and phoned Hans from the moving company to tell him she had left the key under the flower-pot by the front door.

Then she cast a final look up at the building, before calling for Jonas and Dina so they could all head back to Dragør.

15

"I gather you were over in Esbjerg this weekend," Superintendent Willumsen said, stopping Louise in the corridor after the Monday-morning conference in the lunchroom. "Don't count on time off in lieu, even if Rønholt did promise you overtime."

"I'm not counting on anything," Louise replied curtly, turning into her office and switching her computer on.

"What's he doing with himself?" Willumsen inquired with a nod toward Lars Jørgensen's empty chair.

Her work partner hadn't come in yet. She told Willumsen he had to collect his twins at their mother's and take them to school.

"He'll be here by ten at the latest," she said, fully aware that she was waving a red rag in Willumsen's face.

"It's like a rest home for pregnant nuns, this department," he moaned before turning his attention back to Louise. "We don't have the resources for you to be running around wasting time on cases that don't belong to us."

She let out a sigh. Her boss was notorious for roping people in from HQ's other departments if he happened to be short, but was always less than inclined to lend anyone out himself.

"What I choose to do in my spare time is my own business. You were on vacation last week, so I couldn't have asked you anyway," she said, trying her best to sound ironic.

Willumsen sat down on the low bookcase inside the door. Only then did she realize Lars Jørgensen had managed to get to the bottom of his pile of case folders. The shelf was cleared—he must have even taken the lot down into the archives. Job done. So much for Willumsen's rest home. Willumsen himself, however, was of course oblivious. He was just chewing her out to be on the safe side.

"Rønholt wants to borrow you for one more day to go through the Milling case. Claims it needs a fresh pair of eyes."

Louise looked at him in anticipation.

"I told him no. You shouldn't be wasting your time on it. The girl's missing, that's all there is to it. The case is cold. She'll turn up herself if she wants to," he proclaimed, resolutely folding his arms in front of his chest.

Louise tipped back in her chair. "That's where you're wrong," she said quietly, trying not to get his back up. "Jeanette Milling didn't disappear of her own accord. There's absolutely nothing to indicate she did. My view is she fell victim to a crime."

Willumsen shook his head. The dark sheen of his hair shimmered in the light, the little knot of his tie drawn tight against his throat. His vacation had done him good, she realized suddenly. He had seemed so tense recently. Pressured and uncomfortable. She guessed things were more serious with his wife than he was letting on. Or maybe he himself wasn't well. As trying as it was, Louise was perfectly capable of making allowances for his gruff demeanor and blunt words, as long as he didn't drive the whole department mad with his insufferable moods.

"She didn't disappear of her own accord," she repeated. "Anyway, you've no need to worry about lending me out, because I've already read the case file. I borrowed it when I was over at Rønholt's on Friday and went through it over the weekend. I don't suppose he reckons anyone ever works more than they get paid for."

Willumsen smiled feebly. "So you think something happened to her?" he said, dropping his arms to his sides.

Louise nodded. "A drowning accident maybe, but then you'd think her body would have washed up by now," she said. "But whatever happened to her, there's no doubt at all in my mind that she didn't just decide to walk off."

"All right, I'll get in touch with Rønholt myself and tell him what you think. He won't have to bother me anymore after that," Willumsen concluded with some satisfaction, barely concealing the fact that he would be chalking the kudos up to his own account for her having read through the report on her own time.

"You do that," said Louise, studying him with anticipation when he remained seated on top of the bookcase. Clearly he was about to bring something else up.

"I saw in the paper this morning the police down in Roskilde are suspecting old Walther Sachs-Smith of doing his wife in," he said eventually, screwing his eyes up slightly as he asked if she had heard anything about it.

Louise frowned, instantly annoyed with herself at not having looked at the paper herself before leaving for work. After Jonas and Dina had moved in she never usually got around to reading it until the evenings. Most days it tended simply to join the pile on the kitchen floor. She had more than enough to do with making dinner and Jonas's packed lunch.

"Seriously? How did they work that out?" she blurted, shaking her head in astonishment.

"It does sound a bit mysterious," Willumsen conceded. "But if you ask me, so is the fact that Nymand and his people are reopening the case following information given to them by your friend Camilla Lind."

Louise tried to look nonplussed. She had known perfectly well what had been coming and had decided to stay neutral, promising Camilla not to say a word about her meeting with Walther Sachs-Smith. In return, she had insisted on her girlfriend keeping quiet about Louise having been in the know.

Willumsen studied her. "I gave Nymand a ring, just to get the lowdown on what had happened to make them reopen the case."

He folded his arms across his chest again and tilted his head slightly to one side.

"And guess what? It seems they'd spoken to Camilla Lind at your insistence. Which then led them to do some new tests on the blood samples they'd taken after the old woman's death. God knows how she might have talked them into it. It's a very expensive business once you have the foreign labs involved. But all of a sudden there it was, bingo! The results show Sachs-Smith's wife most likely didn't kill herself after all but died from a lethal injection of insulin. Now they reckon the sleeping pills were just to make her drowsy and camouflage a murder."

Louise couldn't think what to say.

"What does Camilla Lind actually know, I wonder?" Willumsen mused, leaning forward with his hands propped against his knees.

"Wasn't there some story about her carrying on with the eldest son when she was over in the States just recently?" he went on, apparently having paid more attention to watercooler gossip than Louise had realized.

"Yes," she replied. "She did an interview with Frederik Sachs-Smith when she was in Santa Barbara."

Willumsen nodded. "I thought so."

"I can't help you any more than that," she said, a feeble attempt at bringing the conversation to an end.

He brushed the matter aside with a swipe of his hand in the air. "Not important. I'd like to speak to her myself. Get her to come in to my office sometime today. I'm curious to know what sort of info she sniffed out over there. She knows something about that family, that's for sure."

"What, so you can gloat at Nymand's expense?"

Louise couldn't help but laugh. Willumsen had always been drawn by the high-profile cases, but she had never before known him to encroach on one that so obviously belonged to another police district.

"Absolutely not," he snapped. "But we'd be able to offer assistance if we knew something they didn't."

She shook her head at him. "I didn't think we had the resources to be offering ourselves out to other people's cases," she rejoined matter-of-factly. "I'll make sure Camilla gets in touch, but only if I can pop over to Rønholt in return."

Willumsen jumped back to his feet with a satisfied nod.

"You do that, then. Tell your friend I'll be available after lunch."

"Walther Sachs-Smith did not kill his wife. I've never heard such rubbish," Camilla burst out angrily. She was seated in Willumsen's office with a cup of canteen coffee. "I've just spent all morning in a broom cupboard at Roskilde Police Station being questioned by a bunch of pinheads staring themselves blind."

She tossed her head shrewishly and glared at Willumsen.

Louise remained silent in the background. Camilla and Willumsen had enjoyed some quite spectacular clashes over the years, but oddly enough for the moment it seemed they were both on the same side.

"You may be right," Willumsen conceded. "But there's a reason why Nymand reopened the case, and that reason came from you."

Camilla folded her hands deliberately on the table in front of her, making no attempt to conceal how carefully she was weighing her words, before nodding and acknowledging that his assumption was correct.

"There was a reason, of course. And a very good one at that. It concerns the Angel of Death," she replied, pausing to consider Willumsen's reaction.

Louise's superior raised an eyebrow and asked Camilla to clarify. "I'm afraid I'm not quite with you there," he admitted.

Camilla shook her head. "Clearly not. Nymand wasn't, either. Every time I mentioned the Angel of Death he cut me off and wanted to know about my relationship to Frederik Sachs-Smith instead. Nymand's convinced Frederik must have put me onto something."

"Did he?" Willumsen rejoined.

Camilla stopped herself and threw up her hands. "I can't go into any detail as to how I received my knowledge. As a journalist I'm bound to protect my sources, as you well know," she said, staring directly at Willumsen across the table. He nodded, though Louise noted the crease that had suddenly appeared in his brow.

"The day Inger Sachs-Smith was killed, the Angel of Death disappeared from her husband's office. It had been hanging there on the wall for twenty-five years and in all that time it had been a well-kept family secret," Camilla explained, leaning slightly forward toward Willumsen as she spoke. "We're talking about a very old Byzantine treasure that ought not to be in the family's possession at all, though the finer points of that discussion aren't entirely relevant for now. The fact is, however, that this icon would be a highly prized target for some very wealthy collectors."

"What did Nymand have to say about this?" Willumsen inquired with interest.

"He'd never heard of it, and who could blame him? I gave him a copy of this."

She produced a plastic folder from her bag and tossed it down in front of him.

Willumsen picked it up and spread the documents it contained out on the table. The sheet at the bottom was a list.

"The figures are in Danish kroner," Camilla said, watching him as he read:

Jackson Pollock canvas: 833 mill. kr.
Picasso's "Nude, Green Leaves and Bust": 630 mill. kr.
The Wittelsbach Diamond: 140 mill. kr.
Blue and white jar, Guan Yuan dynasty: 130 mill. kr.
The Jenkins Venus (late 1st, mid 2nd century): 68 mill. kr.
Hind in bronze (10th century), Umayyad dynasty, Córdoba, Spain: 31 mill. kr.
Mamluk enameled glass jug, Egypt or Syria: 28.3 mill. kr.

"Famous artifacts change hands for the most exorbitant sums," she said, studying Willumsen as she paused.

"These are items sold at auction by Sotheby's and Christie's," she then went on. "All of them registered artifacts that can be bought and sold freely on the open market. Similar antiquities and art treasures without certificate of registration are in a different price class altogether on the illegal market."

Willumsen studied the figures in silence. When he was finished he looked up at Camilla but said nothing.

"What I'm trying to say here is that these things can be very valuable indeed. As such, I think the police should be interested in finding out who removed the icon from Walther Sachs-Smith's office the same day his wife died."

Willumsen nodded pensively. "That could have been Sachs-Smith himself," he pointed out. "Anyway, I don't see how this would alter Nymand's perception of things. If we ignore the possibility of Sachs-Smith having taken his own life after his wife's death and instead proceed from the assumption he killed her and then went into hiding, the most obvious thing would be for him to have secured his most valuable assets first, wouldn't it?"

Camilla shook her head and closed her eyes for a second before looking up at him again.

"What Walther Sachs-Smith had hanging on his wall wasn't the real icon. He wasn't that stupid. It was a copy," she said, explaining how Sachs-Smith had commissioned the reproduction many years previously. "But the fact remains it disappeared on the same day his wife was killed."

Willumsen smiled thinly. "If it wasn't that valuable, then there's not much of a motive, is there?" he ventured, gathering the documents together.

Camilla gave him a look of exasperation. Louise watched as the entire gamut of her friend's emotional register passed across her face. For a moment she looked like she was about to cry, but then she slapped her hands down hard on the table in front of her.

"Just believe me, will you?" she burst out, her coffee cup dancing momentarily in its saucer. "He didn't do it!"

Her outburst made Willumsen jump.

"You're looking in the wrong direction. This is all about the icon!"

The next instant she was leaning into Willumsen's face.

"How much do you know about Carl Emil and Rebekka ousting their father from the board of his company when they negotiated the takeover at Termo-Lux?"

Willumsen shrugged, conceding he knew little more than what had been in the papers the previous autumn.

"The two of them are completely without scruples," Camilla went on. "They're more than capable of going all the way, make no mistake. They've just shown the entire country they hold nothing sacred. Walther and his father built that company from scratch, and yet that pair had no moral issues whatsoever with kicking him out and cheating him out of a fortune in the process."

"I don't know the finer circumstances, but as I recall it he was bought out," Willumsen put forward hesitantly.

Camilla cut him off. "Wrong. This was the meanest, vilest takeover you could imagine, and I for one am amazed they got away with it. My guess is their parents were reluctant to air the family's dirty laundry in public. By rights it should have been a matter for the fraud squad," she added.

"Where does the icon fit into that?" Willumsen looked like he'd lost the thread.

"It all hangs together," Camilla exclaimed. "It shows how little they give a damn. Those two would sell their own grandmother if they could make a buck and get away with it."

"And kill their own mother?" Willumsen queried, aghast. "Is that what you're saying?"

"Insulin," Camilla stated more calmly. "Don't you think it's rather a coincidence the son's got a whole medicine cabinet full of the stuff at home?"

The police superintendent said nothing.

"It's certainly more likely than their father having done it," she said after a moment.

Willumsen got to his feet and stepped over to the window that faced out onto Otto Mønsteds Gade. He stood with his hands buried in his pockets and seemed to be miles away as he rocked on his feet. Then he turned back to Camilla and fixed her in a stern gaze.

"Where is he?" he asked. "You met him, didn't you?"

When no answer was forthcoming he looked across at Louise.

"Do you know anything about this?"

One, two, three, four…Louise tried to count to ten, concentrating as hard as she could while staring back at him and shaking her head. When she'd learned that the Mid and West Zealand Police suspected Walther Sachs-Smith of murdering his wife, she had tried talking Camilla into telling them about their encounter in Hawaii.

Willumsen went over to where Camilla was seated and placed a paternal hand on her shoulder.

"I want you to be fully aware here that you may be in breach of the law concerning the withholding of evidence in a murder inquiry. That's an offense that may be penalized with a term of imprisonment."

He gave her shoulder a squeeze before going back to the other side of the table and sitting down again.

"So where did you meet him?"

Camilla shook her head. Louise had prepared her for the fact that holding back such important information could lead to charges, but she had stood firm and seemed now to be continuing her stance regardless.

"You can stop that right now," she said, unrattled by the reprimand. "I came here because you asked me to, even though you've got nothing whatsoever to do with the case."

She sat motionless for a moment before changing tack.

"But you're right," she said. "I did meet him. Walther Sachs-Smith is alive and well, and do you want to know why he's keeping a low profile?" she asked, spitting sarcasm.

Louise pulled her chair closer to the table, astonished that Camilla was now suddenly deciding to come clean about Walther Sachs-Smith. Moreover, she was quite aware that their meeting with the superintendent had now switched from an informal chat at Willumsen's behest to an interview that would be going straight into the case file in Roskilde.

The line that had formerly creased Willumsen's brow was now gone and he leaned forward in anticipation. "That would indeed be rather interesting," he said with a nod. "Do tell."

"He's keeping a low profile until, with my help, he finds out who gained entry into his home the day his wife died."

"And I take it you're not going to tell me where this meeting took place?" Willumsen suggested.

Camilla shook her head and smiled at him for the first time.

"Correct," she replied. "But maybe now you can understand why I'm so exasperated about Nymand being so blinkered that the only suspect he can think of is Walther."

"But you haven't told him what you just told me," Willumsen came back at her. "I think perhaps you should."

Camilla picked her bag up off the floor, gathering the documents off the table and putting them back in the folder.

"Yes, I suppose I'd better," she nodded, rising to her feet. "But you're going to have to back me up. Otherwise he's going to carry on along the same track."

Willumsen did not reply, but he stood and opened the door for her.

"Thanks for coming," he said as she stepped out into the corridor.

※

"Rather a handful, isn't she?" he said with annoyance after closing the door behind her. "I'm sorely tempted to charge her, just to make her really understand how serious a matter this is."

Louise stepped over to the door. She paused and studied him as he picked up the phone, listening while he asked to be put through to Nymand a moment later.

"You owe me," was the first thing he said, ignoring Louise's presence completely. "She spilled. Walther Sachs-Smith is alive and she's met him. I don't know if he's paying her or what kind of a deal they've struck, but it seems he's got her running his errands for him. She claims he's been forced to keep his head down, but if I were you I'd get someone over to his son's place in Santa Barbara, and that vacation home of his in Hawaii. It wouldn't surprise me one bit if the old man was shacked up there."

Louise marched back to her office and slammed the door shut. She was seething now. Nymand had gotten Willumsen to angle in on Camilla because he'd been unable to get anywhere with her himself, and Willumsen had tricked Louise into helping him out.

"The lousy bastard," she spat, switching off her computer and calling Rønholt in Search to make an appointment.

"He's in conference all day tomorrow over at the National Police. How about Wednesday first thing? I'll make sure there's some nice fresh pastries for you," Hanne suggested. "How does that sound?"

"Fine, thanks," Louise decided.

She wasn't thinking of asking Willumsen's permission.

16

6:52 p.m. Emerges. Walks down street, waits. Carl Emil jotted the words on his pad.

He had been keeping the dancing school under surveillance for almost two hours, and on the few occasions someone had walked past the car he had hidden his face from view behind some documents that lay on his lap for the purpose.

His head was spinning and he felt exhausted after another round of questioning in Roskilde. For several hours the woman detective had come at him about the insulin. How much did he keep at home? How often was it dispensed to him? She had bombarded him, and when he told her, she asked him again.

He had tried to explain that people with diabetes always had to keep a stock of medicine in reserve. He kept some in the car, for instance, and at the office. But the killing had occurred six months ago and he simply did not keep track sufficiently to be able to prove it if there was some he had not taken himself.

He rubbed his eyes and sensed the onslaught of a splitting headache.

Nevertheless, he remained seated, fully concentrated with his eyes fixed on the door of the building. He had also been inundated with reporters phoning and wanting to know what he and his brother and sister had to say about the police suspecting their father of murdering his wife.

"No comment," he had told them from the outset. But after his interview at the police station he had stopped answering his phone altogether. He had even left his cell phone at home on purpose.

The news was everywhere. Splashed all over the newspapers, the lead story on TV and radio. Carl Emil had switched on the news channel before leaving, only to switch it off again just as quickly when helicopter coverage flashed onto the screen, the camera circling over his parents' property. Down on the ground, viewers could indulge in the sight of a couple of photographers who had somehow managed to intrude all the way up to the house, and the estate manager doing his best to keep inquisitive members of the public at bay. He had also noted a single police car parked on the gravel, so apparently they were still there.

Now he was here outside the dancing school. As luck would have it, a big Volvo had pulled away from the curb just as he had arrived, allowing him to secure a parking spot from where he had a clear view of the school's imposing entrance as well as the path leading around to the parking lot at the building's rear.

He had picked up his niece there on a number of occasions after her lesson, but otherwise it tended to be his sister's Filipina au pair Marybeth who brought and fetched. She had dropped Isabella off today, and she would soon be back to collect her again.

Carl Emil studied his niece as she stood waiting. It was dark now, and his eyes followed her as she went and stood under the light of a streetlamp. He knew Isabella was scared of the dark. Her au pair would never make her wait in back, where the parking lot was so dimly lit.

Some five minutes later Marybeth came zipping up in Rebekka's Mini Cooper. She turned into the lot around the back and shortly afterward came scurrying into view holding a cell phone to her ear. She waved to Isabella while still talking, beckoning her toward her.

Isabella had a small sports bag slung over her shoulder and she seemed genuinely happy, dancing a few steps as she skipped along the pavement. She looked like she was bursting with things to tell, but the au pair was far too occupied by her phone call and didn't have time to listen.

Marybeth wasn't exactly the most punctual of the au pairs Rebekka had had in her employment, Carl Emil noted with satisfaction.

As she and the girl began to walk back to the car, he glanced in the rearview mirror and saw the way his niece's dark hair bounced against her down jacket's shiny exterior. For a moment he had been afraid she would recognize his car, even though he was parked on the other side of the street, but she had not looked in his direction and now she disappeared into the darkness and out of his field of vision.

❧

He had been following his niece all afternoon, having made the decision on Sunday evening.

After his meeting with Wedersøe on Saturday he had driven

out to the estate to search for the Angel of Death. He could see the police had been there the day before, but fortunately at that point the media had yet to get wind of the suspicions against his father. That thought at least was a relief as he sat and stared toward the parking lot entrance. Nevertheless, his search had been fruitless. He had looked everywhere inside the main house and had also gone through the attic, the two large wings, and the outbuildings without any sign of the icon. And to be honest with himself he had no idea where else to look.

The problem with his parents' property was that there was no junk piled up anywhere. The estate manager made sure of it. There wasn't a blade of grass out of place, on Walther Sachs-Smith's express instructions. Carl Emil had even been through the barn where the farm machinery was housed, though with just as little success.

He started the car and the climate control kicked in immediately, blasting out its air and causing the pages of his notepad to flutter. He turned it down, glancing up in expectation of the headlights appearing from the parking lot.

He drummed his fingers impatiently on the steering wheel while his thoughts wandered to his sister. He had driven over to her on Sunday afternoon to tell her about the wreath he had received. To begin with she refused even to listen to him, but when he mentioned the silk sash with the gold lettering she grudgingly acknowledged it could seem like a death threat.

REST IN PEACE.

The message was hard to ignore. And yet she quickly turned it around, wondering if she herself might in any way be in peril.

How typical, Carl Emil thought, feeling the anger rise up inside him once again. She could take advantage of him when there was something she wanted, yet wash her hands at the slightest unfavorable complication. She had snapped at him and told him it was only fair that he should be the target if anyone really did want to harm them. By putting the Angel of Death on the market he had confirmed to anyone who was even slightly awake that the icon was in the family's possession.

⚘

The idea had taken shape while he had been sitting in Miklos Wedersøe's office, and later, as he drove home from visiting Rebekka, it became increasingly clear to him that if they were to secure his sister's help he would have to get to her in some way. He realized rather quickly that her only weak spot was her daughter.

His niece attended dancing school on Mondays, Tuesdays, and Thursdays. It was a somewhat strenuous program for an eight-and-a-half-year-old child, Carl Emil thought, but he knew Isabella was keen on it.

The routine was always the same: She would arrive and be dropped off at five fifteen and spend approximately an hour and a half in class before being collected again.

It was usually the Filipina au pair who drove her, Rebekka seldom managing to get home early enough. He failed to comprehend why his sister felt she had to work as much as she did. Termo-Lux had no need for her as CEO with all the other executives drawing their huge salaries to make the wheels go around, but his sister devoted herself anyway, her entire identity seemingly dependent on the title. She loved it when the gossip magazines referred to her as Denmark's most beautiful businesswoman.

It had been a long time since he himself had stopped going to work every day at the company headquarters in Roskilde. Now he concentrated on being prepared for the board meetings, and Wedersøe was instructed to inform him if there was anything he thought Carl Emil needed to be involved in. Decision making and the like.

But for the last forty-eight hours he had been focused entirely on his eight-year-old niece.

He adored her, and always had. Sometimes it felt like he was closer to Isabella than to his own mother. Often, they did things together that Rebekka would never dream of doing with her. They had gone on trips to theme parks like Lalandia and Djurs Sommerland, and to Disneyland in Paris. The latter especially had been thoroughly enjoyable.

They were taking their time, he thought, a spike of unease jolting him back to the matter at hand. Was there some other way out of the parking lot that he wasn't aware of? Or had Marybeth clocked him after all?

At that same moment a pair of headlights swept over the curb as they pulled out of the lot. Without signaling, the Mini turned out onto Helligkorsvej and set off in the direction of Byvolden.

Recognizing the vehicle straightaway, he ducked down across the passenger seat and waited until they passed. He gave them time to vanish from sight beyond the first curve of the road before turning the Range Rover's ignition and pulling out in their wake. There was no panic. He knew where they were going, so he drove sensibly and kept his distance.

He opened the window slightly and lit a cigarette, sucking in the smoke until the ember glowed red in the dim light, savoring the rush of nicotine that immediately settled his restless nerves. He had been so close to losing focus while he waited.

The darkness made the imposing homes of the Sankt Jørgens-bjerg area seem like oases, issuing their rays of warmth out into the cold of winter. There was little traffic; the roads were quiet as he entered the roundabout by the Viking Ship Museum without braking, his thoughts circling on Isabella. He needed her if he was going to convince his sister to help find the icon.

Before the Angel of Death they would be absolved of all their sins, he thought to himself, his eyes on the red taillights up ahead.

What crap. Wedersøe had dug up a pile of material about the icon and its history, but Carl Emil had barely been bothered to read a word of it. It was quite sufficient for him to know how much the Angel of Death was worth in cash.

Half a billion kroner, if he split with his sister. The figure made him dizzy.

When he had spoken to Wedersøe earlier in the day, the attorney had told him his American contact had phoned, anxious to have the deal confirmed. Fortunately, Miklos had succeeded in keeping him hanging on and they had won a couple of extra days to get things sorted out.

He thought about the wreath again. It took quite a bit to unnerve him, yet he realized he was not a courageous man, and he certainly was not unaffected by someone leaving a coffin display outside his door. Maybe he was getting paranoid, but he found it spooky nonetheless that it had been left there the day after the police had started investigating his mother's death as a murder. He asked a couple of his friends if they by any chance had been around to his apartment, but if they knew what he was talking about they certainly had not let on.

All this was distracting, and all of a sudden he found himself too close to the Mini Cooper when it pulled up at a red light. He had not seen the flashing turn signal and had been unprepared when the vehicle had switched into the turn lane. His foot left the accelerator and stamped the brake, though too late for him to be able to pull up behind, forcing him to draw up alongside them instead. And there they waited, window-to-window. When the lights changed he would have no option but to carry on straight ahead.

He swore under his breath and flicked his cigarette out of the window. He felt observed, and fought the urge to put his foot down and speed off. He leaned his elbow against his side window, concealing his face behind his hand and staring at the road. Then the lights changed and the Range Rover's turbo thrust him forward as he pressed down on the accelerator. Having passed through the lights, he considered turning back and trying to catch up with them again, but swiftly dismissed the idea.

He decided it didn't matter. He knew Marybeth picked his niece up from school and drove her home, and that just after five she would drive her to dancing school and collect her again ninety minutes later.

He had it sussed and could just as well go home and wallow in a hot bath. He felt cold and his body ached from sitting in the car for so long. He turned the radio on and put his foot down, the Range Rover responding like an arrow as he headed for the highway.

⚜

He pulled up at the curb outside Sticks'n'Sushi on the Strandvejen and inhaled three cigarettes while pacing the pavement and waiting for his meal. He added two beers and a tin of wasabi peas to the order and paid in cash. It was one of the things he had decided to do from now on: He didn't want anyone being able to trace his movements, so instead of using his credit cards he withdrew cash from the bank. He put the bag of takeout food down carefully on the passenger seat and climbed in.

The radio was playing the Rolling Stones. Carl Emil cranked the volume up and drummed on the wheel as he turned toward Tuborg Havn. For the first time since Saturday morning the feeling was absent: the sense of an iron fist gripping him by the neck, steering his actions without him knowing who it was holding him so firmly in their talons.

He sang along as he entered the underground parking facility and was still humming to himself when he cautiously lifted the bag out of the car so as not to disturb its contents. He wondered whether to go out a bit later on. Though it was only Monday there was sure to be someone he knew at the wine bar, but then again he had no desire to be bothered by journalists and decided against it.

He sang to himself as the elevator slid up through the building. The doors opened. As he stepped out, the bag of sushi dropped from his hand onto the landing's dark terrazzo.

In front of his door was a headstone, the block letters of his name painted crudely on its surface:

CARL EMIL SACHS-SMITH
   Born 06.06.1972
   Died 18.02.2010
   Rest in Peace

Someone had decided when he was going to die. He had less than three days.

He picked his bag of sushi off the floor and found his keys in his pocket. When he closed the door behind him he was crying.

17

No," Camilla repeated and stared at Nymand wearily. "I have absolutely no reason to believe that Walther Sachs-Smith is responsible for the murder of his wife. But it doesn't seem to matter what I say, does it? You don't believe me anyway."

The chief superintendent cleared his throat. "That's not entirely true," he protested. "I believed you enough to have the new batch of analyses carried out—"

"Yes," Camilla cut in, "and I was right, wasn't I? So try at least to entertain the assumption that what I'm saying now might be right, too."

Following her talk with Willumsen in his office, she had been summoned to the Mid and West Zealand Police in Roskilde at nine that morning. They had already been through the formalities about her risking being charged for withholding information, and

Nymand had eventually accepted that she was entitled up to a point to protect her source.

"You don't really think Walther Sachs-Smith would be asking you to direct your attention to his wife's death if it was he who had killed her?" she asked, looking him in the eye.

Nymand did not reply.

"I'm willing to tell you all about my meeting with him, but I'm not going to say where we met. It's got no relevance."

"Very well," said Nymand, tipping backward in his high-backed swivel chair.

"Walther Sachs-Smith was present at a board meeting on Fyn when he received a phone call from the family housekeeper informing him of his wife's suicide attempt. At that point the ambulance crew had yet to arrive on the scene, so Inger Sachs-Smith had not yet been pronounced dead," Camilla began. "Naturally, he broke off his meeting immediately, but while he was in the car he received another phone call. His wife had failed to respond to any resuscitation attempts."

Nymand nodded while she spoke. So far everything she had said was already in the report.

Camilla wondered for a moment whether she ought to have contacted Walther to square with him how much he wanted her to tell them.

Too late now, she thought. Besides, there was no sense in holding anything back if she was meant to relieve him of a murder suspicion.

"His attendance at the board meeting has been confirmed by the others who were present," the chief superintendent put in.

Camilla nodded without comment.

"He disappeared after the service on the day his wife was put to rest. Having thanked the mourners, he drove home and packed a small suitcase. He left some personal documents and his wallet on his desk and went directly to the airport, taking with him his passport and a couple of credit cards allowing him access to his foreign bank accounts."

"Why?" Nymand interrupted. "What reason did he have to leave in such a hurry?"

Camilla folded her hands in front of her and took a deep breath.

"He already knew when he was called home from Fyn that Inger had not taken her own life, but to begin with he was unable to make sense of it. It was only that same evening when he withdrew to his office with a bottle of whiskey and his consuming grief that he discovered the icon was missing from the wall."

She paused as she noticed the same crease appear again on the chief superintendent's brow.

"There were any number of valuables on the Boserup property that a thief might have made off with. Anyone unfamiliar with the history of the Angel of Death would be highly unlikely to have targeted the icon."

Nymand had no time to interject before Camilla went on, relating the story of how the art treasure had fallen into the hands of Walther Sachs-Smith's family and how for almost forty years they had retained the secret of its continued existence.

"The day Inger died he was scared," she explained. "He realized someone was after the icon, and he knew that whoever it was had killed his wife in order to get their hands on it. That's why he elected to leave the country as soon as the funeral was over."

"And the original icon is still in existence?" Nymand inquired.

Camilla nodded. "What's more, he intends to exploit the fact in order to lure his wife's killer into the open," she said. "However, that won't be an option until you realize that his wife was indeed murdered and that the two things are connected."

Nymand nodded pensively now.

"Benefit of the doubt, I suppose," he mumbled, before adding somewhat more clearly: "He's always come across as a very decent and honest businessman, so it's not that I don't want to believe him."

"Anyone not knowing about the Angel of Death would be bound to suspect him, it stands to reason," Camilla prompted. "But you have that information now."

He acknowledged that she was right.

"Is he really somewhere abroad? Or is he still in Denmark?" Nymand probed, leaning forward in his chair. "And how would he be intending to go about this?"

Camilla shook her head, unwilling to answer the first of his questions, unable to answer the second.

"It would certainly make our inquiries a lot easier if we could talk to him ourselves."

She nodded and told him she was perfectly willing to facilitate the contact, but that she would have to speak to Walther first and let him make the first move.

"Does he have any idea himself who might be after this icon?"

"He has a list of names, people with a conceivable interest. He's willing to send it to you, but not before you're convinced there's a connection. There are a number of international collectors, fanatics he calls them, who have shown an interest in tracing the object. He keeps himself informed on the subject and has collected all the articles that have appeared in the professional journals. I'm not sure if there's anyone he actually suspects, though."

"Tell him we'd like to speak to him and that we're naturally very interested in pursuing any lead he might provide as to his wife's murder. However, we need something more to go on if we're to get started."

Camilla was just about to stand up when Nymand took a deep breath and continued:

"Remind me again of your own private involvement in the Sachs-Smith family."

Her jaw dropped in surprise and she fell back in the chair, wondering if she ought simply to ignore the question. At the same time, she was annoyed by the fact that he still seemed to be doubting her even after she had been straight with him about what she knew.

"My involvement is no more than I've already stated. I met the man and listened to what he had to tell me. I've no other ties to Walther Sachs-Smith than that."

"It was more his eldest son I was thinking about," the chief superintendent clarified.

"I'm not involved with his son, if that's what you mean," she said curtly.

Nymand raised an eyebrow.

"As I understood it, the two of you were seeing each other at some point, is that right?"

"At some point, yes. But not anymore," Camilla replied, rising to her feet to escape the piercing gaze that now drilled into her private sphere. She strode to the door and opened it, only then turning to say good-bye, and shutting it quickly behind her as she left.

In the corridor she paused for a moment and closed her eyes. She had been prepared for the eventuality that he would ask her about Frederik and had even worked out what she would say in reply. But when the question came it had thrown her completely.

She walked toward the staircase, descending to the big glass entrance doors that led out into the parking lot.

She missed him and thought about him all the time, no matter how much she tried not to. They had been so good together when she and Markus had stayed with him in Santa Barbara. He had come over to visit her twice after they came home again, and now he was doing everything right, calling her and sending her flowers.

It was his quiet demeanor that drew her so compellingly. His equilibrium. The way he was so much more than simply his rich father's son. Indeed, he seemed so unaffected by his family's wealth, trusting instead his own singular talents. She had fallen for all these things, but he was still so far away. It was going to hurt once they got around to realizing that geography would work against them. She had decided to spare herself the pain.

But hurt did not diminish for being self-inflicted.

She sat for a while in the car before feeling ready to drive home, toying with the idea that perhaps she ought to pull out of this whole business concerning Walther and the death of his wife, and put the family behind her once and for all. Every time she returned to the matter of his father and the agreement they had made, she thought of Frederik, too. But it was no good; she couldn't just pull out of a promise. Besides, she was already at work on the articles.

18

There were three messages for Naja Holten when she stopped by reception on Tuesday morning. All three concerned the premiere of her new movie. The film company's PR department wanted her to confirm some interviews that were being slated for immediately after her return home so they could appear in the newspapers on the day of the premiere. Breakfast TV wanted her, too, and the national broadcasting company DR was inquiring about a phone interview for the TV news that same evening.

There was a message from Jesper as well, asking her to call. He missed her.

The cold blast of the lobby's air-conditioning made the tiny hairs stand up on her forearms, so before sitting down at the guest computer to reply to her press secretary she popped back to her room to pick up a cardigan.

She tossed her bag on the bed, picked up her cell phone, and went back out.

It was more a feeling, an instinct rather than any physical sense, that alerted her. Was someone lurking there, at the end of the corridor? She closed the door behind her and stood still for a moment. But there was no one in sight.

Shaking her head as though to dismiss the thought from her mind, she turned and started back toward reception, sensing her fright subside as she went. At the bend in the corridor she glanced back over her shoulder to reassure herself there was no one there, not even a shadow in the dim light.

She purchased half an hour's Internet time, instructing her press secretary to arrange her schedule for the days surrounding the premiere as she saw fit. By the looks of it she could expect to be rather busy. The thought pleased her, and although as ever she felt apprehensive about the upcoming reviews, she realized she had rather a good feeling about what lay in store.

She checked her Facebook, rereading her status about warming up to the premiere with sangria and flamenco, smiling at all her likes and the comments from friends wishing her well and saying how much they were looking forward to it.

"Señorita Holten?" a man inquired in Spanish, stepping toward her and holding out a very large bouquet of flowers.

Naja rose to her feet and nodded. She had no idea what else he said, but accepted the flowers with astonishment. The girl in reception beamed at her, the same one who had checked her in on arrival.

"Boyfriend?" she asked, gesturing toward her floral compliment.

Naja gave a sheepish shrug as she removed the little card that was attached to the cellophane with sticky tape.

Now it begins! Five-star review in Woman's Weekly *next week—hurrah!*

"Yes!" Naja exclaimed, and almost punched the air with joy. The flowers were from the PR department. She could see the text was cut from an email. *How kind of them*, she thought.

Now suddenly she was looking forward to going home again and smiled to herself at the thought of the people in the film company's office whose contacts had tipped them off in advance about the review.

She decided to celebrate, and with the flowers in her arms she strode off immediately to book a table at the hotel's expensive restaurant. Passing by the small indoor fountain she encountered the man who had been standing behind her in reception the day she arrived. He looked away before they made eye contact.

She stood for a moment before a waiter came to ask how he might help her. The fat reservations book lay open on the counter and she noted how busy the place would be, but if she was prepared to dine rather early they could manage a table at six. She arranged a vase for her flowers before going out onto the patio and ordering a drink topped with a cocktail umbrella.

"The new stove came yesterday," said Jesper when she phoned home. "But the stupid delivery guy left it at the curb. It weighs a ton, so I haven't gotten it inside yet."

She laughed and could hear the dog in the background wanting to play, as always when they were on the phone.

Her drink arrived and she had them charge it to the room.

She missed them madly all of a sudden. Jesper had taken time off work to get the kitchen organized while she was away, and she loved him for it.

"Your mother's invited us for dinner on Saturday, so I was thinking I could come and pick you up at the airport and then go straight there. How does that sound?"

"Fine," she said, and had the feeling that she had already been away far too long, even though it had only been three days since she came.

"I got some wine in, just in case you want to invite some people back after the premiere," he said.

Again, she marveled at how well he knew her. A few days before she left she had told him there was no way she would have the energy to throw a party after the formal celebrations the film company would be laying on. But it was her movie, and of course she would celebrate. The news of the first review had already vitalized her. She told him about the flowers and the message from the PR department and could almost hear him smile.

"You knew!" she exclaimed.

"Hmm," he admitted. "What's more, I know *Politiken* is planning a big feature article, so you've got every reason to celebrate."

She blew a kiss into the receiver and told him how much she was looking forward to coming home. Then she finished her drink and decided to go back to her room and soak in a hot bath before dinner.

The wind was cool when a couple of hours later she started toward the restaurant, and though it was still early it was already turning dark. The sun descended toward the sea, and the twilight was slowly engulfing the pool area. From a distance the restaurant looked like a grotto filled with candles that flickered invitingly. She followed the walk that edged the hotel parking lot before turning down onto the little pathway that led to the entrance.

She did not see the shadow, yet sensed immediately the sudden snap of breath at her rear, unable to react swiftly enough before the cloth was pressed down over her nose and mouth. Seeking to lash out, she realized her arms were held immovably at her sides. Desperately she tried to kick her legs, only for her strong assailant to tighten his grip and quash her every effort. The bitter smell of ether stung in her nose and caused her to gasp for air, but she found her respiratory tract blocked, and her arms began to tingle and turn numb. The twinkling entrance of the restaurant up ahead dissolved before her eyes, the pungent liquid sending her tear ducts into alarm, abandoning her to fog.

Thoughts flashed in her mind: the movie, Jesper, their dog and cat, the new kitchen. Everything she had been so looking forward to coming home to.

During all the many hours she had spent with the laptop on her knee, immersed in her manuscripts, her creative mind had concocted all manner of scenes. Often, she had found herself moved by the stories she wrote, and occasionally she had delved so deeply into her characters' thoughts and emotions they had seemed almost to become a part of her, inseparable from her own being. Yet never in all her life had she imagined that death would be so lonely an occurrence.

Her thoughts merged and vanished as the night drew close around her. Naja Holten felt fear, then lost consciousness and slumped in the arms of her attacker.

19

Her skin glistened as if she had just stepped out of her bath when he finished rubbing in the body oil. Meticulously he wiped his hands with a clean towel and scrutinized the results of his work to make sure there was nothing he had missed.

Not that it was actually necessary to finish the job in this way; it had just occurred to him at some point how fine it would be, like concluding a sentence with a neat full-stop.

He had not done so with the first of his women, having simply transferred her directly into the display cabinet once the silicone had hardened underneath the heat lamps. Her skin had been satisfactory enough, if lacking somewhat in luster. Actually, it had been rather dry and neglected-looking, he had begun to think, and that was when it had occurred to him to apply body oil.

He went into the next room, switched on the ceiling light, and satisfied himself that all was ready. He had assembled the display case and mounted it on the podium he had draped with black velvet. He paused and absorbed the moment.

Her final destination, he thought, returning to the gurney. Now she would rest, preserved for time to come, and all thanks to him. Her body transferred easily to the display case, but as he leaned forward to carefully lower her into position, she almost slid from his arms and her shoulder left a greasy smudge on the inside of the glass. He averted the danger deftly, his hand moving swiftly beneath her to grip her by the neck.

There was no give in the hardened silicone, and the oil made it difficult for him to hold her in place.

Abruptly, he froze. It felt almost as if she had moved in his arms. As if from some unimaginable beyond she had tried to resist and flee his grasp. Instinctively he released her, allowing her to slide down into the display where she then lay askew, her hair dangling untidily over the rim.

He knew it was silly, and yet he glanced quickly about the room as if in some rational attempt to locate the source of the unfamiliar fear that had suddenly come over him, the ridiculous notion that the woman was alive and reacting to her fate.

Shaken, he went out into the room containing the acetone freezer, finding a bottle of household spirits on the chemical cart and pulling a microfiber cloth out of the drawer. Now her fair hair was tarnished by the body oil on his hands. He poured some spirit onto the cloth and dabbed at her locks, rubbing the scalp gently to remove the substance, though with no satisfaction at the result: A tuft of blond hair stood out, not nearly as silky smooth as the rest, despite his having washed her hair while she lay under the heat lamps, even applying conditioner for that perfect sheen.

Angrily he tossed the cloth onto the floor, immediately taking a series of deep breaths to calm himself. It was imperative he keep a cool head now. He had taken such care throughout the entire process, and everything had turned out exactly as he had wished. Yet now, suddenly, he was losing his head, and there was no one to blame but himself. Here, in the final stages, he had begun to waver, his thoughts wandering this way and that. He realized the fact, but felt powerless to make them stop.

He stepped up to the wall and leaned momentarily against the cold brick for support. It occurred to him that he might have collected fine wines like so many other men with a passion and money to spend on it. Perhaps he might even have gained some of the same pleasure, passing through his cellar, noting with satisfaction the labels of his many vintages. But he knew his desires did not extend in such a direction. The pleasures might well be similar, but vintage wines were too banal, collectible to anyone, providing they could afford it.

His collection by contrast was unique. No one else in the world had what he had in his cellar. The joy that gave him was the ultimate satisfaction. Now and then he would imagine owning his own island with no access permitted for anyone. He would be gripped by the fantasy of moving freely amid the beauty he had created around him without having to hide it all away under the ground. And when he closed his eyes he was almost there in his mind: his very own paradise.

Many times he had indulged himself online, searching for such a place. But private islands cost money. He was a wealthy man, certainly, but twenty to forty million dollars was completely beyond his means.

He opened his eyes again and beheld his women, and all of a

sudden it struck him that he had never before seen them for what they were: four corpses laid out in his cellar. He had always enjoyed them as individual works of art, each with its own particular expression and warmth. And there was the erotic aspect, too, the artist's ever-compelling motive.

But here they were, four corpses in their transparent coffins, and the exquisitely illuminated room transformed at once into a burial chamber whose walls seemed almost to be closing in on him. Instinctively he moved toward the door, his chest and shoulders rising and dropping as he again endeavored to take deep breaths and return to some semblance of control.

Don't panic. Stay calm.

He knew that nothing had changed merely because his perspective had altered. He had to pull himself together. Had Picasso destroyed his earlier works at his every development as an artist? Of course not, and thankfully so.

Yet he had to acknowledge that he could no longer resist. He had tried. Certainly, he had tried. But still the Angel of Death had returned to him. Now that it had been confirmed that the icon was still in existence, he had to have it. He needed to own it, to take it into his exclusive possession. There was no turning back. He could no longer fight it, and his thoughts continued to revolve around one thing only: how to create the perfect setting for its display.

Black velvet, as he had used to set off his glass cabinets, would be quite insufficient. The religious artifact required more light, and from every conceivable angle. It would hang in his cellar, yet the figure in the glass had to be coaxed to the fore, to cast its ring of light before it, just as it had done inside the Hagia Sophia all those centuries ago. He had already imagined how utterly compelling an experience it would be to step into its presence.

He closed his eyes once more and saw a large, illuminated room, white and Spartan; on the far wall would be the Angel. It occurred to him he needed to investigate backlighting if he was to achieve the desired effect, and as he stood there he found himself overwhelmed by a near-irresistible urge to break open the bricked-up windows and let the light flood into the entire cellar. Suddenly there was something claustrophobic that had not been there before. But there was something else, too: There was an emptiness.

His eyes passed over the rectangular freezer, the chemicals lined up on the stainless steel trolley, the gurney. These were objects that had filled his life and thoughts. He felt a stab of grief run through his being, like the pain of a failed love affair. A terrible longing for something good that had come to an end and was now impossible to recall.

He left the room and closed the door of his exhibition, resolving there and then to discontinue the project and shut everything down, the sordid rooms with their vile equipment. All at once he found them repulsive. It all had to go.

The project had been gratifying while it lasted, bestowing joy on his life and occupying his thoughts so completely. But he realized now that he had come to the end and needed to move on. Nothing was lost. He still possessed his women. But the fifth display case would no longer be required.

He would have to contact his supplier. He would pay for the one who perhaps even now was on her way, but the supplier would have to get rid of the body himself.

Right now though, he needed to concentrate on one thing only: keeping a cool head. After the first failed endeavor, he knew it would be no easy matter to secure the icon. But he was prepared now to go all the way and would not yield until the Angel of Death was his.

20

Carl Emil's hands were shaking. He tightened his grip on the wheel and glanced at the time. It was too early to drive to the dancing school, so he pulled in up a side street a short distance away and counted the minutes. He rolled his window down and lit another cigarette.

He had thought the procedure through so many times in the last twenty-four hours, it had become a looping sequence in his brain. On his way he had stopped off at the bank and took out some more cash, not knowing how long it would take before he found the icon.

Restlessly he flicked his half-smoked cigarette into the road and looked again at the time. Ten minutes. His plan was to park outside the school just after half past six. Now he hoped the au pair would not be on time for once.

He had spent the day making his final preparations. He had bought a few items of clothing for Isabella—some underwear and nightclothes—before driving out to the Fona electronics store in the Lyngby mall. It was a busy place, and no one would remember him being there. Standing in front of the shelves, he had spent some time selecting games for the PlayStation he normally used to play race-car and first-person-shooter games. Eventually he decided on a couple that looked like they were for girls, and then the newest SingStar complete with two mikes so they could sing together. He didn't want Isabella to endure any hardship just because he was trying to put pressure on his sister.

With the games in his basket he had moved on to the movie section. She would need something to pass the time when he wasn't there. *Dirty Dancing* or *Strictly Ballroom*. *Saturday Night Fever*. Anything to do with dance. He hoped she was old enough to watch them, and picked some *Hannah Montana* just to be on the safe side.

He took a deep breath. He wanted them to have a nice time, to lounge about on the sofa, eating takeout and candy. She loved that, but her mother hardly ever had the time.

It was now or never. He thrust the car into gear and pulled away from the curb, more nervous than he had imagined. Slowly he drove up to the junction and flicked the turn signal.

All the wrong thoughts suddenly flashed through his mind. What if he got stopped by the police? What if someone crashed into him?

It mustn't go wrong. It had to work.

The sight of the headstone outside his door returned to him. He saw the lettering, the stark white of his name on the stone. Someone wanted him dead the day after tomorrow. He had forty-eight hours to find the Angel of Death, and although he had found it hard to think clearly these past few days, he knew exactly what he would do the moment he found it. Everything was agreed with Wedersøe.

They would drive out of the country so that the icon could not be traced. Using the airport was out of the question. Wedersøe had already made arrangements for a car with German license plates to be waiting for them in Hamburg. From there the plan was to drive on to Luxembourg, where their contact was arranging for the deal to be completed. And when it was, he would no longer care about death threats. He would be out of there, and with a billion in his pocket he would never need to return to Denmark again. Nor to Rebekka, for that matter.

He had the keys to a house on the Rue des Prés and could avoid the Luxembourg hotels. There was no reason to register anywhere else but the bank where he would set up his account.

He pulled up at the curb a short distance from the arched entrance door of the dancing school. Children were already coming out along with their parents, but Isabella as usual would be expecting to be one of the last to be collected.

A little boy emerged and stood in the doorway, scanning the arriving cars.

Rain began to spot the windshield. *Damn!* Carl Emil thought. If it started raining harder his niece would stay inside. He hadn't thought of that. Then he saw the lights in the tall windows being turned off one by one.

The boy was still standing in the doorway when Isabella finally appeared. He wondered if the boy had been waiting for her.

He drummed his fingers against the steering wheel. It was a bad habit, but he was unable to keep still.

The two children stood there larking about. The boy was throwing his bag in the air and catching it again, most likely an attempt to impress her.

All of a sudden a car sounded its horn and came toward them, its headlights flashing once. The boy dropped his bag but picked it up quickly again before scurrying over the road without looking. Isabella was on her own now. She waved at the car; it flashed its lights back at her.

Carl Emil rolled forward a few meters, his heart pounding in his chest, and felt the sweat emerge on his brow. He pulled up alongside the parked cars at the curb, jumping out and forcing a smile as he called to his niece. "Where's my little dancer, then? Have you had a nice time?"

"Calle!" she exclaimed with obvious delight, immediately running up to him. "I was really good today *and* I've got new shoes."

He opened the door on the passenger side and helped her up into the tall vehicle, taking her bag and tossing it onto the backseat.

"Marybeth never said you'd be picking me up today. Can we go to your place for a bit before we go home?"

How easy children were, he thought. She looked up at him, full of trust and bubbling with excitement as they drove off.

"Of course we can," he replied, running his hand over her hair. "Your mom called from the airport. She was very sorry she couldn't tell you herself, but she had to go to Hong Kong for some meetings. I said it was okay, so she gave Marybeth some time off."

"That's so typical of her," Isabella said precociously, shaking her head exaggeratedly as if she were used to having to deal with her mother and her work.

"She sends you all her love and told me to give you a big kiss," said Carl Emil with a smile.

"Does it mean I'm staying with you until she gets back?"

"Yes, it does. And do you know what? We're going have a great time as well!"

"Yippee!" she burst out gleefully. "But what about school? I don't have my school things with me."

All of a sudden there was concern in her voice. Carl Emil reached across and tousled her hair.

"We'll just have to play hooky, then, won't we?" he replied, feeling the adrenaline pumping through his veins. He needed to calm down and act normally. "What are you hungry for? Pizza or Mexican?"

"Pizza! With shrimp and ham!"

"Same as usual, then," he said, feeling his cell phone thrum in his inside pocket. He had muted it and hoped she wouldn't hear it vibrating.

"Yes, and you'll have pepperoni and extra onions like you always do, I suppose?" she rejoined, and instantly he felt more relaxed.

Arriving home, he glanced nervously around the underground parking facility before picking up the pizzas and her bag from the backseat. Crossing to the elevator she took his arm and he swung her in the air, a game they had played ever since she was little. Three swings one way, then all the way around.

"Ow, ow," said Carl Emil, sounding like she was breaking his arm. And they laughed, just like always.

He let her press the button, but on the way up he froze. Suddenly he felt like he could no longer breathe, the muscles in his throat relaxing only when he realized there was nothing waiting for him on the doormat.

The phone in his pocket thrummed again as he closed the door behind them. He was reasonably sure it was his sister.

21

S he's gone!" Rebekka yelled into his ear once he had collected himself and answered her call.

The pizzas were on the table steaming up their boxes, and Isabella had set out the plates and glasses.

"Who is?" he asked as calmly as he could, closing the door of the living room behind him.

"Isabella! She wasn't there when Marybeth came to pick her up from dancing school."

"Maybe she just went home with one of the others?" he asked, sitting down by the big window and looking out over the harbor.

His sister's voice was strident and dry, brittle almost, he thought, as if it might crack at any moment. Her words were breathless bursts.

"I've been waiting for her to call, but there hasn't been a word.

I've tried calling the dancing school to hear if anyone's seen her. I thought maybe she lost track of time if some of the professional dancers were rehearsing. But there's no one there to pick up the phone and the office is closed."

"What about her dancing teacher, have you tried calling her?"

Now her voice did crack. "I don't even know her name," Rebekka almost whispered back. "I'm never there, it's Marybeth who goes with her."

There was a lull during which his sister did not cry but was merely silent.

"I'll come over," Carl Emil said. "You get over to the dancing school and see if she's there. Maybe she just forgot the time like you said."

The envelope was ready, and had been since the afternoon. It was on the shelf in his wardrobe.

"I'm scared," his sister breathed. "What am I going to say to the police?"

"I'll leave right away," he said. "We'll find her, I promise."

He went into the kitchen and sliced the shrimp-and-ham pizza into six equal pieces, placing two on a plate and filling a glass with cola.

"Listen, sweetheart, I'm afraid I've got to pop out for a couple of hours," he said, noting immediately the disappointment in the girl's face. He knew she didn't like to be alone when it was dark outside, and sure enough her fingers had already found their way to the ruby heart she had been given by her grandmother when she was small. Her little comforter, his mother had called it, promising her grandchild that if only she clasped the heart tightly she could be sure her grandmother would be with her in her thoughts.

What am I doing? Carl Emil wondered, anguished by the way

the child found solace in the heart that hung from its little chain around her neck.

He put the food down on the table in front of her and smiled. "Come and see what I've bought you," he said, leading her into the room he had made up for her and tipping the contents of the carrier bag out onto the bed.

The day before, he had disconnected his cable TV, making sure she wouldn't zap into a news program when searching for the kids' channels. He had no doubt her picture would soon be everywhere once it became known that one of the country's wealthiest families had fallen prey to a kidnapping.

He had unplugged and removed his landline, too, in case she missed her mother all of a sudden and wanted to call her. Not that he thought she knew the number by heart, but he felt it best to be on the safe side.

Naturally he had also considered how to persuade his sister to let the matter drop once he had found the icon and Isabella had been returned. However, it was not an issue that kept him awake. She could be difficult, certainly, but she was by no means stupid. Rebekka would never put herself in any situation that involved opening the curtains on what went on in the family away from the public glare. Faced with a choice, she would prefer by far to keep her mouth shut.

Carl Emil was convinced she would not pursue things any further after he was gone and the girl was back home where she belonged. He would even assist her in constructing a suitable explanation to prevent it getting out that her brother had deceived her because she was pigheaded enough to think she could alienate her entire family and scrape its fortune into her own coffers.

"*Dirty Dancing*!" Isabella exclaimed, holding up the box for him to see. She could hardly contain herself, her eyes already darting among the other movies he had brought her; she'd already forgotten all about her ruby heart.

Carl Emil got up off the bed and after inserting the disk in the drive he showed her where to press PLAY and PAUSE.

"It's the same as the one I've got at home in my room, silly," she said with a laugh. "You gave it to me yourself for my birthday!"

"That's right; I forgot," he said and shook his head. His mind was elsewhere. He needed to be off so he could get there before his sister got back from the dancing school.

"There's more pizza in the kitchen. I've cut it into slices."

He went into his own room to get his jacket and the envelope. He had not touched his own pizza. He felt the adrenaline rushing through his body, and the knot in his stomach had long since taken away any appetite he might have had before. His thoughts were on one thing only, which was to make the plan work. Someone wanted him dead the day after tomorrow, and now Rebekka was going to help him get his hands on the Angel so he could get away.

He went back in to Isabella's room and blew her a kiss. But the opening credits had started and she was already well on her way into Patrick Swayze land.

❧

As he drove past his sister's house he saw that the only lights were in the kitchen and the part of the basement where the au pair lived. The rest of the big house was dark.

Rain lashed through the air. He had not even thought of taking an umbrella. The only thing on his mind had been to get going. He had decided to park the car a bit farther down the road and would have to think up an explanation for why he was so wet. If she even asked.

He hugged the neighboring property's meter-high hedge as he went, avoiding the dim pools of light that fell from the streetlamps and caused the rain to shimmer against the asphalt.

He had not thought of what he might do if his sister came home before he got there. He would just have to deal with it. Improvise.

He held the envelope under his jacket. If he left it on the porch up against the front door it would not get wet, he thought, reaching the driveway and noting that Rebekka's Mini Cooper had yet to return. The big Audi was there, but if she wasn't at work she always used the Mini.

He stood for a moment and stared toward the light. Seeing no movement, he crept forward, following the outer wall of the house to the front door where he left the envelope and turned away, neither glancing around nor straightening up.

All he could think about now was getting away.

He reached the Range Rover before seeing the turn signal flash. She came toward him from the direction of the town, signaling briefly as she turned off Frederiksborgvej.

Two minutes, he said to himself. It had been that close.

He waited a few minutes before turning the ignition and drawing forward.

❦

The front door was wide open when he drove up to the house and pulled in. The light was on in the hall, and when he stepped inside his sister was sitting on the staircase that wound its way up to the first floor.

The envelope was on the floor at her feet and she was cradling a little Nokia in her hands. Nothing fancy, just a regular, basic phone.

He had thought through her possible reactions right from the start when he had begun to plan the operation, and he knew that everything depended on how he dealt with her now. And yet when he saw her sitting there with such panic in her eyes, all his preparations fell by the wayside and he forgot completely what he was going to say.

Rebekka held the phone in her hands as if it were an object she had never seen before, and he watched silently as she pressed a couple of keys to see if it was switched on.

The display lit up and she sat there quietly, staring at the tiny screen as she read the message that had appeared. After a moment the phone dropped from her hands.

"They've taken her," she said in a small, strangled voice, without looking up. "They've taken my daughter."

Carl Emil stepped forward and sat down beside her on the stair.

"I can't call the police," she said flatly.

She began to cry, leaning her head on his shoulder and weeping.

"But you must," said Carl Emil. "We'll call them right away."

22

When the phone began to thrum on Louise's bedside table, she was miles away in sleep. Jonas was going in late, so she had set the alarm for eight. It was now seven thirty.

"Morning," said Thiesen when she answered.

She sat up immediately. When the head of the negotiation unit phoned at this hour it could only mean they had an incident.

"Morning," she replied, flustered.

"Rick, we've got an abduction situation and I want you and Palle," Thiesen explained as she swung her legs out of bed. "An eight-year-old girl. Vanished from her dancing school yesterday evening. The mother received demands a couple of hours later. The chief super in Roskilde just got in touch. We're getting down there on the double so we can be set up and ready the next time there's word."

Louise had not negotiated in a kidnapping case before. Usually they were called out to suicide threats, people who had to be talked down from parapets and bridges, or perpetrators who had holed up somewhere and were refusing to come out. Sometimes they dealt with psychiatric cases trying to pull off a suicide by cop—forcing a situation to the point where the police had no option but to open fire. Only once before had she been involved in a hostage situation, a failed bank robbery in Amager where the robber had withheld three of the staff.

What she liked about the negotiation unit was how they intervened between perpetrator and police. When she worked with Thiesen she was no longer an investigator; she became instead a mediator trying to solve a conflict.

Jonas, she suddenly thought. She had been intending to get him off to school with a minimum of fuss and had arranged for Melvin to be there when lessons ended so they could gain some idea of when he was coming home.

Louise had tried talking to him several times now, but all he did was shut her out and stare at the ground. She had tried again the night before, and eventually he had gotten so angry with her he had yelled in her face and told her that she wasn't his mother. Louise conceded that he was right but also reminded him that coming to live with her had been his choice. Before she had time to apologize he had gone off into his room and slammed the door behind him.

At a loss, she had gone downstairs to see Melvin and suggested they both be more attentive and try a bit harder to be there for him.

"Is it a bad time?" Thiesen asked in response to her sudden silence.

"No, not at all," she replied swiftly.

"The address is in Roskilde, Frederiksborgvej. I'm on my way to the vehicle, so I can pick you up if you want," he offered, explaining that the girl's mother was the daughter of Walther Sachs-Smith. "Given the size of the family's fortune we should probably be prepared for demands to rise," he concluded.

The wooden flooring felt cold under Louise's feet, and the sight of her long, tangled hair in the mirror reminded her she had an appointment with the hairdresser. She would have to cancel.

"You mean it's his grandchild?" she burst out in surprise. "When did this happen?"

"The girl vanished after her dancing lesson. Someone snatched her before the au pair got there," Thiesen repeated, adding that Nymand and his people were in charge of the investigation.

"Are they asking for a ransom?" Louise asked, sensing adrenaline displace her fatigue.

"We're not sure yet," Thiesen admitted. "The contact so far has only been brief. When the mother got home after looking for the girl at the dancing school she found an envelope at the front door with a cell phone in it. The kidnappers sent her a message on it."

"What did it say?"

"It said *The Angel of Death for your daughter*."

Louise left a note for Jonas along with some money so he could buy his own lunch in the school cafeteria. She would call Melvin later on. Their downstairs neighbor was no early bird, and she decided to give him time to get up first.

She threw some clean clothes into a weekend bag along with her toothbrush, some cookies, and what fruit was left in the bowl, then closed the door behind her and went down to wait for Thiesen.

She had no doubt the story would be given maximum attention by both Police Headquarters and the media. Not that it worried her much. What did concern her, however, was that the kidnapping seemed to confirm what Camilla had told them. If they were dealing with the same people who had killed Inger Sachs-Smith, then the little girl's life was in imminent danger. Louise felt sure that whoever was responsible was convinced the family was still in possession of the priceless icon.

"Do you want your bag in the back?" Thiesen asked as the big Mercedes van pulled up in front of her and he jumped out to give her a welcoming hug.

Louise shook her head and climbed into the front, dumping her bag at her feet. At first she had been uncomfortable with the way her colleagues in the negotiation unit always hugged when they met up on a job. After a while, she understood it had to do with the intimacy and trust that always existed among them. They worked so closely together, both physically and mentally, that it gradually occurred to her how natural a convention it was.

"Palle's on his way," Thiesen went on. "And I've called Ole, but he's in Aarhus and can't get off the job he's doing over there, so I've put him on standby in case we need him."

The unit was drawn together from colleagues in various police districts across the country. Most were investigators or team leaders, and all had their own particular strengths. Palle Krogh, for instance, could maintain a clear overview of even the most complex situations. The unit's vehicle was fitted out with a small table in the back, the seats could be turned around, and there was even room for a bulletin board across most of the window space on the vehicle's left-hand side. The last time Louise had worked with Palle they had sat in the back negotiating with a robber who refused to come out of a house in Copenhagen's well-to-do Frederiksberg district.

"The Special Intervention Unit has been alerted, and they're ready to go in as soon as we know where the girl is," Thiesen continued. "Do you want to be number one?"

Louise nodded. She had been hoping to be the one who would guide the girl's mother through her contact with the kidnappers.

"Do you know much about the Sachs-Smiths?" he asked.

"Not really," she replied, going on to tell him about Camilla's encounter with Walther Sachs-Smith.

"So someone was already looking for the icon six months ago," she concluded, explaining that their colleagues in Roskilde had just reopened the case and were now investigating the death as a murder.

"How the other half live." Thiesen nodded pensively. "Do we know if Camilla Lind is still in touch with Sachs-Smith?"

He did not seem particularly surprised to hear that the wealthy businessman was still alive out there, taking the information in stride.

"I think so," Louise said, without knowing how much they actually spoke.

"But he'd be informed about the kidnapping, I take it?"

She shrugged. "If Nymand's in charge of the investigation I'm sure he'll have been in touch with her. He knows there's a connection between the two at any rate, so I assume he'll have asked her to make contact with him."

Louise leaned back against the headrest and found it strange that her friend had yet to phone if she already knew about this new and rather serious turn of events.

23

They've got your grandchild," Camilla said when Walther Sachs-Smith finally called her back. She had phoned him on the new number he had sent her in an email, which up until now he had not been answering.

Following her first interview at Roskilde Police Station and the meeting in Willumsen's office, she had written to him and informed him the police now suspected him of his wife's murder. That same evening he had responded with a new email saying that he had left Hawaii and providing her with the new phone number. Moreover, he would be shutting down his Hotmail account and promised to get back to her from another address once he had gotten settled in his new location.

Despite the allegations against him she sensed he still felt sure the police would help him as soon as they began to believe his story.

And now they do, Camilla thought. She sat curled up in a corner of her sofa. Markus had left his phone behind when he had gone off to school. It was in his father's name and she was using it now to make the call. Her own lay on the coffee table in front of her, but she was too scared to use it. Maybe she was being paranoid, she thought, but after the meeting with Willumsen it wouldn't surprise her if Nymand were tapping her phone.

After she received Nymand's voice mail, she'd started calling Walther's number at five-minute intervals.

"I'm coming home," he told her.

She could hear how shocked he was.

"I'll get to the airport right away and find a flight."

"The police would like to speak to you."

"Call them and tell them I'm on my way. But even if I'm lucky and find the flights there's no way I can get back to Denmark tonight. Tomorrow, more likely. Perhaps not even until Friday."

Suddenly he sounded so much older than Camilla remembered, his voice thin and tinny, devoid of strength.

"Do you need help with your tickets? I can book online if need be," she offered.

For a moment he was quiet. Camilla heard only the sound of his breathing until he cleared his throat.

"I just don't understand," he said instead of answering her question. He spoke so softly she could hardly hear him. "How could it come to this all of a sudden?"

He paused a moment, silent again, before going on:

"In all these years there's never been the slightest trouble with that icon. The few inquiries I've received have never been aggressive or threatening in any way. I wish now that I'd handed it in. The Angel of Death has no worth to me other than its sentimental value. To my father it was the history of the object that meant something, that was where its value lay, and I respected that after he was gone. I was always aware it was a highly sought-after piece and that there were collectors out there who would very much like to acquire it, but I never imagined it would come to this, that people would be willing to commit murder to lay their hands on it…"

His voice trailed away.

"I realize this may be asking a lot of you, but it's for my grandchild's sake, you understand," he said.

Camilla sat up and swung her feet back to the floor. "I'd like to help," she said immediately, unsettled by his despair, which came through clearly even though he was on the other side of the world.

"I don't want the police jeopardizing my grandchild's safety in any way," he continued more firmly. "They may be planning some kind of action to free her, and of course they would be interested in arresting whoever is responsible."

"Absolutely," she said. It was a highly plausible scenario.

"No harm must come to Isabella under any circumstances," he reiterated. "For that reason I shall not hand over the icon to the police. Doing so would be inviting its exploitation in some risky operation. What I want is for Carl Emil to be in charge of the exchange. Then at least we can be certain he'll do everything in his power to ensure the child's safe return. My son has always been devoted to his niece."

"We might not have any say in the matter," Camilla began, only to be cut off.

"I shall call the police myself and explain my wishes to them."

She resisted the urge to smile at the man's authority in a situation in which he hardly had a card to play.

"But I will ask you to collect the Angel of Death."

"Me?"

"Yes," he said. "It would be too much of a risk to have Carl Emil drive out and pick it up. If they're targeting his sister, I'm sure they'll be keeping an eye on him, too."

"Yes, you may be right," Camilla conceded after thinking it through.

"Do you know where the estate is?" he asked.

"I've got a GPS in the car," she said, jotting the address down in the margin of her newspaper. "But what if the icon's not there?"

"It is, believe me. Otherwise they would not have taken my grandchild."

"No, you're right."

"In the hall you will find a key to the wood house, a small brick building at the rear of the main house. When you open the door you will see there is a gap under the floor to keep the firewood aired. The icon is concealed there."

He gave her the code for the front door, and Carl Emil's cell number.

"Call me if you have difficulty finding it."

"Do you want me to take it to Carl Emil's address or your daughter's?" she asked.

Camilla sensed him thinking about it before answering.

"Take it to the Hotel Prindsen in Roskilde and check into a room there. I'll reimburse you, of course. Their parking lot is at the rear, so you should be able to take it inside without drawing too much attention. Leave the icon in the room until the exchange is set to take place."

He paused.

"Do tell me if this is too much to ask," he added after a moment, sounding rather humble all of a sudden.

"Not at all," she replied, already on her way into the bedroom to get changed. It had been a long time since her pulse had raced so fiercely, and she would have been lying if she claimed not to be enjoying it.

"I'll phone your son as soon as I'm at the hotel."

"Thank you," said Walther Sachs-Smith, and then he hung up.

24

The fjord lay dense and black behind the white house, where a pennant in Danish red and white hung limply from a flagpole. Thiesen pulled up next to the carport and together they walked up to the front door. It was opened by a young Filipina who ushered them inside and took their coats.

Nymand appeared from a door at the far end of the hall, explaining that Rebekka had fallen asleep in the sofa in her office, so they had withdrawn to the kitchen to allow her some peace.

"A counselor has been with her. Just left."

Louise nodded and greeted the chief superintendent, who was holding a small black Nokia phone in his hand.

"There's been no contact since yesterday," he told them, gesturing for them to follow him into the kitchen as he spoke, revealing that the phone in his hand was the one that had been left in the envelope at the front door and that its display still showed the kid-nappers' demand.

"We need a place to set up in the house," said Thiesen, looking at Nymand. "Do you want us in the office or in the living area?"

"I'll leave that to you. There's room enough both places."

Thiesen looked at Louise. "Where would you prefer? You're the one who's going to be looking after her while it lasts."

Louise nodded and went back into the hall to find the living area.

"Left-hand side," Nymand called after her.

The living area comprised three rooms, all looking out onto Roskilde Fjord. The first was a dining room; the two others were furnished with comfortable sofas and matching armchairs, and the room in the middle had a television.

She crossed cautiously to the office on the other side of the hall and opened the door. The view was just as impressive here. Be-sides the desk there was a small conference table and bookshelves on all the walls, as well as a sofa on which Rebekka lay asleep with her back to her.

Without a sound, Louise withdrew and went back into the kitchen.

"We'll use the two living rooms," she decided. "I'd like to get her out of the office and put her in less formal surroundings. Is that okay with you?" she asked, looking at Thiesen, who had just opened the door for Palle Krogh. Tall and rangy, Palle entered car-rying a big box he had brought from the incident van. It would be his job to coordinate all the information they received and keep a record of exactly what was said every time they were in contact with the kidnappers.

They accepted the au pair's offer of coffee and then asked her to leave again and close the door behind her before they began taking stock and Palle started to unpack.

"What do we know about this icon they're asking for?" Thiesen asked, looking at Nymand.

"We know it probably exists, but neither Rebekka nor her brother Carl Emil has any idea where it might be. It seems their father is the only person who knows."

"And what do we know about him?" Thiesen went on, without mentioning what Louise had already told him.

Nymand sighed heavily. "Primarily that we most likely were wrong in suspecting him of killing his wife. The rather serious development on our hands now would seem very much to indicate that whoever is trying to get their hands on the icon also committed that murder, as Sachs-Smith has always maintained, according to the journalist Camilla Lind. We're doing our utmost to trace him and hope very much we're going to have him home again as quickly as possible. Walther Sachs-Smith is our strongest card if we're to give the kidnappers what they want."

"Have there been other threats against the family since Inger Sachs-Smith's death?" Louise asked, glancing at the Nokia that lay on the table. It could ring at any moment, and she was anxious to speak to Rebekka so they could agree how best to deal with the situation when the call came. If it came at all, she corrected herself, and looked back at Nymand.

"None we know of," he said and shook his head. "Neither the sons nor the daughter seem to know much about the icon at all. They knew the reproduction that hung on the wall of their father's office, but that was it."

"Do we know for certain an original exists?" Thiesen put in from across the table.

Louise nodded. "I'm certain we can take what Walther Sachs-Smith told Camilla to be true. Have you spoken to her?" she asked, turning to Nymand.

The chief superintendent shook his head. "Not since this. I've left several messages on her voice mail, but I'm still waiting for her to call back."

Louise got to her feet while he spoke. "What time did you call her?"

"About eight-ish. I explained briefly what had happened and asked her to make sure Sachs-Smith contacted me as soon as she'd informed him. But she hasn't responded. Does she have any other numbers you know about?"

"I'll see what I can do," Louise promised and was just about to go when she stopped in her tracks and asked if anyone had spoken to the girl's father.

Nymand nodded.

"He's been informed. I've got two men with him now and nothing would seem to indicate he's involved in any way. He's pretty shaken up, as you can imagine."

The little Nokia made no sound, its display simply lighting up as a new message came in. It lay there on the table and for a moment, it seemed none of them was sure what to do. But then Thiesen reached out and picked it up.

His eyes darted almost imperceptibly from side to side as he read the message on the little screen before looking up.

"They want the icon tonight at nine," he said, putting the phone down.

167

"As soon as you have yourselves sorted out and ready here, I want a statement put out saying we're interested in the girl's whereabouts," said Nymand.

They needed the whiteboards and flip charts up so Palle could map their contact with the kidnappers. Every word would be written down, every time noted, so Louise could keep track of what was going on, and within the hour surveillance equipment would be concealed about the house so they could be sure Rebekka Sachs-Smith was not communicating with anyone without Louise's knowledge.

Thiesen nodded. That was Nymand's domain; the negotiation unit had no prerogative there.

"We've already drawn up a statement to the press, it's ready to go. I'll call a conference sometime this afternoon," Nymand went on.

Louise paused in the doorway. It felt strange for her not to be a part of the investigating team. The first thing the detectives had to focus on was scrutinizing the family to make sure there was nothing going on that they hadn't been informed about. It was not uncommon that people very close to those affected were involved in an attempted extortion.

But that didn't have to be the case here, Louise thought. When an heiress of one of the country's wealthiest families was kidnapped, anyone at all could be involved. The ransom was a big enough motive on its own.

None of that was her concern now, though. She was not looking for the icon or even for a perpetrator. Her sole task was to provide Rebekka Sachs-Smith with the right things to say when the kidnappers made contact again.

"I'll go and wake her up," Louise said. "We need to be ready when they come back with their instructions."

Thiesen nodded and followed her into the living area.

25

Carl Emil hadn't slept properly. He bent down to pick up the tray he kept next to the dishwasher, then took a glass out of the cupboard and some chocolate milk from the fridge.

Negotiation unit, he thought to himself, switching off the oven after heating up some rolls for Isabella's breakfast. He wondered what they did. His sister had said they had taken over half the house.

He would have to go there. Not knowing what was going on made him restless. He had not heard a word from them since he sent his message. Maybe they were waiting for something more from him, but he felt unsettled by Nymand having called in a special unit. He had to get down there and find out what their plan of operation was.

"Morning, little wonder," he whispered, sitting down on the edge of the bed with the tray on his lap.

"Morning," his niece replied sleepily and rubbed her eyes. Her long hair fanned out over the pillow as she turned onto her back and peered up at him.

Carl Emil bent forward and kissed her on the cheek.

"I've got to go to the office for a couple of hours. Here's some breakfast. And look what else."

He placed the PlayStation games he had bought on top of her duvet and studied her reaction as she picked them up one by one and beamed.

"Thanks!" she said excitedly. "Is it today we're skipping school?"

He nodded, hoping she wouldn't ask why he was going in to the office if they were supposed to be staying at home. Fortunately she said nothing and was already tearing the wrapper off her new SingStar.

"I'll be back around lunchtime," he said, with a nod toward the kitchen. "There's plenty to eat in the fridge if you get hungry."

She nodded absently, putting the games aside in favor of the TV remote.

"I think I'll watch *Dirty Dancing* again," she said.

He nodded and smiled. "You do exactly what you want, but don't forget your breakfast."

❧

Miklos Wedersøe's big Mercedes S65 was parked outside Rebekka's front door. The black van would be the police, Carl Emil surmised, as he pulled up in the Range Rover behind his sister's two cars.

Wedersøe himself appeared in the doorway as he walked across the gravel.

"We've got to talk before you go in and meet the police," he said, pulling Carl Emil aside. "Obviously, we've had to tell them about the Angel of Death, but they don't know about the offer we've gotten for it."

Carl Emil nodded and took deep breaths again to steady his nerves. "We have to tell them that, right?" he said. "They'll need to know about the wreath and the headstone, too."

His plan all along was for the police to link the kidnapping with the death threats he had received and investigate on that basis. The headstone gave him one more day to live. He very much wanted the police to take those threats seriously.

"Certainly," Wedersøe nodded. "As long as you're prepared to tell them our plans to sell the icon illegally. You could go to prison if they decide to charge you."

"Charge us both, you mean," Carl Emil hissed back, incensed at his attorney's angle on the matter. "You're the one with the contact, remember."

Wedersøe dropped his hand to his side and nodded.

"It wouldn't exactly be good for business," he mused. "But at the moment, your niece comes first. None of us could have foreseen that whoever was after the icon would take a child hostage."

Carl Emil's thoughts were a fog as he tried quickly to weigh up the pros and cons. He had a lot to lose if the sales agreement did come to light. There was more to gain if they kept it to themselves and simply informed the police that the family was in possession of the priceless artifact and left it at that.

"We won't tell them," he decided eventually. "It wouldn't give them any advantage anyway. We don't even know where the threats are coming from ourselves."

Wedersøe nodded and looked like he agreed.

"But I will have to tell them I made inquiries among potential buyers to find out what it might be worth," Carl Emil went on. "If I don't say anything about it, Rebekka most certainly will. We can show them the inquiries my father received over the years. They need to know there have been several people on its track."

Again, the attorney agreed with him, smoothing a frustrated hand over his bald head. "Your sister's at her wit's end in there."

Carl Emil walked up to the imposing front door and stepped inside. He tossed his jacket onto a high-backed chair in the hall and followed Miklos into the living area.

❧

His sister was sitting on a sofa with her legs drawn up underneath her. Her face was puffy with tears, her hair tangled and loose over her shoulders. She looked like she had slept in the clothes she was wearing: black trousers and a crumpled blouse.

She looked so vulnerable, shrouded by fear and grief.

He went over and bent down in front of her, drawing her toward him. She allowed him to put both arms around her and rock her gently without resisting.

"They want the Angel of Death tonight," she breathed into his ear.

She was no longer crying; her breathing was calm and almost unnoticeable. Only when his back began to ache did he release her and straighten up again, stepping across the room to shake hands with Nymand, who introduced him to a woman officer from the negotiation unit. The others were in the adjoining rooms, and he gave them a brief nod of acknowledgment before pulling out a chair.

"Do you have anything to go on?" he asked, looking at the chief superintendent.

"We've got this," Nymand replied, indicating the Nokia. "We're trying to trace it, but it wouldn't surprise me if we hit a dead end there. It'll be pay-as-you-go, and the phones themselves are most likely stolen or from abroad."

Abroad, yes. He had bought them in Nice not long ago on that weekend trip with his friends. He had given them one each and instructed them to leave their own in the valuables box when they checked in at the hotel, effectively banning all contact with work, wives, and girlfriends for the duration. The eight little Nokias meant they could keep in touch with each other all weekend, wherever they happened to wander off, while the surrounding world was kept at bay. He had one of the remaining seven in his pocket now.

"We're leaving the phone with Louise Rick. She'll guide your sister next time there's any contact. That way, I can assure you we're doing everything right in order to return the little girl safely home again."

"My sister informed you about the demand?"

Nymand nodded, the dark-haired woman likewise.

"None of us knows where the icon is hidden," Carl Emil continued. "So I'm afraid to say I don't know how that demand can be satisfied."

"No," Nymand conceded. "It does seem like an impasse, and we're not likely to get much further until we know where it is."

"Are you even looking for it?' Carl Emil replied. "Are you actually doing anything to help us?"

He tried to control his voice. The hours were ticking away, and he had imagined the police would be a lot more active in trying to track the icon down.

"We can't just sit here and wait," his sister said. "We must try and find it."

"I'm afraid leaving the house won't help much," Nymand cut in, rising to his feet as he spoke. "The important thing at the moment is for the kidnappers to get in touch. And your father is already in the process of releasing the icon to us."

"Our father?" Carl Emil burst out in astonishment, while his sister's jaw simply dropped.

Nymand nodded and buried his hands in his pockets.

Wedersøe, who until now had lingered in the background, stepped forward. "I think that might require an explanation," he said in disbelief.

"The explanation is that we're in touch with him and that he's promised to bring us the Angel of Death."

"I don't understand," Carl Emil stuttered.

"We don't know much ourselves yet," Nymand acknowledged, "other than that your father seems to have been staying at your brother's vacation home in Hawaii."

"You mean Frederik knew?" Rebekka asked.

"If he did, he's not letting on," the chief superintendent replied, shaking his head.

"How long have you had this information?" Wedersøe demanded, glaring angrily at Nymand.

"Not long. I received a phone call from him an hour ago. I was going to tell you, of course," he said, adding that their father was now on his way home to Denmark but they still didn't know when he might be able to board a flight.

"So where is he now?" Carl Emil inquired, suddenly feeling a need for air. He thought of Isabella back home in the guest room of his apartment. The movie was probably finished now and most likely she was watching another. He felt the pressure mount inside him as he thought of the headstone outside his door. He needed to get hold of the icon and release the girl. If his father really was coming home, he would be unable to go through with the plan; he wouldn't have the backbone. He realized immediately he was going to have to get away.

"We hope to have him back in the country within the next two days. In the meantime it'll be the job of the negotiating unit to keep the kidnapper hanging on. However, once your father has secured the icon I feel confident the child will soon be home again."

Two days.

Carl Emil's throat felt dry as he stood outside on the gravel a few moments later, collecting himself before driving home and making his niece some lunch.

26

We need proof of life before promising them anything," said Louise, her eyes fixed firmly on Rebekka Sachs-Smith.

The woman's dark hair was now gathered loosely at the neck, and she seemed almost transparent.

"You must promise me my daughter's coming home again," she said as if oblivious to Louise's words. "I keep seeing her in my mind. Such a sweet girl, and I was never there for her. I don't even know the name of her dancing teacher."

Rebekka buried her face in her hands and sat there motionless.

"We have to prepare and be ready," Louise explained calmly. "We don't know if they'll decide to phone next time, and if indeed they do phone rather than sending a text, you're the one who has to answer."

"But I can't," Rebekka spluttered despairingly in a sudden burst of tears.

"I'll be listening in and I'll help you."

"What am I supposed to say?"

"You're to say that you're doing your very best to get them the icon, but they have to understand it'll take time. Time is very important, we need to win ourselves time. But you must tell them that you've accepted their demand."

Rebekka looked up at her. "But we don't know where it is!" she sobbed.

"No," said Louise, shaking her head. "But we will soon. Your father's in touch with the police. For the moment, you and I need to concentrate on maintaining a productive dialogue with the people who have your daughter. Don't promise them you can get the icon, just keep telling them you're doing your utmost to secure it and that you need some more time. And again: Don't promise them anything at all before they can provide us with some proof of life, as we call it. You must ask them for proof that they have your daughter and that she's alive."

"How?" Rebekka replied, hardly voicing the word, her face glazed with tears.

"Ask them a question they can only answer if Isabella tells them what to say."

"Like what?"

"Like a pet name; has she got a pet name?" Louise prompted. "Or maybe something that happened at dancing school? Something special she would remember if someone asked."

Rebekka shook her head, but then her face brightened slightly as if suddenly she had an idea.

"I'll ask about Greta Garbo," she decided, explaining that it was the name of an old doll to which her daughter was very attached.

"Good," said Louise, getting to her feet again to inform

Thiesen, but then at that same moment her phone rang. Seeing it was Jonas, she excused herself and went into the hall.

"Hi," she said, fleetingly worried by him calling her during school hours, only then realizing it wasn't Jonas at all.

"Sorry to bother you," his class teacher said, causing Louise to instantly regret having answered. This was not the time for another dressing-down.

"Jonas has just been taken to the emergency room," his teacher explained.

"The emergency room?" Louise exclaimed in fright. "What's happened?"

"It seems he got himself into a fight. Now he's got himself a split eyebrow."

"Jonas? In a fight?" Louise repeated incredulously. "If Jonas has been injured it's because someone's been picking on him. He's not the fighting type."

It was the last thing in the world she could imagine.

"I'm afraid it was Jonas who started it," the teacher stated matter-of-factly.

"Who's with him at the hospital?"

"His math teacher drove him there, but obviously he can't stay with him for long. I'm afraid you'll have to collect him yourself."

"Yes, I will," Louise replied. "I'll be there as soon as I can."

"Can I just suggest that you need to take this rather seriously?" the teacher went on. "If it carries on like this, the class won't be able to have him much longer."

"Now, you listen to me," Louise put in immediately. "If there's any failure here, that failure is at your end entirely, in the classroom. And in that case you should be doing everything in your power to make sure the class addresses whatever it is that obviously isn't working. Jonas is a conscientious student, he does whatever's asked of him. He's not violent in any way whatsoever, as you well know. I'm not saying it's your fault if the children don't get along, but it certainly is your responsibility to be aware of any problems that might have arisen and to get to the root. If Jonas is behaving the way you say he is, then clearly something in the class isn't right."

Now it was the teacher's turn to interject.

"The only thing that isn't right is that Jonas Holm doesn't know how to behave."

Louise hung up promptly, trembling with rage.

She couldn't even call Jonas if his phone was still at school. Instead she rang Melvin, who immediately offered to pick him up from the emergency room. With a voice full of concern he asked about what had happened, how the boy possibly could have gotten himself into a fight, but Louise was unable to tell him much apart from the fact that apparently he was having problems at school. She had no idea why, because he wouldn't talk to her about it.

Melvin promised he would have a word with him and ask him about it, but Louise still felt dreadful not being able to collect him herself and be there for him when he needed her. His face must be a mess.

Louise felt the need for some fresh air. She dropped the Nokia into her pocket in case it rang. On the gravel outside she gulped the cold air into her lungs and had just sat down on the step when her own phone rang.

Her first thought was that it was Jonas's class teacher again, so she was surprised to hear Ragner Rønholt's voice at the other end. The head of the Search Department had never called her private number before, and she was rather taken aback to discover he knew it at all.

"Not interrupting, I hope?" he asked, without waiting for an answer. "We've got another young woman who seems to have disappeared from her hotel in Marbella. No one's heard from her since yesterday afternoon and the hotel has confirmed the bed and towels haven't been touched since housekeeping was there yesterday morning."

Louise pricked up her ears.

"She hasn't been gone long, especially if she's there on her own," she replied, surprised that he was even considering they had a case.

"True," he conceded. "But I think we can safely assume this one wouldn't be planning to go off of her own accord. She's a film director, you see, and her new movie is having its premiere next week. Immediately before she went missing she was in touch with her film company and her partner, and both are saying she was looking forward to coming home."

"Who reported her missing?"

"The film company's PR section contacted her partner. She was supposed to be doing a live phone interview with DR, for the TV news at six thirty, but when the journalist called her there was no answer. Obviously, DR called the press secretary right away and since then they've been trying without any luck to get hold of her. The partner called in last night and reported her missing."

"A film director, you say. Anyone I'd know?" Louise asked.

"It's Naja Holten."

Louise had begun to feel cold. She got to her feet, an image of the red-haired director clear in her mind.

"Who spoke to her last?" she asked, stepping inside.

"Her partner, boyfriend it seems, was in touch with her yesterday afternoon. Said she'd booked a table in the hotel restaurant, only didn't show up. No one's seen her since," Rønholt replied, pausing for a second before going on. "I called the Spanish police this morning, and the guy on the Jeanette Milling case promised to have a look and see if there were any more Scandinavian women missing in the area. I told him that if there turned out to be a connection between Jeanette and Naja Holten, there might be others."

"Has he called back yet?"

Louise heard Rønholt take a sharp breath. "He rang an hour ago. It seems that in the last two years four Scandinavian women have gone missing down there, all aged about thirty and all of them reported missing while vacationing on the coast."

"Four?" Louise exclaimed, casting a glance into the living room where Rebekka seemed to be asleep on the sofa again. "And no one's tried to link them in any way before this?" she asked, withdrawing again and stepping into the office where she sat down behind the big desk.

"It seems not," Rønholt replied. "Their cases have only gone out to police in their respective countries. Two were from Sweden, one from Norway, and then Jeanette from Denmark. No one seems to have posited any links among them. I've been trying to get hold of Grete Milling. She might be able to tell us if there were any connections among the four women."

"Try calling my downstairs neighbor," Louise suggested. "It wouldn't surprise me if he knew where she was. They've been getting to know each other, I think."

She gave him Melvin's number.

Louise got up and was about to end the call, but Rønholt had one more question.

"You've seen Jeanette's flat," he said. "Was there anything there that gave you any reason at all to think she might be part of some network, or was somehow in contact with women in the other Scandinavian countries? A reading group, perhaps, or some other such thing. Anything at all."

"I can't say there was, no. Not that I can think of. But then I wasn't really looking."

"No, of course not," Rønholt replied, swift to understand. "It would just be such an unpleasant development if it turned out they were connected in some way."

"You're telling me," Louise acknowledged. "Do you know anything about how the others disappeared, what circumstances were involved?"

"Only that they all traveled alone and vanished without a trace from their hotels."

"I don't like this at all," said Louise. "In fact I rather hope it's just coincidence, because if these cases really are connected it sounds to me like it could be very nasty indeed."

"I agree," said Rønholt and promised to keep her posted.

27

Camilla drove down the long, narrow approach, which was lined on both sides by sturdy trees. Beyond them, the bare winter fields extended toward the surrounding woodland. The big white manor house loomed up in front of her. Reaching the courtyard with its whitewashed pillars marking the entrance, she took her foot off the accelerator of her Fiat Punto and turned in.

She knew the Sachs-Smith property only from pictures in the newspapers, and as she pulled up in front of the main house her first thoughts were of an English country mansion. It was a splendid building with windows as tall as patio doors and a front entrance with wide stone steps that fanned out from a main door flanked by boxwood in big, elegant stone planters.

She parked and got out. The courtyard in front of the main house featured a circular lawn with a little fountain in the middle, and the whole area between the two detached wings extending at right angles from the main house was covered with the finest gravel.

The small stones crunched under her feet as she approached the front door. The place seemed empty without in any way appearing abandoned. Walther had told her the estate manager lived in one of the adjacent houses and looked after the family's farming interests. Camilla glanced around. Seeing no other houses from the main steps, she guessed he must have meant one that lay farther away, toward the woods.

She had already found the scrap of newspaper on which she had noted down the code when suddenly she remembered the key. Walther had explained to her that there was an extra key in the fountain. She would have to feel around for it in the cold, murky-looking water.

Stand with your back to the house, he'd said, *on an axis going from the front door to the middle of the fountain, and you'll find it.*

Camilla went over and rolled up her sleeves, almost immediately finding a small, hard plastic box with the key inside. She returned to the front door, pressed in the code, and turned the key. Nothing happened. A red lamp flashed in the alarm cabinet. She checked her scrap of paper again and pressed in the six-digit code once more, but the red lamp kept flashing. She stepped back, her thoughts milling. After a second she got out her cell phone and called Walther's number, hoping to catch him before he got on a plane.

His deep voice answered straightaway. Camilla could hear the bustle of what could have been an airport in the background.

"The code doesn't work," she said, raising her voice so he could hear her through the noise.

At first he didn't answer, but after a moment he cleared his throat.

"They must have changed it," he said. "You'll have to call Carl Emil. No, wait, I'll call him myself and get him to ring you back. Otherwise he'll be suspicious and give you a hard time. What number are you calling from?"

Camilla told him the number, and after ending the call she went down the steps and walked around to the back of the house. A brick archway with a black wooden door led between the main house and the wing to the garden. She went through and immediately saw the whitewashed structure that had to be the wood house. As she approached, she saw that the door was ajar. She ran up and opened it wide. It was obvious that someone had been there already: The neat stacks of wood were in disarray.

She paused and glanced around. The only sound to be heard was a few crows perched in the trees. The wind was cold and damp, but there was no rain yet, though the sky was heavy with clouds. She began removing the logs that lay in the doorway, tossing them back inside before eventually crouching down.

The floor was slightly raised from the ground, just as Walther had said. Camilla knelt and reached underneath. It was there. She could feel the rough iron of the frame through damp cloth and began to pull.

And then she paused.

A car came tearing up to the front of the house, the gravel crunching under its tires as the driver braked hard. She heard a man's voice call out: "Who's there?"

She scrabbled to her feet and closed the door. Her hands were dirty, and glancing down at herself she saw that her trousers were wet and stained with grass. She wiped her hands quickly on her jacket and went back to the gate in the wall. A red pickup had pulled up in front of the main door. A man wearing a fleece was peering inside her Fiat.

"Hi," she called out, switching on a smile. "You wouldn't be the estate manager, by any chance? Rebekka said I'd probably run into you."

She stepped up to the gray-haired man and put out her hand.

"My name's Camilla Lind. I'm doing a series of articles on preparing gardens for the spring. I spoke to Rebekka Sachs-Smith last week and she said I could stop by and have a look around, see if I could get an angle on the article."

He accepted her greeting, but withdrew his hand quickly.

"And when might you have spoken to her?" he probed suspiciously. Camilla's reply was preempted by the sudden appearance of a helicopter.

"I must ask you to leave the property," the man said loudly so as to be heard above the noise, making moot any explanation she might care to offer.

She was about to protest, but he cut her off immediately.

"You've got no business here. You're trespassing on private property."

"I'm not trespassing at all," she objected, feeling the plastic box in her pocket with the key inside it. If the estate manager discovered she had taken it he would almost certainly call the police.

He pointed up at the TV news helicopter. "That's the second time today they've been here sending their reporters snooping. As if that's going to help the poor girl any."

At the same moment, Camilla's phone rang and she stepped away to answer it. Although she hadn't spoken to him before, she recognized his voice straightaway. It reminded her of Frederik's and she felt a stab of emotion, even though the two brothers had little else in common.

"I understand you've spoken to my father," Carl Emil began, pausing as the helicopter passed overhead before retreating back over the fjord toward the town. "He asked me to give you the code."

"Your father's estate manager has just ordered me to leave the property, so to begin with it would be a great help if you could explain to him that I've got business here."

"And what is your business exactly?" he asked.

"The garden series I'm researching," she replied, handing the phone to the estate manager, who listened for a moment before grunting a brief reply and handing it back to her.

Camilla put her hand over the phone's mike. "Is it okay to go back into the garden again?" she asked.

The man nodded. "Can't be too sure at the moment," he mumbled by way of apology before turning back to his car.

"No worries," she said and lifted her hand in a wave.

"What has my father actually told you?" Carl Emil wanted to know once she returned to the phone.

"He's afraid the police are so intent on catching the perpetrators that it's going to compromise security when the exchange is made. Therefore he's asked me to collect the icon on your behalf so you can ensure the kidnappers release his granddaughter."

"Is it somewhere on the property?" he asked immediately. Camilla could almost hear him hold his breath.

"Yes," she replied briefly, going back toward the garden again before suddenly halting as he barked into her ear:

"Wait there until I arrive."

"No," she said, turning back and walking over to her car instead. "Someone might be following you. We can't take that risk."

She stopped him just as he was about to protest:

"I'll call you once I've got it," she said, and hung up.

She got into the car and started the engine before turning the vehicle around and reversing up to the garden gate. She ran to the wood house and flung the door open, dropped to her knees, and with both hands began to drag the icon out into the open.

It weighed more than she had anticipated. The backs of her hands scraped against the coarse underside of the wooden flooring and began to bleed. But gradually it began to move.

The Angel of Death was wrapped in a large cloth that was musty and damp, speckled with green mold.

Having dragged the first edge into view, she gasped for breath, her heart thumping so hard inside her chest she felt dizzy. She got to her feet and crouched, endeavoring to maneuver the heavy object toward her bit by bit. But it felt increasingly like it was stuck, as if the cloth was catching on something farther in. She heaved again, ripping her skin once more against the wood, when suddenly it gave and the icon came free.

Carefully she drew it out onto the lawn. A large, heavy rectangle, like an oversize stable window, she thought, glancing at the wing building whose iron-framed panes were half the size and yet still seemed imposing.

She manhandled the object upright, stooping to lift it and carry it out to the front of the house in a series of small, shuffling steps, a searing pain running through her hands.

Having negotiated the gateway, she leaned the icon up against the wall in the courtyard and opened the trunk of the car. She had already put the backseats down but found herself now unable to lift the object inside, edging it instead over the lip of the trunk space and carefully shoving it the rest of the way inside.

The sweat ran from her brow by the time it was done, and with filthy hands and blood trickling down her fingers she jumped into the car and drove away over the gravel with the stones kicking up audibly against the undercarriage. Her phone had rung while she had been struggling to extract the icon. Now it rang again, but she ignored it and accelerated away up the tree-lined driveway, her heart still pounding, sweat pooling under her hair at the neck.

She could not help but glance back in the mirror, but there were no other cars on the narrow road. She lifted her foot slightly from the accelerator, moderating her speed and wiping her face and hands with a scarf she had dumped on the passenger seat. She considered phoning Walther, but decided to concentrate on finding her way to the Hotel Prindsen.

Ten minutes later when she turned off the Stændertorvet square and passed the rear of Djalma Lunds Gård, her nerves had more or less settled again. She made a right into the hotel parking lot, continuing into the inner yard and finding a vacant slot in the row of diagonal spaces. She flipped the sun visor down and looked at herself in the vanity mirror, running her hands through her hair and applying some gloss to her lips before leaving the car and going inside to get a room.

28

"Police and the observation unit are searching the area surrounding the dancing school," Louise repeated when Rebekka Sachs-Smith again jabbed a finger at her and accused them of not doing enough to locate Isabella. "We've got personnel all over the city out looking for her."

"Who says she's even in the city?" came the despairing response.

"No one's saying she is," Louise replied calmly, having already anticipated Rebekka's charges. She knew they were a reaction to the powerlessness she felt and tried to answer as best she could. But she did not allow herself to be carried away by Rebekka's deep-seated frustration.

She had just returned to the living room after having spoken to Rønholt. The information he had passed on to her ricocheted in her mind, but she needed to keep her focus. The little girl had been gone almost twenty-four hours now and the details of the exchange needed to be in place before the kidnappers made contact again.

The mood in the living area was thick with concentration.

"Your father called Nymand," Louise said to Rebekka. "He's on his way home."

"From where?" she wanted to know. "Where's he been all this time?"

"I'm afraid I don't know," Louise replied, ignoring the woman's aggressive tone. "But he has assured us that the Angel of Death will be available this evening. Your brother will be informed once it's been retrieved."

Rebekka began to cry silently. "He should never have gone away. How could he even do that?"

Now it was her father she was blaming. Louise shut her mind to them, but the accusations poured out, as irrational as they were unpleasant.

"I understand this is hard, but believe me, we'll get your daughter back, all of us together, without any harm," she said comfortingly.

"How do you know she isn't harmed already?"

The woman's anger was again vented in Louise's direction but abated as quickly as it had arisen as she sank back into the spacious armchair and closed her eyes.

"I'm sorry," she whispered.

"That's all right," Louise said, and glanced up at the board next to the sofa.

At 1:21, they had received the instruction to have the icon ready at 9 p.m.

At 1:30, Louise had messaged back asking for proof of life—the name of the doll Isabella had been given by her grandmother.

At 1:32, the kidnappers had texted again: *Greta Garbo*.

As Palle wrote the message times on the board, she had sent a new text asking for a photo of Isabella.

It had yet to come.

"What will they do to her?" Rebekka whimpered, addressing no one, then exploding suddenly in an outburst of rage, hammering her fist down into the armrest of the chair: "That fucking icon!"

"What is it about the icon, Rebekka?" Louise inquired as if nothing had happened, sensing for the first time during the hours they had been together that something significant might be on the verge of being revealed.

Rebekka's eruption had been so sudden and swift it was hard to know for sure if it had occurred at all.

"Nothing," she said calmly. "I just fail to see how it can be so important that someone would take my daughter for it."

"What's the story behind it exactly?" Louise went on, trying to sound interested without coming across as too inquisitive.

"It was a coincidence it even fell into our hands," Rebekka replied wearily.

"Has it ever been appraised?"

"No," she answered, clenching her fist briefly, but long enough for Louise to notice. "But to a fanatic collector, I suppose it's priceless."

"But you haven't actually had a figure put on it?" Louise said.

Rebekka shook her head. "We've never had any plans to sell it, and as far as I know there's no certificate attached that would mean it could be sold aboveboard. To be frank, though, I've never bothered to look into it."

"But those kinds of objects do change hands quite often," Louise ventured. "Illegally."

Rebekka gave a shrug.

"Why aren't they sending that photo of her?" she snapped, changing the subject in a flurry of agitation.

"They're just playing for time. It's not that important. But we'll have a problem on our hands if we don't have the icon by nine o'clock."

The Nokia vibrated harshly on the table.

Confirm exchange 9 p.m., the display said.

Louise got to her feet and went to consult Thiesen, who was sitting in the far room with Palle. Besides updating the boards, Palle Krogh collated the stream of information from the Roskilde Police and together with Thiesen picked out what Louise would pass on to Rebekka and what for the time being they would keep to themselves.

Although Thiesen was in charge of the negotiating unit overall, for this operation he had appointed himself as tactical adviser to the three-man negotiating cell he had been instrumental in setting up. He stood up and followed Louise back into the living room where Rebekka was seated.

"Do we confirm?" Louise asked as he stepped over to the window and stared out at the fjord.

"In my estimation, it's too early," he said, having considered the issue for a moment.

"Of course we confirm!" Rebekka burst out, leaping to her feet. "You tell them we're sticking to the agreement. If my father promised to retrieve the icon, then that's exactly what he's doing!"

"We confirm nothing until we have the icon," Thiesen determined, turning to Louise. "You must keep them hanging on. Ask again for a picture of the girl and tell them we can confirm nothing until we know she's alive and well."

Rebekka slumped back into her chair. She was pale, but no more tears were forthcoming, and no more outbursts.

Louise sat with the little Nokia in her hand and worked out what to say before her fingers began to type in the words:

Unable to confirm until photo received.

To begin with they had considered allowing Rebekka to type in their messages herself, but had eventually agreed that Louise would handle such practicalities. The media had already broadcast the fact that the negotiating unit was operating from the child's home.

She sat for a moment and read the text through before pressing SEND. It was the first time she had communicated entirely by text messages in a negotiation situation.

Nymand's people were hard at work on a trace, but such things took time and were a highly complicated matter when pay-as-you-go was involved.

Cannot guarantee child's well-being if deal unconfirmed within hour.

Rebekka sat up in her chair as the new message beeped in. Louise smiled at her reassuringly.

"They know it takes time," she said to her, returning immediately to Thiesen to confer.

"They're issuing threats now," she whispered, showing him the message. The two of them exchanged glances without speaking before Thiesen gave her a nod and Louise sat down on an armrest to write back.

Isabella your responsibility. Deal off if harmed. Proceed or stop?

Louise sent the text and sat for a moment with the phone resting on her thigh as she looked out over the water.

She felt her pulse rise and knew the message she had just sent could be a very unpleasant turning point. The best thing was always to negotiate face-to-face where you could decode the body language, read their faces, and use gestures to shade your words. Second best was to speak on the phone where you could read the tone in their voices. Text messages were a much more difficult medium. The words were so stark and irretrievable and could never say enough.

She went back into the living room and sat down in front of Rebekka. Neither of them spoke, but Louise could tell by looking at her that she had sensed something had happened. Something not very good.

Her gaze was a shadow, but she remained silent, watching Louise from her chair as the stillness gradually became oppressive.

Then suddenly the Nokia beeped again and Rebekka jumped.

Proceed, said the text. A moment later it was followed by a photo.

Louise got up and went over to the armchair to show Rebekka the image of her daughter smiling obligingly against a nondescript white background. It was not an exuberant smile, by any means, but neither was there any fear to be traced in it. All it revealed was that the person taking the photo had asked her to smile.

"Oh, thank God," Rebekka gasped, clutching the phone in both hands, an immense outpouring of relief despite the brevity of the utterance. For a moment she sat there silently, pressing the phone to her chest, then studying the photo again before handing it back to Louise.

29

He could no longer think straight and could hardly sit still. Restlessly, he went about the apartment hoping his unease would not transfer to Isabella, who was in her room watching *Strictly Ballroom*. The dancing movies absorbed her attention completely.

The whole thing had taken an unexpected turn. Carl Emil had not even entertained the idea that his father might suddenly emerge. Nor had he been able to foresee that a journalist he had never heard of would appear out of nowhere and remove the icon from his parents' property.

He flopped down on the sofa and closed his eyes.

At this moment an unknown woman was driving around with his billion kroner in the back of her car. She had promised to phone him back, but he had heard nothing. All along, he had been anticipating that the police or Rebekka would produce the icon, after which he would make it disappear again.

If only this journalist woman would call him back he might still be able to slip away before the exchange was set to take place. His thoughts swirled. He put the phone down on the sofa, buried his face in his hands, and tried to focus. He needed to work out his next move.

"Calle!"

His niece called for him, but before he had time to get to his feet his phone rang.

He grabbed it and jumped up.

"Yes?" he answered sharply, stepping over to the window where he leaned his forehead against the glass and looked down on the harbor. A couple of seagulls bobbed about.

"I'm at the Prindsen in Roskilde," said Camilla.

Carl Emil closed his eyes. "And the icon?"

"The icon's here, too. Are you coming?"

"Calle!" Isabella called again. She was standing right behind him.

He swiveled around and put a finger hurriedly to his lips to make her stay quiet.

"I'll set off straightaway," he replied calmly into the phone, sig-naling with a nod that she could go back to her room, he would be right with her as soon as he had finished his phone call.

His palms sticky with sweat, he dropped the phone into his pocket and dashed into the bedroom, where he grabbed his brown weekend bag out of the cupboard. Quickly he stuffed it full of trousers, shirts, and underwear before deciding simply to buy whatever he needed later.

"Are you going away now, too?" Isabella asked with obvious unease, watching him from the doorway.

Carl Emil had not heard her come in and forced a smile. "No, no, not all," he reassured her. "It's for one of my friends; he needs some clean clothes, that's all."

"Why does he need clean clothes?" she wanted to know.

Carl Emil's thoughts raced in his mind. Couldn't she just shut up for a minute and go back to her movies?

"Because," he said after a second, racking his brains to come up with an explanation, "he fell out with his girlfriend and has to sleep at the office for a few days."

"Does he have to sleep on the floor?" she asked.

"No," Carl Emil answered, shaking his head. "Luckily he's got a sofa in his office, but he's run out of clean clothes and needs to change."

He made sure the Nokia was in his pocket. It was muted, but he could feel it against his thigh if it vibrated. Leaving it behind by mistake didn't bear thinking about.

"Okay," said his niece, turning around in the doorway. "What time's dinner?"

He glanced at the clock: It was nearly four thirty. All he could think about was getting out the door, and he was unable to hide his annoyance. "There's loads of food in the fridge," he snapped. "Snacks in the bottom drawer, and popcorn. Take what you want when you get hungry."

"Aren't you coming back?"

He paused and told himself this was no time to sound irritated with her. Instead he crouched down in front of her with his hands on her shoulders and nodded.

"Yes, yes," he said. "Of course I'm coming back. I just have to pop out, that's all. As soon as I'm home again, we'll give your mom a call, all right?"

His niece nodded, her dark eyes fixing him in their gaze.

"Is she home now?"

"I think she's on her way. But we can ask her when she's coming to pick you up."

"But I want to stay here with you," she complained. "We haven't even tried SingStar yet!"

Carl Emil smoothed her hair with his hand and smiled at her as he nodded. "We've got lots of time for SingStar," he said with a stab of guilt, and got to his feet.

She followed him into the hall and waved as he picked up his weekend bag and his keys. Outside on the landing he turned around and locked the door behind him.

⁂

As he drove the Ranger Rover out of the underground parking he tried to form a plan. How was he going to approach it?

The main thing was to get the journalist out of the way first. He had no idea if his father had promised her anything or how they even knew each other. Everything had happened so fast, and he was still rather shaken by their father suddenly have turned up like that.

He pulled onto Tuborgvej and headed toward the highway. The traffic was congested, and the thought of taillights holding him up all the way to Roskilde tensed him up.

What the hell was he going to do? He needed to keep the dialogue going with Rebekka and the police who were with her in the house, and in principle he still had until nine o'clock. As long as they had yet to confirm they were in possession of the icon, he could remain passive. The ball was entirely in their court at the moment; it was he who was waiting for them.

He realized he was driving too fast and took his foot off the accelerator. It would be idiotic if he got stopped now. Thoughts teemed inside his head. He would have to move the icon; he knew that. But where?

All of a sudden it occurred to him that he had not for a moment considered that someone might be following him. He scanned the rearview mirror, but the rush-hour traffic kept the cars strung out in a long, unyielding line, so spotting anyone who might be on his tail was basically impossible. Without signaling he swerved over into the next lane. There was a clamor of angry horns as he cut across the middle and positioned himself in the slow lane to make sure he could slip away at the next exit.

Høje-Taastrup and Sengeløse. He carried on without slowing down and had almost passed the exit when quickly he flicked the turn signal and lunged onto the tail of a black station wagon. Swiftly he assessed whether to take a left onto Roskildevej or else head through Sengeløse and into the town from the Jyllinge side. He took a right, thinking it would be easier for him to keep an eye on the cars behind him if he stuck to the minor roads.

Again he concentrated on keeping calm. At some point during the evening he would send a text to Rebekka and explain to her where her daughter was. By the time she received it, he would be out of the country.

As he turned toward Herringløse he felt confident there was no one following him. He pulled to the side and texted the journalist woman.

On my way, he wrote, hoping she would not become impatient and start ringing his father. His father! Was he on a plane at this very moment? Abruptly he felt himself overwhelmed by the emotions that had been packed away all these months when they had thought their father to be dead. His stomach knotted, and as he reached Gundsømagle he was forced to pull over again and collect himself.

He missed the old man and wanted to see him again, but he knew he never would. Once he had the icon he would have to break off all contact. It would be his turn to be missing.

Until now he had only thought he would be walking out on Rebekka. And Isabella, but he could live with that. Sacrifices were inevitable if he was to live a life in freedom. It couldn't be any different, he told himself, and pulled back onto the road.

Reaching the lights, he turned left toward Roskilde.

Clearly, there would be things he would have to forgo; it stood to reason. On the other hand, he would be a very wealthy man indeed.

❦

"Room one-oh-one, would that be first floor?" he asked the young fair-haired girl in reception.

She nodded, and he could feel her eyes on his back as he went toward the staircase. She had recognized him, but there was nothing he could do about it, he told himself, and took the stairs two at a time.

The journalist opened the door straightaway as if she had been standing behind it waiting.

"I saw you through the window," she said, putting out her hand.

Carl Emil shook it and studied her. Tall, blond, he noted, his eyes then darting briefly about the room. The icon was easily located, leaning up against the desk, wrapped in a dirty sheet.

He stepped inside and immediately began unpacking it as the journalist closed the door behind him. He felt like something was stuck in his throat, impeding his breathing.

"I've just had a message from your father," she said, helping him remove the cloth. "He'll be landing in Copenhagen first thing tomorrow morning."

Carl Emil wasn't listening. He tipped the icon forward to remove the cloth from its rear, supporting its weight against his body as he did so and allowing the cloth to drop to the floor before leaning the artifact back against the desk and stepping away to admire it.

It was truly magnificent, yet seemed in a way far too striking for where it was. Obtrusive, almost. He moved the chair to the side and went and stood over by the window. It looked like the one his father had kept in his office. Exactly like it. Yet the experience was incomparable.

The colors of the glass seemed that much more striking, he thought, the religious content brought so much to the fore that it was almost disquieting. But then he thought of the myth. Whoever prayed before the icon would be absolved of their sins. He could nearly believe it. The effect was so potent. Perhaps one day he really would be forgiven.

Carl Emil gave a heavy sigh. The journalist was now standing at his side. She said nothing, but stared at the icon in front of them.

"It's beautiful," she said after what seemed like a long time, and sat down on the bed.

He nodded.

"How do you think the kidnappers knew about it?" she asked him.

"From the history books, I imagine," he answered, sensing an equilibrium now, in contrast with his hectic unrest of before. "I'll drive out to my sister and tell her we've got it, and then hopefully everything else will go off without a hitch and my niece can be returned unharmed."

Camilla nodded.

"I think my father would like to keep this quiet for a while, allow us to catch our breath as a family before the media get wind of what's happening," he went on.

"That's my impression, too," she said, adding that Walther had called Nymand himself to say he wanted his son to personally take care of the impending exchange. "As it happens, the negotiator who's with your sister now is a good friend of mine. She's the one who's in contact with the kidnappers. I could get in touch and tell her, if you like."

He felt his pulse leap again.

"No need," he replied quickly. "I'll get out there and talk to them in person, explain that we'd like to take care of the matter ourselves. But I'd like to thank you for what you've already done."

He tried to smile, aware of how feeble it came across.

"How do you actually know my father? You obviously know him rather well or else I doubt he would have involved you to this extent."

"Well enough for him to trust me, at least," Camilla said, rising to her feet and picking up her coat.

Only then did he notice the wounds on her hands and the stains on her trousers, but he refrained from comment. Nor did he inquire as to where the icon had been hidden. He stepped over to the door and opened it for her to leave.

"Thank you very much indeed for your help," he said again, and shook her hand good-bye.

If he were to take the death threat seriously he had perhaps seven hours left to live, he pondered, sensing immediately that he took it very seriously indeed. He felt like a hunted animal, though he had no idea from where the threat had come, much less who to keep an eye on. The thought rotated in his mind and made it hard for him to focus. All he knew was that he had to get away, and soon.

After the journalist left, he had closed the door behind her and stretched out on the bed. He tried to compose himself and maintain perspective but felt the only thing he wanted to do was to carry the icon down to the car and vanish before anyone could get to him. At the same time, he knew that such rash behavior was not what was required. Things had to happen in the right order, he told himself, pulling his phone from his pocket before sitting up with the pillows in his back and calling Rebekka's number.

It rang four times before she answered.

"I've got the icon," he told her. "You can confirm now that it's with us."

He could almost hear the relief that rippled through his sister's body.

"Where is it?" she asked.

"It's safe and close by."

"Thank God," she breathed without pursuing the matter. "Thank God."

The text came after five minutes.

The Nokia thrummed with his sister's message, sent by her negotiator, informing the kidnappers that the Angel of Death was now in the family's possession and that they were ready to make the exchange. They asked for instructions and a meeting place.

The unrest he felt was like electricity, his body struggling against the urge to flee. Again, his courage failed him. Just as it always did, when he was halfway there. It seemed to be his lot to be unable to carry a matter to its conclusion, he thought, comparing this to the several occasions when nerves had gotten the better of him and he had failed to show up for an exam.

But this time would be different.

He stretched out his foot and felt the icon with his toe. He had to get hold of Miklos, he thought, aware of how he faltered, his nerves wriggling in his chest, tentacles of fear clutching coldly at his diaphragm. But he had obtained the icon as promised. Now Wedersøe could deal with what remained.

He sat up straight on the bed, reached out for his phone, and sent a message:

I've got the Angel. Prindsen, rm. 101. Get over here now.

30

He was angry as he approached the rest area outside Slagelse. In fact he was seething. The supplier had not disposed of the body. It was still in his car and he was refusing to get rid of it. He wanted his money according to the agreement.

The air was streaked with sleet, the road wet and treacherous, prompting him to keep his speed down.

The evening before, he had phoned to make sure everything was all right. He had imagined the supplier would be coming from Germany somewhere. He had even offered to up the price, sensing the man's reluctance, but his Spanish contact had responded by simply hanging up.

He would have to try again. There was no way he could run the risk of ending up with a woman's corpse on his hands. The ones in his cellar were different. This one was to be disposed of.

He had half an hour until the agreed meeting time at the rest area. He wondered how the man might be persuaded. As the time approached he found himself willing to pay whatever price might be demanded. He would offer any amount of money to make sure that the supplier would be the one to get rid of the body.

He pressed the call-back function on his phone and proposed putting off the meeting for another hour so as to allow the supplier to find some suitable back road where it might be done.

"No," came the curt reply. "I want my money. You order, I deliver."

Immediately he felt he could no longer control himself. His anger welled up inside him and he raised his voice into the receiver.

He had not intended to lose his temper, yet his emotions had momentarily gotten the better of him. He turned the wipers to fast, spelling it out once and for all that unless the supplier got rid of the body he could expect no payment.

The man at the other end responded angrily. The ensuing bombardment of Spanish invective forced him to hold the phone away from his ear for a moment.

He was about to respond in kind when the man's voice suddenly broke off. To begin with he thought the connection had been lost, but then came a screech of tires followed by a hideous grating of metal, and then the crash.

The impact was a tumultuous clamor in his ears as the supplier's vehicle slammed the crash barrier. Shocked, he dropped the phone and heard the man's tinny scream issue from the receiver as the car was crushed.

He took his foot off the accelerator and pulled onto the shoulder, his emergency lights blinking. His heart hammered in his chest as he closed his eyes and leaned back against the headrest. He tried to work out how far the supplier would have gotten. Nyborg, he guessed, but maybe he had been ahead of schedule and had crossed the bridge already.

He tried to steady his breathing, inhaling deeply before deciding to carry on and find out where the accident had occurred. Reluctant to drive over the bridge and be picked up by the CCTV, he nevertheless felt he had to do something. The body was still in the supplier's car, and his own cell phone would be easily traced by the police.

"Shit," he seethed as he switched on the radio. He found the traffic information and waited for a gap so he could pull out. At the same time, he realized it was the first time in days that the Angel of Death had been supplanted from his thoughts. But now she returned, an insatiable lust ablaze inside him. He would not allow the supplier's misfortune to ruin everything. Still, he needed to know what was happening.

He put his foot down and cut into the fast lane, speeding toward the giant span of the bridge, every muscle tense with rage.

The bulletin came as he approached the Vemmelev exit.

"Reports of a serious solo accident on the eastbound lane of the Storebæltsbroen. Motorists crossing the bridge on their way to Zealand are advised to proceed with caution. Emergency units are on their way to the scene…and we're informed now that the bridge has been closed to traffic while rescue work takes place."

"Damn it!" he spat, realizing that police would already be there.

He flicked the turn signal immediately and veered off the highway at the exit. There was no sense in continuing now.

He turned right and drove back toward Slagelse, pulling off to the side of the road after a couple of minutes to get some air. Outside the car he lifted his face to the sky and let the sleet cool his brow while he racked his brain. It was by no means certain the police would check the trunk of the vehicle at first. It might easily be some time before they discovered what was in the back, so perhaps he had a head start.

As he got back in, his phone beeped loudly on the floor. He was so taken aback he almost dropped the key, and a moment passed before he felt able to bend down and retrieve the phone. When he did, he stared at the message on the display:

I've got the Angel. Prindsen, rm. 101. Get over here now.

⚭

For a long time, he simply sat and stared. A moment ago the icon had seemed so far away, but now it was close, so very close. He smiled and took a deep, satisfied breath.

Before clicking into his seat belt he found a church recital among the CDs in the glove compartment, Michala Petri on the recorder, accompanied by Lars Hannibal, and seconds later the music flowed soothingly from the Bose system's ten speakers. He turned the car around and went back to the highway, accelerating down the ramp in the direction of Roskilde.

He felt himself relax as the car picked up speed. He ran through the checklist in his mind, satisfying himself he had everything he needed. The silicone hardener was in the trunk together with the tubs of silicone he had planned to take with him to the recycling station and dump in the chemicals bin.

The streets of Roskilde were empty. It was as if the whole town shut down when the shops closed at five thirty. He pulled into the inner yard behind the hotel and parked parallel to the wall, sitting for a moment to steel himself before getting out and stepping around to open the trunk.

The hypodermic was concealed in the space meant for the spare tire, wrapped up in Kleenex. He removed the tissue carefully and wiped the long needle before unscrewing the top of the small, transparent bottle of hardener and filling the syringe.

31

He knew the hotel well enough to know that room 101 was one of their so-called Nordic rooms in the new wing. He slipped in through a side door so as to avoid reception and walked briskly up the stairs.

The room was the first on the corridor. He was expected. No sooner had he knocked than the door was flung open and Carl Emil drew him inside, closing it just as quickly behind them.

Miklos Wedersøe studied his client: His hair was tousled and his crumpled shirt untucked. Carl Emil was pale, disheveled, and clearly at his wit's end.

Instead of making any comment the attorney stepped forward to the great glass icon that was leaning against the desk.

How divine it was, he thought, hardly listening as Carl Emil twittered on about his sister, how he had texted her and called off the exchange at 9 p.m., and about his niece, who was at home in his apartment in Hellerup.

Miklos sat down on the bed, his ears ringing, his eyes unable to move from the colors in the glass. That same compelling effect that had drawn pilgrims in droves to the Hagia Sophia, he mused.

"Have you informed your contact?" Carl Emil wanted to know, now restlessly pacing the floor. "Is the car ready in Hamburg?"

"Yes, of course," Miklos replied, though it was far from true. He had not had time to make the necessary calls. After he had received the message from Carl Emil he had focused only on getting back to Roskilde as quickly as possible. "What about the girl?"

"She's fine."

It surprised him that Carl Emil had mustered the courage. Granted, he had said all along that he would make sure his sister fell into line in the event that she refused to help them of her own free will, but *courage* was not a word he connected with Carl Emil Sachs-Smith. Rather, he was gullible and naive, doubtful qualities that nevertheless occasionally had their own advantages.

It had certainly been the case the day he had obligingly handed over the key to his parents' property along with the code for the alarm, having readily believed that his attorney needed to pick up some of his father's papers. They had both been under the impression that his mother had accompanied her husband to Fyn. As it turned out, she had not. All of a sudden she had appeared in the doorway of the office in her nightdress and dressing gown and stood staring at him, clearly wondering what on earth he was doing.

Foolishly he had been caught in the act, the icon already in his hands. That was before they understood it was only a copy.

His surprise had been so great that he had struck the woman. Not once, but several times. His first thought had been to take her back home with him to the cellar, but she was far too old and quite unlike the others. It was not until he carried her up to the bedroom that he discovered the sleeping pills.

He crushed them into a powder on the bedside table, dissolving them in the half glass of water that was there before forcing her to drink.

The rest had been easy. He knew there was insulin in the bathroom. A tiny jab was all it took.

He had taken care of a problem, and now he would do so again.

◆

"Come on, let's get it downstairs," Carl Emil said again, his silly, screeching voice returning him abruptly to the present. "We'll take your car to Hamburg."

Miklos merely nodded. How telling it was that the little rich boy would expect to use someone else's car.

"Were you thinking of taking it like that?" Miklos indicated the fusty, damp-stained cloth that lay on the floor, scuffed halfway underneath the desk.

"Have you got any other suggestions?"

"Why not take the sheet off the bed? We can leave the other one in your car before we go."

He watched Carl Emil as he stepped into the corridor and called the elevator up to the first floor. It would be stupid not to accept some help carrying the icon to the car, he thought. On the other hand there was bound to be someone downstairs who recognized the Sachs-Smith son. Especially now that his sister was all over the media.

Miklos pulled the cover off the bed and tossed the duvets aside so he could remove the sheet. When Carl Emil returned to the room and stepped up to the icon he was prepared, throwing the sheet over his head from behind and instantly twirling it around Carl Emil's throat.

He might not even need the hypodermic, he thought, pulling the material tight with both hands.

Carl Emil thrashed and lashed out. Miklos felt a searing pain as he received a vicious kick to the shin, yet managed to keep his distance as he hauled him over to the bed and forced him down.

A gurgling rattle issued from Carl Emil's throat as his fingers desperately scrabbled at the material in which he was being strangled. But Miklos's hands were unyielding.

Resistance ran its course, and then it was over: His arms flailed one last time, then dropped feebly to the bed.

He did not much care for the wheezing of the larynx, nor indeed for the tremulous shudder that jolted through the torso and limbs. The body was lifeless, and yet in the grip of the nervous system's final flourish, so impossible to decode: Was he dead, or was it still too soon?

He could take no chances, certainly not now, and pulled the sheet still tighter.

All movement subsided, and yet he persisted. His eyes returned to the icon. Its astonishing colors and the image of the archangel Gabriel holding his long, white lily. So emotional was the experience of beholding that the figure seemed almost physically to enter his being. Its sparkling silvers and blues, the scintillating shimmer of dark and light.

He felt no pity for Carl Emil. He had given him no choice. Everything had its price, and he would not be alone.

He remembered the myth.

The Angel of Death, collecting the souls and returning them to God.

32

Rebekka was paler than before. She stood clutching the door for support, and for a moment Louise was afraid she was about to pass out.

"Why are they calling it off all of a sudden?" she asked, her voice a sliver of despair.

She had kicked off her flat shoes and her feet were now bare. It was as if she passed restlessly across the herringbone parquet without actually touching it.

"They know we've got the icon. Why won't they give me my daughter back?"

Louise chewed on her lower lip and shook her head. "I don't know," she replied in all honesty.

She had just had Rebekka's ex-husband on the phone. Jeffrey was in a terrible state and wanted to come over to the house so he could keep up with developments firsthand. The suggestion had caused Rebekka to break down all over again.

Thiesen had stepped in and closed the house off for as long as the negotiation unit was present, so now one of Nymand's officers had been assigned to stay with the girl's father, trying to calm him down while keeping him up to date.

The tension was getting to Louise, too, though she tried as best she could to keep it at bay. She sat with the Nokia in her hand. The message was brief and it was impossible to read anything into it other than what it said:

9 p.m. canceled.

She had replied asking for a new time. Palle had instructed her carefully: With the kidnappers calling things off so abruptly it was vital she hold back on forcing any new agreement before the morning; they needed time to fully prepare themselves so they could ensure that nothing happened to the girl.

"Buy time and keep a level head," he repeated, his hand on her shoulder.

Marybeth had been taken in for questioning at the police station but had now returned and had put some soft drinks and a plate of cookies out for them on the coffee table. She went around the living area switching on the big floor lamps with their elegant silk shades as darkness descended. A soft light spread through the rooms, and the girl drew the heavy curtains and switched on another lamp on the bureau.

"I think we need to get hold of your brother and tell him the exchange tonight is off," Louise said, closely observing Rebekka's reactions. She saw that her shoulders had drooped and the look in her eyes was different in some way. Ever since Louise had entered the house, Rebekka had clearly been in a state of shock. Apathetic, she had sat staring into space, and it had been impossible for Louise to gauge what was going on behind her empty eyes. Until now that state had been interrupted only by sudden outbursts of rage in which she flared up at some piece of information, ripping into whoever happened to be nearest or taking Nymand to task for not doing enough to find her daughter.

Her moods fluctuated, though mainly she seemed hardly to be present. Now she appeared even more despondent, as if something inside her had abandoned all hope of Isabella ever coming home again.

"He said he was going to come, but that was over an hour ago. And now he's not answering his phone," she said with barely any emotion, sighing as if she were used to such behavior on her brother's part.

She crossed the floor and sank back into an armchair.

"Can't you try his number?" she asked, looking at Louise imploringly.

Louise was momentarily taken aback but nodded even so. What good would it do her calling him? She went in to Thiesen in the other room and picked up the list of contacts. Palle had drawn it up when they'd first arrived. There was a little asterisk in black ink marking those they were monitoring.

Carl Emil Sachs-Smith's number was tagged with just such an asterisk.

She called the number, only to be directed immediately to his voice mail. She left a message telling him to call back, then put the phone down on the table with a shrug.

"Still no answer," she said. "Do you know where he was when he called you?"

Rebekka shook her head. "All he said was that everything was fine, he had the icon and it was nearby, so he could be here soon."

Louise nodded and went back to Thiesen and Palle in the far room.

"Anything on his phone?" she asked.

Thiesen shook his head. "It must be up and running now, though. I'll get them to check."

"No contact," Louise said with a sigh. "With either the kidnappers or the brother."

She ran a hand worriedly through her hair and could tell she wasn't the only one who felt concerned. Thiesen's lips had tightened, and a little frown had appeared.

"To hell with these text messages," he snapped. "Have you tried calling?"

Louise nodded. "It's switched off. Either that or there's just no connection. Maybe they turn it off when they're not using it. Presumably they realize we'll be trying to find out where they're calling from."

Thiesen nodded and rubbed his temples absently with the tips of his fingers.

"Does Nymand know the exchange is off?" Louise asked, looking at Palle, who dealt with all communication with the chief superintendent.

"I think so, let me just check."

He picked up his cell phone and called the number, but was shaking his head even before finishing the call.

"No," he said into the phone, "we haven't received any new instructions, we're just waiting."

"And Sachs-Smith senior's in transit, so we can't get hold of him, either," Thiesen added across the desk.

Louise nodded.

"How did Carl Emil get hold of the icon, do we know?" she asked, looking at her colleagues in turn.

"No idea, but the old man phoned Nymand from nowhere insisting his son take care of the exchange. If the chief super would promise him that much, he'd make sure the icon was retrieved and ready at the appointed time."

Louise leaned against the windowsill, listening with the increasing feeling that something was wrong. There was a hidden agenda somewhere, but she couldn't work out what it was and the fact was beginning to annoy her.

It was there in Rebekka's eyes and in Walther Sachs-Smith's decision to make the exchange without police involvement, though he must have realized there would be quite some risk in doing so.

"I don't know how he got it organized, but it must have been over the phone," Thiesen mused. "Now we just need those bastards to give word again."

Louise nodded and suddenly felt rather sure she knew who had retrieved the icon.

"I need to step out for a bit," she said, grabbing her coat and asking them to keep an eye on the Nokia for a few minutes while she was gone.

※

"They've called it off," Louise said into the phone when Camilla answered her call.

"Called what off?"

"The exchange. The icon for Isabella Sachs-Smith."

"What about the girl? Is there any indication she's still alive?"

"None; it's been ages since we last heard. They've gone completely silent. And we can't get in touch with Carl Emil, either," she explained, waiting for a second to allow her friend to pitch in with some information, but Camilla said nothing.

"Where's the icon, and where's he?"

"How long have you been trying to get hold of him?" Camilla asked instead of answering the question.

Louise could hear noises in the background, a door being closed, followed by footsteps.

"Are you outside?" she asked.

Another door, this one heavier, an entrance door slamming shut, and Camilla running.

"Where are you going?"

"Have you tried calling where he lives?" Camilla asked breathlessly. Louise heard her getting into a car, the ignition being turned and the engine starting.

"Camilla, you know where the icon is. Where are you going?"

"Give me half an hour, I'll call you back."

"No, absolutely not. Tell me where you're going. The girl's eight years old and we've got no contact. You've got to work with us on this. Rebekka's not saying anything and there's obviously something going on that we don't know about. Something they haven't told us."

"What do you mean?"

"I just know there's something going on that we haven't been involved in, and if you know what it is you'd be completely irresponsible keeping it to yourself."

"I don't know what you mean," Camilla responded.

"How many people know where the icon is now?" Louise probed in a more settled voice.

"None."

"I'm scared there's something going on that you don't know about, either. I think there are several people involved and most likely they've taken you for a ride."

"I don't know what you're talking about. No one's taken me for any ride. I've spoken to Walther, and yes, I know where the icon is. And my guess is that Carl Emil is with it, so give me half an hour."

"You tell me where it is and tell me now, otherwise I'll put a search out for your car," Louise insisted, fully aware she had nothing on Camilla that would warrant such an action. "Maybe you know where the girl is, too? If you do, perhaps I can have her picked up and returned to her mother while you're off playing Wonder Woman?"

"That's enough!" Camilla retorted, finally sounding like Louise had gotten to her.

"She's eight years old," Louise repeated, stressing every word.

The response came after a silence:

"The icon's in a room at the Hotel Prindsen, and a couple of hours ago Carl Emil was, too."

33

He wasn't normally the kind of person who allowed himself to stress about matters. He did not care for it, and nothing good ever came of it. But now was different.

The Angel of Death was in the trunk of his car. He had moved the silicone tubs up in front of the passenger seat. His heart thumped in his chest and he was sweating. He had no idea how much time he had before the police put a warrant out for his arrest.

He had to prioritize. And priority number one was to make sure he was safe. He needed some leverage in case he had to negotiate.

Before getting into the car he satisfied himself again that he had the keys he had taken from Carl Emil's coat pocket.

Beads of perspiration dislodged from his neck and trickled uncomfortably down his back. He caught a glimpse of himself in the rearview mirror and looked quickly away.

How unlike him his reflection seemed. A flustered, discomposed individual, flushed and sweating. The very sight made him sick to his stomach.

He filled the car with music and drove out through the gate, leaving the hotel behind him. For a brief second he took his foot off the accelerator and closed his eyes, savoring the tones that enveloped him so warmly, then sensing the first spark of pleasure. It was a stubborn pleasure that encroached upon his unease like weeds taking over a garden. The only difference was that in this case it was the opposite: The pleasure was good, and the good smothered the bad.

He breathed in deeply and exhaled gently as satisfaction kicked in.

He had done it.

Now all he needed was to take care of the remaining practicalities, though to be honest with himself this did not worry him unduly. The job was almost finished, he reasoned, and he drove away from Roskilde.

❧

He had been there so many times before and was quite familiar with the parking facility in the building's basement. He knew, too, where to find Carl Emil's dedicated space.

Slowly he drove the big Mercedes down the ramp and passed along the row of parked cars.

He found no pleasure in such concrete and would never choose to live in such a building himself, where privacy was forever compromised by one's proximity to other occupants. The office environment was different and did not bother him in the same way, though at the office he was never himself. His home provided him with a vast and vital mental space. Space in which to enjoy and savor.

It was what life was all about.

Enjoy and savor.

He took the elevator up and let himself in. The apartment was silent and for a moment he was struck by doubt.

Was there something he had missed? Something he had failed to understand?

He closed the door carefully behind him and glanced into the living room with its panorama view of the harbor, noting how tidy everything was. He continued toward the kitchen, passing Carl Emil's bedroom on the way. The door was ajar, the wardrobe open, a mess of clothes and other items strewn out over the bed.

He glanced quickly into the empty kitchen before moving on to the guest room and opening the door.

She was lying on the bed, fully dressed and asleep on top of the duvet, a bag of chips at her side and the TV still switched on.

His eyes passed over the DVDs and computer games. Some clothes lay folded in a neat pile next to the dresser. Brand-new clothes, with the price tags still attached.

No time to dwell, he told himself, slipping his hands under her back and lifting her up.

"Calle," she mumbled, stirring sufficiently to rub an eye, then returning immediately to sleep.

She lay in his arms, oblivious as he began to walk, her small body giving a start as he closed the front door behind them and stepped into the elevator.

He had not considered what he would do if she began to scream, nor did he care to think about it as he crossed through the basement to the car.

There, at the Mercedes, he knew he needed to put her down. Gently he let her slip from his arms onto the concrete, supporting her weight until she lay flat and his hands were free. He unlocked the door, but the chemical tubs on the passenger side would hamper his plan. She would just have to sit with her legs on top of them, he told himself, then leaped in fright when the scream came, as shrill as it was sudden.

Her terrified voice ricocheted off the concrete walls, piercing into his ears and forcing him to put his hand over her mouth.

Instinctively he flung the car door open, gripping her tight with both hands and bundling her inside as she screamed again, so loudly he feared his eardrums would be perforated by the strident, earsplitting tone.

It all happened so quickly he had no time to check if anyone had seen them. The girl thrashed so wildly and her scream was so excruciating he thought he would go mad.

He had been thinking he would tell her he knew her mother and uncle and that they had asked him to collect her. It would have worked, he was a good and persuasive talker—it was how he earned a living.

But now it had gone wrong and it was imperative he shut her up.

He slammed the car door and saw the way her hands immediately scrabbled to open it again. It was already locked, of course, but before he could reach the driver's side she was over the wheel, pressing down on the horn and setting off the alarm at the same time.

Sweat burst from his pores again. He yanked the door open and hurled himself at her, wrenching her away from the wheel. In his pocket he still had the hypodermic with the silicone hardener he had not needed at the Hotel Prindsen.

The fleeting realization was a lapse in concentration and he was too slow to stop her before she bit deeply into his hand, causing him to yelp with pain. Her teeth were like ice picks thrust into the flesh of his hand, and though he tried to pull away they kept their grip.

He had lost control. Rage rose up inside him, as suddenly and as violently as on previous occasions when he had used the hypodermic.

He hit her as hard as he could in the face and she relented.

※

She lay in a heap on the passenger seat, her eyes closed. He had taken the chamois from the glove compartment and stuffed it in her mouth, tied her hands and feet with strips torn from the sheet he had taken from the hotel to protect the icon.

It had all happened so quickly, and yet he had no sense of how much time had actually passed. Now he would drive home and make ready. Collect himself and calm down. He nodded with resolve, his thoughts already focusing on how best he might exploit the Sachs-Smith grandchild now being firmly in his possession. There was no doubt in his mind that right now she was a considerable asset.

Briefly, he considered driving back down to Roskilde, taking Carl Emil's Range Rover, and making a dash for it out of the country.

But then what about his women?

And the Angel of Death that was to complete his exhibition?

It was quite wrong; the very thought was anathema to him. Everything had become so untidy, and now his hand was bleeding, too.

34

This time, Camilla didn't care where she parked as she pulled up at the Hotel Prindsen. Seeing that the police had gotten there first she simply abandoned the car inside the lot entrance, ran through the yard and up the steps to the glass door. There she was halted abruptly by a man who called her name.

She wheeled around and saw Nymand come panting behind her.

"It's on the first floor," she said, waiting for him to catch up.

"My people are trying to get access now," he said, with a nod toward reception.

He was clearly annoyed by the receptionist's apparent reluctance to hand over a key at the police's request.

"I booked the room, so they can give the key to me," Camilla replied, striding toward the desk without noticing the way Nymand initially stood transfixed, gaping at her in astonishment.

With the key card in her hand she stopped on the landing and waited for him again as he hauled his heavy weight up the stairs, clutching the banister for support.

"I retrieved the icon from the manor on Walther Sachs-Smith's instructions," she explained, Nymand responding only with a breathless nod. Most probably he had already worked that out, Camilla thought to herself, bounding up the final flight.

As they came out into the long corridor she put her ear to the door and listened, but the room seemed quiet. All she could hear was Nymand's wheezing in her wake.

She knocked cautiously.

No answer.

She knocked again, harder this time, but when there was still no response she inserted the key card into the slot and moved aside to make way for Nymand, who stepped forward and opened the door.

Carl Emil Sachs-Smith lay sprawled across the bed on his stomach. His face was turned toward the window, but from where Camilla was standing she could clearly see the way one eye was wide open and staring unnaturally into the darkness. His arms were splayed out at his sides as if he had fallen from a height.

Nymand had put the light on but as yet he remained just inside the door. Camilla stood on her toes to peer over his shoulder.

She knew already. It was obvious.

The Angel of Death was gone, and the dirty cloth in which it had been wrapped when she had retrieved it from the family estate lay in a heap under the desk.

She stepped back slowly, allowing the police in to do their job. She paced the corridor then sank down at the far end with her back against the wall before phoning Louise.

"Carl Emil is dead," she began. "His body's in room one-oh-one at the Hotel Prindsen and the icon's gone. Nymand just got here."

"Oh, Christ," Louise said at the other end and hung up.

Camilla sensed her friend's exhaustion. They had yet to talk about what was going on with Jonas. Markus had told her about the fight he had been in after he got home from school that day, but she had not had the chance to ask what it had been about. Now more than twenty-four hours had passed since the little girl had disappeared and Camilla felt run-down, not so much physically as mentally.

She thought about Frederik. He was there all the time, among all her other thoughts. She had called him and told him his father was on his way home to Denmark.

She had wondered why he had not sounded more surprised, but on the other hand she had always had an idea he never really believed his father to be dead. If he ever did, he had certainly never seemed particularly affected by the fact. Only now did the thought occur to her that he probably had people keeping an eye on the house on Kauai. If so, then they had surely reported back to him that an elderly gray-haired man had been observed sipping chilled white wine on the deck these past few months.

She missed Frederik and longed to feel his tanned and sinewy arms around her. And now Carl Emil was lying dead in this hotel room and she would have to call him again. She owed him the courtesy. Or perhaps it was more because she needed to hear his voice?

Still slouched against the wall, on the plush hotel carpeting, she found her phone and pressed the number.

"Hi," she said when he answered, and began to cry as she told him about his brother. "They don't know where your niece is. Carl Emil is dead and the icon is missing."

At first her words were a shock.

"Where are you?" he asked, prompting the longing she felt inside to well up again.

She took a deep breath and tried to regain control of her voice.

"I'm sorry I had to tell you this over the phone," she said instead of answering his question.

"Where are you?" he repeated.

"At the Prindsen. We just found your brother. He's lying on the bed."

"I'm on my way," said Frederik. Camilla struggled to make sense of what he meant.

She saw Nymand coming toward her.

"What do you mean, on your way?" she asked, getting to her feet.

"I just got into Copenhagen. I was in London when you called this afternoon."

"But why didn't you tell me?" she began, only to stop short when she saw the expression on Nymand's face. "Listen, I'll call you back," she promised, and hung up.

"What?" she breathed, staring at Nymand in fearful anticipation as she walked forward to meet him.

"The contact phone the kidnappers have been using is in that room with him," he told her gravely. "They've cut off all communication and have taken off with both the girl and the icon. You've got to tell us exactly what's been going on and who you've been talking to."

35

Louise sat on the sofa with her arms around Rebekka. She had stopped trembling but was still crying, quietly and with her eyes closed.

They had been sitting the same way since Louise had informed her of her brother's death.

"He was threatened," Rebekka suddenly whispered. "Several times."

Louise straightened up as best she could while still keeping a comforting arm around the grieving woman, as if any further withdrawal would cause her to change her mind and fall silent again.

"Threatened? In what way?"

"Someone said they were going to kill him."

Louise took her arm away now and asked Rebekka to open her eyes. "What do you mean?"

"I don't know much about it," she mumbled without looking up.

"Please tell me as much as you know," Louise said, resisting the urge to shake some life into the woman. "Your brother has just been killed and your daughter has been kidnapped. You have to tell me what you know."

Rebekka sat motionless, then slowly told her about the coffin display that had been left outside Carl Emil's door.

"He was scared," she said. "I could sense it the day he came and asked for my help."

"How did he think you could help?" Louise asked, furious with herself for not having pursued her suspicions that the police were being kept in the dark.

"He wanted the Angel of Death, the real one. We didn't know the one in the office was a copy or that the real one was so priceless."

Rebekka buried her face in her hands.

"How much is it worth?" Louise demanded, holding her breath.

"More than a billion kroner. But I was against selling. The threats came shortly after they received an offer."

"I'm sorry you obviously didn't trust us enough to tell us this earlier," Louise said, struggling with the anger that rose up inside her but deciding not to tell Rebekka that doing so might have saved her brother's life.

"There was a second death threat a couple of days later," Rebekka went on, finally looking Louise in the eye. "Someone left a headstone outside my brother's door. It was inscribed with his name and date of birth as well as the date of his death."

She paused for a moment before going on.

"He was at his wit's end."

Louise could well imagine. She tried to restrain her anger.

"If someone had a headstone made, we should be able to find out where and who ordered it," she said, rising to her feet.

"No," Rebekka said immediately. "It wasn't a proper headstone, just a flat rock with the words painted on."

"When did it say he was supposed to die?" Louise probed, fixing her eyes on her.

"Tomorrow," Rebekka answered. "Or rather today," she corrected herself, realizing a new day had already begun.

Louise shook her head, but said nothing.

"Isabella went missing," Rebekka offered defensively, avoiding Louise's gaze. "I had to concentrate on my daughter."

Louise did not respond, going into the far room instead to wake up Thiesen, who sat dozing in a chair. He stood up immediately and followed her back into the living room.

"It turns out Carl Emil Sachs-Smith received death threats during this last week," Louise explained after they had drawn a couple of chairs over to the coffee table.

Rebekka did not seem to be listening. She had leaned her head back and had closed her eyes.

"Apparently, there was a plan to sell the Angel of Death, and that may have been what sparked the threats and later the kidnapping."

Rebekka nodded and with eyes still closed explained to them that she had been convinced all along that everything that had occurred had been the result of Carl Emil having revealed the secret of the icon in the family's possession.

"Had he found a buyer?" Thiesen inquired in a tone that prompted Rebekka to snap open her eyes.

"Yes," she replied. "It was all going through our attorney and an American contact of his in New York."

"Illegally," said Palle, who had entered the room. "Which presumably is why no one has mentioned this before."

Rebekka nodded. "I didn't want to sell."

Louise hesitated, unsure for a second if she ought to tell her of the disastrous turn of events that had occurred. Clearly, she had yet to fully comprehend the gravity of the situation.

"Nymand and his officers found the kidnappers' phone in the hotel room where your brother died." She then said, pausing and looking at the girl's mother compassionately, "We no longer have contact with your daughter."

For a moment the four of them sat staring at each other without speaking, until Rebekka began to shake her head.

"No!" she said. "No, no, no!"

The heartrending scream that followed shattered the silence and forced the two men to look away. At that moment, the doorbell rang, and Thiesen jumped thankfully to his feet to answer it.

Though it was well past midnight, Palle had somehow managed to find a crisis counselor on call from the Sankt Hans psychiatric hospital. It had been Thiesen's suggestion that Rebekka receive immediate help.

***

After instructing Marybeth to remain with Rebekka while she slept in the living room, so she wouldn't wake up and find herself alone, Louise gathered up her coat and waited for Nymand and one of his men to come and collect her. Before they were informed of Carl Emil's death she had been so tired she could have slept standing up. Now her fatigue had vanished.

"You're sure you're not too tired?" Palle inquired as he came out into the hall with Rebekka's spare keys to her brother's apartment.

"I'm fine," she replied quickly. It was just after 2 a.m. Thiesen had suggested they go home and get some sleep, but as long as they had no idea of the little girl's whereabouts Louise had no intention of going home.

The negotiation unit was no longer needed. With the icon already gone, they had nothing left to bargain with. Louise felt herself overcome with frustration and a deflating sense of failure, so when Nymand suggested it might be helpful for her to go to Hellerup, the choice was a no-brainer.

※

"His flat's up on the ninth floor," Louise said as they passed through the darkness toward the entrance door. "Did anyone actually get hold of that attorney?"

"No."

Nymand shook his head and seemed weary. His movements were slow and heavy, and it occurred to Louise that this was now his second night without sleep. He had been on the job ever since Rebekka reported the kidnapping.

"He wasn't home, but my people are going to try again first thing. He needs to tell us about their plans to sell the icon and who was involved."

"There can't be that many customers for such an incredibly expensive piece," Louise mused as the elevator landed with a gentle bump and the doors slid aside.

"Probably more than one would imagine," the officer who had driven them back to the capital posited. He handed her a pair of thin latex gloves. "I've heard that in the UK a handful of the most established dealers have been known to pool their resources and make a purchase if a customer has shown interest in a certain artifact. After the sale they divide the proceeds among them. I'm sure the buyers are there."

Louise wriggled her hands into the gloves and went to unlock the door.

The apartment was dark. They stood and listened for a moment before opening the door wide and stepping inside to switch on the lights. Two rows of recessed lights in the ceiling illuminated the hallway from above, their light falling on the coats that hung from the hooks on one wall and the sports bag dumped just inside the door.

Nymand ventured inside the living room while Louise and the other officer continued down the hall. She turned the light on in the bedroom and saw an untidy bed with clothes strewn all about, as if they had been wrenched indiscriminately from the wardrobe. Nymand's man had gone on into the kitchen and switched on the lights there.

They began to search through the apartment in silence until the officer suddenly called for them to come.

"Look here."

He had opened the door of the room that was opposite Carl Emil's bedroom.

The bed was unmade and there were DVDs of dancing movies and little girl's clothes all over the floor. Over by the wall was a small red shoulder bag.

Louise went over and crouched down to open the bag.

"We need to go through this place with a fine-tooth comb. There must be something here to indicate where those death threats came from," said Nymand from the hall, only to fall silent as he stepped into the room.

"What have we got?" the chief superintendent asked immediately.

"It looks like there's been a child here," the officer replied.

"It was Carl Emil all along," said Louise, aghast, carefully picking up Isabella's dancing shoes from the bag. She put them down on the floor and smoothed the little dress. "He's been keeping her hidden here."

She turned around in shock and looked up at them.

"He's dead, but where is she?"

❦

Leaving had been hard. After he came home following his excursion to Carl Emil's apartment he had taken a bath and changed into a pressed shirt and trousers before applying a dressing to his injured hand.

Sinking her teeth into him like that had been her big mistake.

Now he had packed a bag with only the most necessary items and gone down into the cellar to bid them farewell.

Saying good-bye had not been easy, but he knew there was no other option. The four women in his life were now a chapter in his past. A very costly chapter, certainly, but what did that matter now? Next time he would throw his passion into something even more exotic.

Uniqueness cost money and he would always look back on

these exquisite female bodies with exquisite satisfaction. If only he had been able, like other artists, to share the beauty of his creations with an audience. Such opportunity, however, had never been available to him, he told himself as he sat in the car on his way across Zealand. Several popular exhibitions had toured the world presenting the human body in all its intricate detail and yet none could boast anything like the perfection of his own collection.

But they had always been for his eyes only and he found this to be another strength, raising his achievement still further in his estimation. He had always felt this to be true, though naturally it rankled somewhat that he would never harvest even the smallest recognition for his consummate works of art.

His first thought had been to burn the house down and vanish, leaving nothing behind. It would have been an easy matter with all the flammables he kept stored in the cellar. But he knew he was unable to go through with it. He could never bring himself to destroy what had meant so much to him and brought him so much joy and pleasure. Therefore he had decided instead to leave the women as they were. Maybe then the world might yet discover what he had created.

Vain? Perhaps. But he had come to the conclusion that he had nothing to lose by letting them stay where they were. He had moved on. And as ever, it was best not to look back.

Moreover, he had realized there was nothing else he could do but sell the Angel of Death, and his contact in New York had made arrangements for him to meet up with his buyer in a small town not far from Hamburg. With the icon in the car and the police on his tail he had no desire to spend any more time on the road than was necessary.

His contact had also confirmed that he would receive a down

payment of five million euros in cash on delivery of the icon. The rest of the sum would be deposited in a closed account in New York, to be transferred to his own account in Luxembourg as soon as the buyer had taken receipt of the artifact.

It was all sealed.

He had never asked for it all to turn out the way it had. He had hoped to be able to keep the icon in his cellar. To begin with, the fact that circumstance had forced him to leave the house behind had felt like failure. Now he chose to think of it as a new start. With the proceeds from the icon's sale he would be able to purchase his own private island. From there, the possibilities were endless.

He looked forward to this new beginning with almost childlike excitement, serenely confident that the next chapter in his life would be quite as fulfilling as the last. From that perspective, things had turned out rather well indeed.

Now he would devote himself to purchasing his very own paradise where he could do whatever he wanted and nothing would need to be concealed.

The thought of the little girl passed fleetingly through his mind. She had been quite a handful. Had she been better behaved he might not have been forced to tie her up, and bolting the hatch might easily have been sufficient. But now it was done.

Besides, it was best that way. No one would look for her down there. And they would find her only if he required them to.

36

W e've found her," said Rønholt. It was Thursday morning and Louise was standing in the doorway of the Homicide Department's little kitchen.

"Isabella?" she replied incredulously, putting the coffee jug down on the counter.

"No," Rønholt replied apologetically, as if he had momentarily forgotten the case that still occupied all Louise's waking hours. "No, Naja Holten."

"Is she dead?"

Louise stepped into the lunchroom and pulled out a chair.

"As good as," he answered. "She's been admitted to the Rigshospitalet in a coma following a serious car accident yesterday on the Storebæltsbroen."

"Does that mean she wasn't missing after all?" Louise exclaimed in surprise and thought immediately of Grete Milling. She had yet to speak to Melvin and had no idea if Rønholt had managed to get hold of Jeanette's mother the day before.

After she had gotten home late in the night she had looked in on Jonas, who lay sleeping with a dressing on his gashed eyebrow, but she had not had the chance to speak to him, and she wasn't sure whether her downstairs neighbor had managed to have a word with him, either.

Not until this morning had she been able to ask him about the fight. Initially he had not been willing to talk about it. But then after a short pause it had all come out. He told her that some boys in the class were constantly on his back and acknowledged readily that he had been the one who had started the fight. But she had been unable to coax him into telling her why they were picking on him or what it was they were saying.

"I'm afraid we're dealing with a very serious incident indeed," Rønholt went on. "Without the accident we might never have found her at all."

"Was she thrown from the vehicle?"

"No, she was in the trunk. The rescue unit only discovered her when the truck came to collect the wreck."

"In the trunk?"

"The doctors say it looks like a failed murder. She'd been poisoned, but whoever did it must have underestimated the dosage. To my mind it was only down to error that she was still alive when the car crashed. She was wrapped up in a carpet, so tightly she ought by rights to have suffocated. Everything seems to indicate her assailant thought she was already dead."

"Is she going to pull through?"

"Hard to say. The driver was killed on the spot. The car was

Spanish registration and all he had on him was a Spanish driver's license and a wad of euros, no other documents at all."

"What about the driver's license?"

"False, of course," Rønholt replied. "The rescue unit found a cell phone under the passenger seat, though."

"And?"

"There was a Danish number in the list of calls. We can see he was in contact with that number even as the accident happened."

"Have you done a trace?"

"The number belongs to one Miklos Wedersøe of Sankt Jørgensbjerg, Roskilde."

"The attorney!" Louise burst out in astonishment. "Have you spoken to him?"

"He wasn't in, and his car was gone, too," Rønholt replied. "I wanted to ask you if were in touch with Wedersøe at any point yesterday?"

"No," said Louise. "Nymand's people stopped by his address last night to inform him about the hotel killing. He wasn't in then, either."

37

W e need to check this attorney from A to Z," Willumsen said as soon as the Homicide Department had been asked to assist on the case. "And Rebekka Sachs-Smith is going to start talking. *Now.*"

Louise nodded and glanced at her colleagues. Michael Stig sat restlessly drumming a pen against his knee. Toft had already raised a hand more than once to get him to stop, but two seconds later he was at it again.

To give her some credit, Rebekka Sachs-Smith had already talked, at least up to a point, having told them about how her brother and their attorney had been planning to sell the Angel of Death to a buyer in the United States.

The mood was tense and Willumsen had barked into the corridor to call them all together, as he did only when there was a breakthrough in a case or some poor soul had been picked out for a public reprimand. His forehead glistened and he seemed altogether a lot more agitated than usual. His face looked like he was on fire.

"Wedersøe was the last person to be in touch with the deceased," he began, and for a moment Louise was confused. Was he talking about the Spanish car driver now?

"The printouts from Carl Emil Sachs-Smith's phone have just come in," he went on. "The two of them, he and Wedersøe, were texting each other while Carl Emil was at the Prindsen."

Louise couldn't get her head around this at all. What had Wedersøe been up to?

"More to the point, however, Nymand just finished up going through the hotel's CCTV. Guess who left the Nordic wing at eight nineteen?" he said, modulating his voice into a flourish as beads of sweat trickled from his temple.

No one said a word, just sat there gaping at him as he perspired. Louise wasn't listening.

Willumsen continued: "Miklos Wedersøe. Captured on film leaving the elevator while lugging a large, unwieldy object wrapped up in a sheet."

"The icon?" Michael Stig offered with a hint of triumph, for a moment putting his infernal drumming on hold.

Willumsen nodded and wiped the back of his hand across his brow.

"That certainly has to be our assumption," the head of investigation replied, now getting up from his chair.

Louise offered to open a window, but Willumsen dismissed the suggestion with a wave of irritation.

"Police in Roskilde are taking care of the scene and interview-

ing witnesses. We've got the attorney on camera, but I want forensic evidence that he was in that room. Who wants to go out to
Wedersøe's house?"

Willumsen glanced from Louise and Lars Jørgensen to Michael
Stig.

"I'll go," said Stig, finally putting his pen down, only to be
brushed aside.

"No," said Willumsen, deciding the matter himself and pointing to Lars Jørgensen. "You and Rick," he said. "Seeing as you're
here today. Or maybe you're clocking out early?"

Lars Jørgensen sighed. "I'm here and working," he said.

Louise frowned and sent Willumsen a glare. He still had difficulty comprehending that Lars Jørgensen worked reduced hours.
To begin with, the superintendent had been so offensive toward
him that Louise's work partner had burned out from stress and
had to go off sick. However, due to a lack of resources in the department Willumsen had grudgingly accepted the situation, and
now the part-time arrangement was fully integrated into their
schedules.

"You're on the autopsy," Willumsen said firmly, with a nod in
the direction of Michael Stig.

38

Less than an hour later, Louise and Lars Jørgensen passed through the narrow streets of Roskilde's Sankt Jørgensbjerg district. Jørgensen was behind the wheel while she sat in the passenger seat keeping an eye on the house numbers as they passed a row of low, half-timbered homes.

Naja Holten had still not woken up from her coma. Rønholt had just checked with the Rigshospitalet, but it was evident that she had been the victim of a very serious assault and the consultant doctor from intensive care thought it a miracle she was still alive. At the moment, they were waiting for the results of their tests. Apparently it was too early to say whether she had suffered brain damage from the poison, so Rønholt had no idea if he would even be able to question her once she woke up. *If she woke up*, Louise thought to herself.

"Next one down," she said, pointing to a white detached residence set back from the road with a small garden out front.

First, they had stopped off at Wedersøe's office in the town center, only to be told no one had been informed he was going to be absent. His secretary was at a loss to explain why he had not turned up. It seemed it wasn't like him at all to miss his appointments.

"Turn up the driveway," Louise instructed, thinking it best to park out of the way. There was no sign of the big Mercedes she had seen at Rebekka Sachs-Smith's house the day before.

The weather had turned cold and her breath frosted in the air as they got out of the car. She went up to the white-painted front door and rang the bell, waited a second, then rang it again. When no one came, she knocked a couple of times for good measure with the heavy brass knocker, which was cast in the shape of a lion's head and positioned beneath a small, diamond-shaped window.

Lars Jørgensen stepped over a row of shrubbery and peered in through a window.

"Were there any other Danish numbers in our Spanish guy's contacts?" he asked, moving on to the next window.

"No, only Wedersøe's. The rest were Spanish, but the Search Department is trying to identify the driver through Interpol. His photo and dental records have already been sent down to the Spanish police. The car was hired in Málaga."

"What were they doing, I wonder."

Louise gave a shrug and rang the bell again.

"There's no one here," Jørgensen said, returning after having looked in through the last of the windows at the front of the house.

"Flemming Larsen examined Naja Holten this morning and he thinks she could have been in the trunk of that car all the way from the Costa del Sol. His assessment was that it was only because she was unconscious that she survived so long. There probably wouldn't have been enough oxygen if she'd been breathing normally," he told her, gesturing for her to follow him as he walked on.

They went around the side of the house and peered into the kitchen.

"Nothing here, either," he noted and buried his hands in his pockets. February's cold nipped at their cheeks. Louise shivered.

It was 11 a.m. and there had been no sign of life from the attorney since the day before. Louise called Rebekka Sachs-Smith to hear if she had been in touch with Wedersøe since Louise had left her house. Rebekka had not been informed about Naja Holten, so Louise inquired only if she might have an idea as to Wedersøe's whereabouts.

"She's gone," said Rebekka, obviously not caring about the family attorney. "My daughter's no longer in the place she was being held."

Her voice was at once shrill and fatigued, as if it were only being kept together by the anxiety and fear that were so plain in her tone.

"What makes you say that?" Louise probed, her eyes watching Lars Jørgensen as he tried the cellar door then gave up with a shake of his head.

"Mona says so. She rang Nymand and told him my daughter was closer than we imagined. But now she's gone."

Rebekka spoke quickly and with insistence, and Louise could hear Marybeth going about her work in the background.

"Mona had no way of knowing it was my brother who'd taken her," she went on.

When they had informed Rebekka that her daughter had been

with her brother ever since she disappeared, she had at first reacted with anger, berating the police for casting aspersions on their family. Eventually she had run out of steam and gone quiet again, shutting out everything and not wishing to hear another word.

"Who's Mona?" Louise asked and was given a story about a psychiatric patient at Sankt Hans who had on several previous occasions proved helpful to police in locating missing persons.

"There was an article about her in the *Roskilde Dagblad*; you can look it up," Rebekka told her.

Louise had more than a little difficulty imagining Nymand swallowing such a story, but it was just the kind of thing the media reveled in.

"A psychic, you mean?" Louise replied dismissively. They had found out for themselves how close the girl had been to them when they discovered she had been held in her uncle's apartment. How this Mona woman could have known about it, however, she was unable to say, since nothing had been given out to the press.

"She says Isabella's afraid. It's dark and cold where she is. You can see the place when you stand under the big arch."

Sure, Louise thought. Attention-seeking tea-leaf readers generally seemed to have no scruples about preying on a mother's fear as long as it meant they could grab some limelight for themselves.

"You could at least talk to her," Rebekka persisted, mentioning almost in an aside that Walther had now come home. "He landed a couple of hours ago and he wants you to put more people on the case."

"We don't have any more people," Louise snapped back, sensing how her lack of sleep suddenly boosted her annoyance levels. "We're working around the clock to find your daughter. You must trust us to do our work properly."

A lull ensued.

"But you aren't," Rebekka said. "If you'd been doing your work properly, my brother wouldn't be dead and Isabella would have been found."

Louise hung up for fear of losing her temper and reminding Rebekka in no uncertain terms that her having withheld information had most certainly hampered the police in their inquiries.

She told Lars Jørgensen about the psychic who had called Nymand. They were always there lurking in such cases, and they knew everything. All they had to do was close their eyes and feel the presence of the spirits, and all details of where and how even the most spectacular crimes had taken place would be mysteriously revealed to them. But they held no water with Louise, although she knew that the head of Homicide, Hans Suhr, took them seriously enough to place their predictions in the pile for further investigation whenever they landed on his desk. "What have we got to lose?" he always said.

He was right, of course, apart from the time they wasted.

"We'd better get a locksmith," said Jørgensen, his phone already to his ear.

She nodded and went over to where the steps led down to the cellar, climbing up onto the low whitewashed wall to look in at a window that was slightly higher than the others. Here she found herself peering into a small guest toilet where a mirror in a gilded frame hung above a little sink, all seemingly spotless and with no sign of recent use.

She jumped down again, only half listening as Jørgensen instructed the duty officer at the Mid and West Zealand Police to send a locksmith out to the address right away. That done, he asked to be put through to Nymand and explained to him briefly that they would be forcing entrance to the attorney's property.

They wandered back to the car to wait for the locksmith. The cold had already numbed their fingertips, and Lars Jørgensen switched the engine on and turned the heater up. As the warm air blasted out into the car interior, Louise began to feel drowsy. She closed her eyes and leaned her head back, and dropped off as easily as if she had taken a sleeping pill.

❧

"Front door or cellar?" said a voice, jarring her back from sleep. A young man was standing in the driveway; she guessed the locksmiths must have sent an apprentice.

"As long as we get in, that's all that matters," Lars Jørgensen answered, striding over to the front door as Louise got out of the car.

The young man considered the lock.

"Not an easy one, this," he said and clicked his tongue with studied skepticism. His hair was long on top and short at the sides, and in his left ear he wore a stud. It looked all wrong against his overalls and black T-shirt. However, after a few seconds and a couple of squeezes of his pick gun, he stepped back with satisfaction: "There we go. Piece of cake, as long as you know what you're doing."

He beamed them a smile while Louise wondered if there were locksmiths who didn't know what they were doing.

❧

The floor in the hallway was black-and-white-checkered marble, classically elegant, Louise observed as they stepped inside. The walls boasted high paneling; a staircase with a black banister and a black stair carpet in the middle wound its way up to the first floor.

Everything else was white. Poul Henningsen's great pendant Artichoke Lamp in copper hung from the ceiling above the staircase.

Louise noted the attention to detail. Not that she expected it would be significant to them in any way, but it helped her form an impression of the person who lived there.

"I wonder if he was single," she mused out loud as Lars Jørgensen came in after having updated Nymand. She thought she remembered Rebekka saying that their attorney was a workaholic of the kind who left no time aside for any private life to speak of, but on the other hand found it quite natural to spend absolutely heaps of money on themselves. She could see how right she was. Over by the fireplace was an Arne Jacobsen Egg Chair, and the TV was by Bang & Olufsen.

There was nobody downstairs. They had gone through all the rooms. The interior decoration, however exquisite, came across almost too perfect. Even the fondest aficionado of Danish Modern would surely find it overdone, Louise thought to herself, following Lars Jørgensen upstairs.

To the right was a bathroom done out in black marble with a huge shower area and a Jacuzzi in the corner. The towels were thick and white, plush bordering on decadent, making her think of a luxury hotel.

Maybe he was gay, she thought. There was something feminine about the room, and there was a scent of lavender in the air, like a soap she kept in her own bathroom at home.

She had thought of him as quite masculine when they had met at Rebekka's, perhaps because he was bald and drove such a big Mercedes—the first impressions he gave could hardly be more potent. The thought confused her as she went through his house.

"Come here," Lars Jørgensen called to her.

Louise followed his voice to the back room that seemed to be the attorney's home office.

On a notice board next to the desk were photographs of Christian icons. THE ARCHANGEL MICHAEL, ANGEL OF THE SUN, a caption said under one. Beside it was another angel, depicted kneeling and clad in a red cloak, lily in hand. Underneath it was written THE ANGEL OF THE MOON, but the words had been crossed out and replaced. Now it said THE ANGEL OF DEATH.

Lars Jørgensen studied it with her.

There was a photo of Roskilde Cathedral, too, and a notice about a meeting of the cathedral parish council along with a contact list of phone numbers belonging to the council's members. The attorney himself was third on the list.

"Is he religious, or what?" Jørgensen wondered, but Louise wasn't listening. On the wall above the desk were four portrait photographs. Four faces in gilded frames. One of them was Jeanette Milling.

Her partner was still going on about the icons on the notice board and the parish council, but Louise was somewhere else entirely. On the desk next to an antique silver box containing writing implements lay a thin gold chain with a ruby heart.

Louise recognized it from photos Rebekka had shown her. At once she felt gripped by fear at these disparate signals she was unable to fit together.

"We've got to turn this place upside down," she burst out a second later, and was already down the stairs before Lars Jørgensen had recovered from the fright. Her partner knew nothing about the ruby heart and had most likely seen nothing menacing about the portraits at all. Nonetheless he leaped into action and followed her downstairs.

"Access to the cellar only from the garden," he barked as Louise scanned the kitchen for the stairs. "Do you want me to call for some backup?"

She shook her head quickly, patting to make sure her service pistol sat snugly in its shoulder holster as she ran out into the hallway. Her every cell prickled with anxiety and made her skin creep.

⚮

Behind the house they entered a neatly kept garden. The leaves had been raked from the lawn, and all was orderly and meticulous.

"It's locked," Jørgensen shouted from the door at the bottom of the steps.

"Get the locksmith," Louise instructed. "He'll have to come back."

Her partner was already calling the number as he ran toward the driveway. Louise followed him and saw him turn the corner. She heard a car door slam and then another, after which he returned with the young apprentice who came walking up with a bottle of cola in one hand and his tool in the other.

It seemed he had been taking his time rather than hurrying back to his boss.

"We've got to get that cellar door open," Lars Jørgensen told him, leading the way around the side of the house.

They stood and waited while the young man went down the steps and muttered a few swear words about it not being one of the easy ones before turning to them with a triumphant little nod.

They flew down the steps and fumbled around in the dark looking for the lights. The windows facing the garden had been bricked up, but it was easy to see they where they had been.

"What's that smell?" Louise asked, stopping in her tracks.

"Maybe he paints," Lars Jørgensen suggested. "It's definitely chemicals of some sort. Turpentine, perhaps."

"It smells more like nail polish remover, only a lot stronger," Louise responded, hurrying toward a wooden door at the end of the passage. She opened it and poked her head into the room, but was unable to see anything at all, apart from the fact that it was quite small and seemed empty. She closed the door again.

"Down here's locked," said Jørgensen from the other end.

"I didn't even check to see if there were any keys upstairs. I'll go and look," Louise said.

She ran up the steps, wondering for a moment if it was wise to split up, but she was already at the front of the house again. Somehow, she had an unpleasant feeling about what they might find behind that locked door.

People's bizarre sex fetishes were not something she cared to learn more about, and if the finicky order of the house's stylish interior was anything to go by it would not surprise her in the slightest if there was something contrastingly messy down there locked away out of sight, she thought, her eyes darting as she looked for a key rack.

She nearly missed the bunch of keys on the kitchen counter next to the sink, yet they seemed almost to have been left there for her to find. She snatched them up and dashed back to the cellar. She found Jørgensen waiting for her in the passage and tried two keys before the third slipped agreeably into the lock.

❧

The reek of acetone was so powerful Louise instinctively covered her mouth with the sleeve of her coat. If anything, it was even

255

more pungent than the smell of a dead body, she thought, tentatively stepping forward toward what appeared to be an oversize chest freezer.

"It looks like some kind of lab down here," Lars Jørgensen speculated, glancing around at the white tiles and the stainless steel table at the end.

"The smell can't have bothered him much," Louise muttered, sensing the chemical grating in her nostrils and throat. She stood for a moment to steady her breathing as Jørgensen stepped forward and pulled on the handle of a door that turned out also to be locked.

She tossed him the keys and studied the gurney that was parked in the passage, listening for any sound and desperately trying to dismiss the flow of images that ran through her mind from recent cases in which children and young women had been held captive for years on end.

"Where the hell's the light?" Lars Jørgensen said.

He had unlocked and opened the door of a room that was completely dark. Louise heard him fumble for a switch.

Then suddenly he exclaimed in fright, jumping back and almost screeching: "What the—?"

Louise ventured forward with the small flashlight she had taken from her pocket.

A second later she screamed.

It wasn't so much the shock of shining the light into the face of a dead woman as it was the fact that the woman was Jeanette Milling.

"What is this?" she exclaimed, stunned by what she had seen.

"I think I've found the switch," Lars Jørgensen said behind her, and a second later the room was bathed in soft, sumptuous light.

Louise stood entranced, unable to move. All she could do was stare at the naked female bodies.

Lars Jørgensen found another switch and an almost theatrical system of spotlights drew all focus to the four corpses.

"Who are the others?" he wondered.

"A Norwegian and two Swedes," Louise replied, thinking of Rønholt's list of women who had disappeared from the same region as Jeanette.

But the girl. There was no sign of the little girl.

Louise wheeled around and ran back through the passage, past the big chest freezer, shouting for Jørgensen to bring the keys. They unlocked the final room and found it empty apart from a large stainless steel bath in the middle of the floor.

Isabella wasn't there. For a second Louise was thankful, though the feeling would not translate into relief.

"Look at this," Lars Jørgensen said, coming toward her with a dark wooden box in his hands.

She had to get up close to see the four pairs of glass eyes inside. The other dedicated recesses in the box were empty. At one point there had seemingly been eight pairs together.

Louise backed away. She needed to get outside and get some air. The feeling of being cooped up in a cellar with four dead bodies knotted her stomach.

She had seen cases where a seemingly normal, stable family man had killed his wife and children one by one and left each in their own pool of blood. That was bad enough. But this was worse, she thought to herself, dashing around the side of the house to throw up. Maybe it was because she had yet to fully comprehend what it was she had seen.

She paused for a moment to collect herself, then called Rønholt and gave him the address.

Louise rushed into Willumsen's office as soon as they got back from Roskilde and told him what they had found in the attorney's cellar. Cold air whipped in through the open window, and Willumsen himself sat ashen-faced behind his desk with reams of paper spread out in front of him.

"Get the others in here," he told her, holding her back for a moment to tell her a woman had called in saying she may have seen a girl fitting the description of Isabella Sachs-Smith.

Louise was still in shock from having discovered the four women's bodies but tried to push the thought aside and focus on the little girl.

"The witness claims she saw the girl being forced into a large Mercedes in the parking area underneath the building where Carl Emil Sachs-Smith lived," Willumsen explained after they were all gathered in his office.

He had risen to his feet. For a second he seemed to drift away, closing his eyes and looking out of sorts. Then he went on:

"She did not intervene, for fear of meddling in something that didn't concern her."

"People these days," Toft snorted with indignation.

Willumsen gave a shrug and looked at Louise. "Time's running out," he said. "The negotiation unit was unfortunately unable to secure the girl's release when they had the chance. Now we need to find out if she's with Miklos Wedersøe. I want that girl back with her mother."

Louise looked down. It wasn't Willumsen's attitude as such that she found provoking; it was more because he never stopped. She tried to dismiss his humiliating criticism, but the fury she felt was also connected to the fact that the remark was merited: They had indeed failed.

"I want a search out on Wedersøe's car," Willumsen commanded, raising his voice suddenly as if there were something he wished to impress on them. "I want every police district in the country out looking for him. Checks on all borders. Men on all ferries and bridges."

Then, abruptly, he clutched his chest and fell to the floor.

39

"Why doesn't Frederik just stay in your bed?" Markus had asked before he went off to school. "You don't have to pretend he's sleeping on the sofa, you know!"

Camilla had been making his packed lunch when he came into the kitchen. Until now she had been doing her utmost to give the impression that Frederik Sachs-Smith was just a good friend who needed a place to stay while he was in Denmark. Apparently, though, her son was not quite as naive as she thought.

She and Frederik had even set the alarm so they could get up ten minutes before she had to wake Markus. As they tumbled out of bed the heady scent of night-long sex still hung in the air of the bedroom and in the duvet they hurriedly bundled onto the sofa in the living room. She only hoped her thirteen-year-old son had not sussed that bit out, too.

She shook her head and went to fetch her laptop but had difficulty concentrating. She kept seeing Carl Emil splayed out on the hotel bed before her eyes. She tried to delete the image from her mind and get to work on the article she was supposed to be writing for *Morgenavisen*.

Although she was no longer a part of their crime desk she had offered them the story when Walther Sachs-Smith had called her shortly after landing at Copenhagen's Kastrup Airport and asked her to find a Danish newspaper that would publish the truth about the Angel of Death.

"I've given the matter a great deal of consideration," he told her, "and the time has come to tell the icon's story. After all that's happened, we can no longer keep it a secret. I want you to reveal how it came into the hands of my father and his family in Poland. I want people to know that we have never sought to conceal the artifact for reasons of greed, but simply because we did not wish to expose my father's poor in-laws to any further harassment. I have lost my wife and now my son. I would like to do everything in my power to avoid anything happening to Isabella."

Camilla hadn't the heart to say that it was perhaps too late. It was obvious to her that the man was crushed. She promised to pen the article and make sure everything came out.

"I shall never forgive myself for my judgment having failed so fatally when I appointed Wedersøe to succeed our former attorney," Walther Sachs-Smith had gone on to say, just as Camilla had thought the conversation to be over. "Things would have looked very different today if he had not been admitted into the family. The strife that has so blighted the company. His predecessor would never have turned my children against me for his own financial gain. I have been angry with my two youngest children, very angry indeed. Yet during these past few months I had looked forward to our one day being able to put all our disagreements behind us. Now I must live with the fact that I never had the chance to be reconciled with my son before he was so brutally taken away. I should not have asked him to take responsibility for the icon. I ought to have foreseen how badly it would all turn out. I'm so terribly sorry to have involved you in all of this."

"I'd like to help," Camilla had tried to say, only for Sachs-Smith to continue.

"I would like you to emphasize in your article that no charges need be brought if only my grandchild is returned to us unharmed. No one should be left in any doubt that the Angel of Death has already cost far too many lives."

❧

Camilla had snuggled into the sofa with her laptop. She was trying to focus on the story and had spread all her notes out around her, including the closely written splashy postcards from Hawaii that now covered the surface of the coffee table, but she was having difficulty getting started.

After her talk with Walther Sachs-Smith, Frederik had come into the living room and sat down opposite her in the white armchair. She had sensed something serious and even before he began to speak she found she had resigned herself to his also having realized that the sensible thing would be to break off their relationship. Even if the sex was good there was still a long way between the United States and Frederiksberg.

"I love you," he said, reaching a hand across the table and taking hold of hers. "Come and live with me."

At first she had no idea what to say. He had completely caught her off guard.

"I can't," she said, smiling to hide how moved she was by his suggestion. "What about Markus?"

So maybe it wasn't all over after all, she managed to think fleetingly, sensing a warmth spread inside her when she realized this was something he had been thinking about for some time. His reply certainly indicated he had been investigating all the possibilities:

"There's a good high school nearby, and an international private school if you think that would be better. We could get him enrolled, it wouldn't be a problem."

Camilla was speechless and could only stare at him.

We could get him enrolled. He made it sound like he wanted to adopt her son. He, who had never had children of his own. But she knew he and Markus had hit it off. She knew, too, that it was because Frederik actually liked to spend time with him. Unlike the boy's own father, who seemed more interested in his new wife and the baby they were expecting that summer. Markus and his father were together a couple of days every other weekend at most now, and even that seemed to be happening less and less.

"I know that he needs to keep up his relationship to his father," Frederik had gone on when she didn't know what to say to his suggestion concerning school. "But the flights are very regular."

It wasn't because she didn't want to reply. She was simply at a loss for words. She still had not gotten used to the idea of money being no object. He was so wealthy that day-to-day finances never came into the picture.

She closed her laptop, finding her thoughts just wouldn't leave her alone. Frederik had borrowed her little Fiat so he could drive to Roskilde and be with his sister and their father. She had been intending to spend the whole day working on the article. But it was no use: She couldn't concentrate.

What on earth would she *do* over there? Frederik had said she could write scripts with him. She could keep her flat in Frederiksberg as a base whenever she needed to be in Denmark.

He seemed to have an answer to her every question. It was obvious to her that he really had thought things through. She thought perhaps that was what made her feel so good about it all.

The prospect buzzed in her mind, like an insistent swarm of insects on a warm summer's eve.

Her phone had been already been ringing for a while before she even noticed.

⁂

"Willumsen just had a heart attack," Louise began, her voice trailing away.

"What?" Camilla exclaimed. This sudden information instantly pushed her own concerns to the back of her mind. "Are you over at HQ?"

"He just collapsed," Louise said, picking up the thread again, her voice thin and feeble. "Suhr tried to revive him while someone called emergency services."

"Is he dead?" Camilla asked incredulously, picturing the dark-haired superintendent in her mind's eye. The two of them had had their tussles over the years. Nevertheless, her stomach knotted.

"No," Louise replied, "there was still a pulse. It was all so awful; he just collapsed in front of us in mid-sentence. Like someone just switched him off."

"I really hope it's not serious," Camilla said, and heard Louise blow her nose at the other end.

"Me, too," Louise replied weakly and blew her nose again, before abruptly changing the subject. "We're pretty sure the Sachs-Smith family's attorney is involved in at least four killings," she said. "He was also captured by the CCTV at the Hotel Prindsen at the time of Carl Emil's murder."

"Oh, my God!" Camilla exclaimed.

Louise went on, "We've put a nationwide search out for him, the public advised to approach only with extreme caution. He may well have left the country already. We've notified police in Sweden and put checks on the border to Germany. Interpol have been issued descriptions of both him and the car."

She added that they were reasonably sure the Angel of Death was in the back of his car.

"What about the girl?" Camilla breathed, thinking once again of the family.

"We don't know," Louise answered. "But I think it's most likely he got rid of her."

Camilla was unable to speak a word as Louise brought the call to an end. All of a sudden Santa Barbara seemed so far away she could barely entertain the thought of it.

Got rid of her?

"Call me when there's news about Willumsen," she managed to say before Louise hung up.

40

Willumsen had been collected by an ambulance. The medics had tried to resuscitate him, but as they sped away they had still not succeeded in restarting his heart, which had apparently stopped since Suhr's CPR.

Shocked and exhausted, Louise shut down her computer after speaking to Camilla and decided to go home and sleep for a couple of hours. Putting on her coat, she felt she ought to call Rønholt and hear if there was anything new, but she simply hadn't the strength. What she needed now was to be off the job, if only for a few hours. The events of the last few days seemed suddenly to bear down on her, and after seeing the ambulance crew dash away with Willumsen like that it had all become too much for her.

She borrowed the keys of a service car from the front office and drove off to Frederiksberg. It had been years since she had felt the kind of fear she did now: the fear of an emotional breakdown. She had been working hard to keep it at bay. And Jakobsen, the department's crisis counselor, had helped her with techniques she could use so as not to experience other people's grief as her own. Of course, she was fully aware she needed to be in her work headspace if she was to be able to think clearly, but right now that distance was very difficult indeed for her to visualize.

So she went home instead.

The flat was empty when she stepped inside the hall. Maybe Jonas had taken Dina for a walk. She had been hoping he would be there when she came in. She glanced up at the time and saw it was half an hour since the last lesson had ended.

She took a soft drink out of the fridge and sat down at the table. She was a poor substitute for a mother, that much seemed clear to her. But at this moment she missed the boy so terribly.

She answered her phone as soon as it rang. It was Lars Jørgensen.

"Willumsen's dead," he said quietly. "He died in the ambulance on his way to the hospital."

Louise swallowed.

"Thanks for calling," she mumbled and hung up. And then she began to cry.

She didn't hear the door when it opened, or realize that Jonas had come in and was standing perplexed beside her. It was only when he crouched down that she discovered he was there.

"What's wrong?" he asked anxiously and put his arm around her. "Is it that little girl?"

Louise glanced around for some paper towels. She didn't care for him to see her in such a state.

Once she had blown her nose and dabbed her eyes, she shook her head.

"Willumsen's dead," she said, sensing how unreal it felt to speak the words out loud.

She drew him close. Jonas knew the superintendent and was fond of him. Willumsen had been anything but the blunt and unpleasant policeman on the occasions he and the boy had met, and while Louise thought she would most probably remember him for his brusque demeanor, she was so upset by the news that her whole being seemed racked with grief.

"He collapsed at work today. It was a heart attack."

"I'm really sorry," Jonas said.

Louise tried to respond with a smile. "Maybe not everyone will miss him shouting, 'What do you think this is, a rest home for pregnant nuns?'"

She choked up again and sobbed, but looked up when she sensed that Jonas was about to say something.

"At school some of them say my parents are lucky to be dead so they don't have to look at me anymore."

Louise gasped for breath.

"They say what?"

He nodded and lowered his head, his hair flopping down to cover his eyes.

She turned to face him fully and put her hands on his shoulders. "Who says that?"

"A few of them," he replied without looking up, clearly uncomfortable with having to tell her.

Louise stood up and held him tight.

"What a nasty thing to say," she whispered.

She could feel the tension in his body underneath his hoodie and hugged him tighter.

"How long has this been going on?" she asked when eventually she let go.

He shrugged without saying anything.

"It started off with Lasse," he said when finally he looked up at her. "After what happened to Signe."

Louise nodded. She had been to pick him up several times when he had spent the night with his friend down by the city lakes, but she had no idea they had fallen out.

"It started with him saying Signe probably didn't mind being dead if it meant she could get rid of me."

Tears welled now behind his long, dark lashes.

Signe and Jonas had been in the same class since they had started school, and in the year before the accident they had been seeing each other a lot. She had been killed one dark evening after running out in front of a car in panic. Her death had hit Jonas hard. He had known far too much grief in such a short time, Louise thought to herself, finding it hard to understand why he had kept quiet about it.

"Now he and a couple of the others are saying Mom and Dad are lucky they can't see me making a fool of myself chasing Eva around."

Eva? Louise thought, trying to put a face to the name.

"Lasse's had a crush on her for the last six months, but she's not interested. That's why."

"Does your teacher know about any of this?"

He nodded and snorted in a way she at first was unsure how to interpret.

"It'd be hard not to know, the way they go around shouting it all over school."

She felt a rush of rage that forced her body into motion, propelling her to the kitchen window where she stood and looked down into the rear courtyard, saddened by the thought that she had so patently failed to see the signs. She ought to have reacted, done something. But she had been immersed in her work.

She buried her face in her hands for a second.

"Is that why you hit him?" she asked, turning to face him again.

Jonas nodded.

"I'll phone that school right away; let me just find the number," she said.

A shadow passed over his face. "No, please don't," he said.

"Why not?"

"Because I don't want to be a snitch."

"But, Jonas"—she stepped up to him again—"putting up with things is fine once in a while. But when there's bullying and someone's saying things as mean as that, your teacher has to step in. And the school executives should be fully informed."

"I'd still much rather you didn't."

Louise studied him for a moment before capitulating with a reluctant nod. Her rage, however, remained.

"Okay," she said with a sigh. "What about Lasse's parents? They should know what their son's going around saying, surely?"

Jonas shook his head quickly.

"I'll manage," he said, and Louise realized he meant it. But she promised herself she would never again allow him to be pushed to the point where he began to lash out physically. She was his adoptive mother and responsible for him; it was imperative she be there for him whenever he needed her.

"Can I stay at Eva's tonight?" he asked, unable once again to look her in the eye, but this time, she sensed, it was more down to regular self-consciousness.

Louise smiled at him.

"If you pack your school bag and remember your toothbrush, *and* make sure Lasse and the other boys see the two of you coming to school together in the morning, then yes, it's okay by me."

41

Miklos Wedersøe had just passed the Padborg exit and was approaching the German border when he saw the blue lights flashing in his rearview mirror. Two patrol cars, as far as he could tell, and it was no coincidence they had appeared at the same time.

They were after him, and they were close. He put his foot down and felt the thrust of the big Mercedes as it seamlessly picked up speed. A hundred eighty, two hundred kilometers per hour and still effortlessly accelerating as he flicked on the main beam and arrowed into the fast lane to shake off his pursuers.

Though his heart was beating fast, he still savored the sheer velocity provided by the vehicle's horsepower—more than six hundred—and the distance it instantly put between him and the two cars behind.

He focused fully on his driving and ignored the dwindling image of his pursuers in the mirror. He was so close to the border now that he had hoped to simply slip through and away. But then, he also had a plan in the event he were thwarted. It was a good plan, he thought, proceeding from the assumption that the police had by now found the keys he had left on the kitchen counter at home.

He was strong, and his weapons were honed.

Suddenly he felt the blood begin to pound in his temples at the thought of the police's own, very real weapons that might soon be trained on him. A Volvo station wagon made to pull out in front of him and he pressed the horn down hard with the flat of his hand, causing the intrusive vehicle to shrink back into its own lane in fright.

He ought to have secured himself a weapon, but he had not had time and would most likely not be needing one anyway, he told himself.

He had the girl.

A moment later he saw them up ahead. The flashing lights coming toward him on the opposite, northbound lane. He noted how the police car sped up the slope of the exit, but he knew it would be unable to catch up with him. He was safely in control in the fast lane, and they would first have to negotiate the highway bridge before being able to join the pursuit in the southbound direction.

The adrenaline rushed through his arteries as it registered that the police would be intensifying their chase now that they'd pinpointed his position.

Abruptly he stepped on the brakes as a truck suddenly crawled into his lane a few hundred meters ahead to overtake a van that was hogging the middle lane. He sensed immediately the futility of trying to bully the huge vehicle back into place; he would have to slow down.

Nervously he glanced back in the mirror and saw the police car now coming down the access road onto the highway behind him.

Several trucks drove in a convoy in the inside lane. It would take time before the one in the fast lane had overtaken the van.

Time was precious and it occurred to him that it might already be too late. His pulse throbbed and his hands were sweaty as they clutched the leather steering wheel. With a quick look back he veered onto the shoulder and put his foot down.

The automatic transmission thrust him forward to pass the convoy of trucks on the inside. He saw he was doing 160 when his brain registered that he was hemmed in. The convoy lay stretched out nose-to-tail; the Mercedes would surely be crushed if he tried to slip in between.

Taking chances was not his forte. He thought of the icon under the quilt in the back and heard the sirens: They were close now.

He accelerated along the shoulder, so squeezed in that he lacked the courage to even glance to the side, forced to fix his gaze on the narrow ribbon of asphalt in front of him. The convoy closed him off from the other lanes entirely and he was unable to see the police cars, but figured they would hardly be alongside yet.

Focus. He was so concentrated that beads of sweat trickled from his bald head without him noticing. Only when they ran over his eyebrows and into his eyes, momentarily blurring his vision, did he release the steering wheel with one hand to wipe them away.

One more truck and the convoy would be behind him. He was going to make it, he told himself, and then, as if to endorse his optimism, the highway opened up ahead.

Filled with relief, he saw that the police cars were still some way behind him. But then, as he swept through the highway's gentle curve, he saw a police roadblock looming up in the distance, stretched out across all three lanes.

The sweat poured from him now, its salt stinging in his eyes. He saw there was no exit by which he might escape before reaching the roadblock. They must have known, he thought rationally, and understood in the same instant that he was trapped.

Glancing to the side, he saw that the steep bank that lined the highway was too much of an obstacle and likewise quickly dismissed all thought of ramming his way through the line of police cars that had been parked bumper-to-bumper to cut off the way ahead. The white vehicles had their blue lights flashing and the police themselves stood in front like a human shield.

Behind him he heard again the shrill scream of pursuing sirens and was immediately jolted back to reality.

There was no escape.

It was as if something inside him turned to steel. He took his foot off the accelerator. A moment before, when he had been stuck on the shoulder and had run a quite indefensible risk, he had felt himself, however briefly, gripped by a sense of rising panic. But it was gone now.

He had the girl, and it would be up to them to decide if she would live or die.

He put his foot gently on the brake.

42

Louise turned off toward the Boserup Forest. Sankt Hans, the psychiatric center, was situated in Roskilde's pleasant suburbs. She saw the big buildings from afar, clustered against the background of the fjord. She followed the signs toward the information desk and parked outside the main door.

"I'd like to speak to one of your patients," she said to the woman who came to help her, handing her a piece of paper with a name on it that Rebekka had given her. "Mona Jepsen."

She presented herself and passed her police ID over the counter.

"Mona isn't here anymore," the woman replied without so much as casting an eye on either the paper or the ID.

"What do you mean?" Louise asked, slightly confused.

"She was admitted when police said they were interested in that little girl's whereabouts," the woman explained, adding that Mona

Jepsen always became rather unsettled by people going missing. "She was in quite a state when she arrived. But today she was feeling much better and asked to be released."

Louise raised an eyebrow in surprise.

"We've known Mona for years," the woman smiled. "She's been in our system here ever since she was young and knows her own rhythm now. She can feel it whenever she won't be able to look after herself, but she also always knows when her seizures are going to stop again."

"Seizures?" Louise inquired, though sensed immediately that any answer would compromise medical confidentiality.

The woman smiled apologetically.

"Do you know where I might find her?" she asked instead.

"Well, either she'll be at home or else she'll have gone to see Gerd," the woman replied, looking pensive for a moment. "I can find the numbers for you, just a minute."

Louise waited patiently until the woman returned with an address, explaining to her how best to get to Svogerslev.

"Thanks very much, you've been a big help," she said, taking the yellow Post-it the woman handed her and going back out to the car.

❧

"Who did you say it was?" the elderly woman answered in a deep, masculine voice when Louise called from her car. At first she thought it was a man, but when the woman called for Mona a moment later she could hear she had been mistaken.

"My name's Louise Rick," she repeated once Mona Jepsen came to the phone.

She heard herself enunciating as if she were speaking to a child who didn't quite understand. "I gather you might be able to tell us something about Isabella Sachs-Smith?"

"She's alive," the woman replied swiftly. "If you've got time I can tell you some more."

Louise felt like an idiot and regretted giving the woman any time at all. She ought to have driven back to Police HQ, but somehow it was the last place she wanted to be. For the moment, at least.

"I'll tell Gerd you're coming," Mona Jepsen added in a bright, clear voice.

Louise thought for a second before accepting. As Suhr always said, what did they have to lose? They still had no trace of the girl, so she was willing to try anything.

"I'm on my way," she said, and hung up.

❧

The houses were red brick and arranged in clusters with little gardens facing the parking area. Louise followed a system of footpaths over to the other side and found the house, the last in a little row.

The woman who came to the door was dressed in dungarees, her gray hair worn in a pageboy style and swept behind her ears at the sides. Her eyes almost seemed to smile behind her wire-rimmed glasses and it did not surprise Louise one bit to learn that the woman, now retired, had once been Mona Jepsen's school psychologist.

"Mona's in the living room," she said, advising Louise that she had two Norwegian Forest cats. "You're not allergic, are you?"

Louise shook her head and thought of Dina at home. She was

really more of a cat person herself, but now they had a dog. For a brief moment, Mik passed fleetingly through her mind. She missed him, but had gradually come to terms with the fact that she would probably never hear from him again.

"Follow me," said Gerd.

The hallway was stuffed with gloomy furniture. A tall sideboard with five enormous drawers stood up against one wall.

Louise took her boots off and followed on behind into a living room that smelled of chamomile tea and herbs. It was pleasant enough, if rather predictably on the mildewy side, she thought, before stopping in her tracks at the sight of Mona Jepsen.

Mona Jepsen was seated at the end of a six-seater solid oak dining table, and Louise was so taken aback she could hardly stop staring.

As slight as a little girl and with white, lifeless hair reaching to her waist, she sat with a number of dead insects arranged on the table in front of her.

Not until Mona pushed her chair back to get to her feet and say hello did Louise snap out of her stupor and put out her hand in return.

At first sight, Mona Jepsen's face suggested youth. As if time were somehow standing still for her, Louise thought, recalling that she had been told Mona was in her mid-forties. Only when she stepped closer did she become aware of the slight droop of her eyelids, the more mature look in her eye than was immediately visible from a distance.

They greeted each other and she thanked Mona for letting her come on such short notice.

"Of course," Mona replied. "I did phone the chief superintendent, but he didn't have time."

Louise could hardly take her eyes off the table.

The insects.

Great, dead things lined up with the care of a stamp collector. All were different, and it seemed Mona Jepsen was in the process of piercing them with needles. On a chair next to the table was a little display board on which the first exemplars had already been mounted.

"I collect them," she said in her little girl's voice that seemed so completely at odds with her macabre enterprise. "These aren't especially rare, but I'd like them framed anyway. This one I found yesterday after I heard about Isabella."

She pointed out a large spider that had now been pressed.

"And a fly, I see," said Louise, pulling out a chair from the middle of the table.

"Yes, there aren't that many insects around in February, so there are always some doubles at this time of year."

Louise nodded.

"The girl's afraid. You must hurry to find her."

Louise opened her mouth and was just about to say something when she noticed the stack of newspaper cuttings in the middle of the table. All seemed to be about Isabella. A shudder ran down her spine and she couldn't help but wonder if the strange and fragile woman with her insects had simply been gripped by the story and fabricated some continuation of it, or whether she really might possess some insight.

Mona Jepsen had sat down cross-legged on her chair. Her baggy harem pants lay in folds around her.

"She doesn't have enough air."

Gerd had now come to the table, too, and pulled a chair out at the other end where she wouldn't be in the way.

"You can trust Mona's intuitions to be true," the retired psychologist said.

Louise smiled awkwardly.

"There was a girl once who disappeared after a concert in the park here," the elderly woman went on. "Mona rang the police and told them the girl was hiding on a boat in the marina. Sure enough, the police found her there that same night."

Louise leaned forward. "Mona, if you have any idea where Isabella Sachs-Smith might be being held, I must ask you to tell me," she said, feeling herself to be suddenly carried away by the conviction in the mysterious woman's eyes.

"I didn't say I knew where," Mona answered quickly, her busy fingers toying with what looked like an earwig. "I didn't say that at all, nothing like. If I knew that kind of thing, I'd have to have your job, wouldn't I?"

She started to laugh.

A nutcase, Louise concluded, annoyed with herself at having given it a try. Still, it would give Lars Jørgensen something to laugh about once this dreadful thing was all over.

"I don't know where the girl is, but if she could look out she would see right across at a big arch. I can feel she's afraid, and it's dark all around her. There's something wrong with her breathing, too. It's like the oxygen's running out."

Louise nodded and stroked the big tomcat that had jumped onto her lap. She was unable to keep her eyes from the diminutive woman, although Gerd had now embarked on a somewhat lengthy speech on the subject of intuition and its conceivable uses.

"It's important you find the right arch," Mona interjected, fixing her penetrating gaze on her guest.

"Why did you admit yourself to the center the other day?" Louise asked her instead of commenting on her visions.

The unburdened look that had been present in her blue eyes vanished, and although she might not have been aware of the fact,

Mona Jepsen's hands dropped underneath the table and she began to shift uneasily on her chair.

Louise sensed immediately that she had touched uncomfortably on a delicate matter.

It was Gerd who answered.

"Mona is very much affected when people go missing, and sometimes it comes over her the way it did when she heard about Isabella Sachs-Smith."

Louise nodded; she knew it was best not to pursue the matter. She got to her feet, stepping toward Mona and offering her hand with a polite suggestion that she would be grateful if Mona would contact her if she felt there was something the police ought to know.

The fragile little woman nodded, her eyes fixed on her insects, and she did not get up when Louise put her card with her phone number on it on the table and left the room.

Out in the hallway, Gerd opened the front door for her and paused while still holding the handle.

"She doesn't often use her abilities, but they're there," she said, her voice full of warmth. "Take it from me, it would be wise to listen to what she has to say."

Louise nodded and thanked her without feeling in any way convinced.

Returning to the car, she checked her phone and saw there were four unanswered calls from Rønholt. He had left a message on her voice mail, too:

"Forensics found insulin pens in Carl Emil's name in the cellar. We're working on the assumption Wedersøe also killed Inger Sachs-Smith. Moreover, they found the same paint that was used for that headstone."

Louise stared into the air in front of her, shaken by the thought that the attorney had resorted to death threats to prompt his client into getting his hands on the icon as quickly as possible.

"The sick bastard," she muttered, reflecting on the case so far. Six lives had been taken. Very nearly seven, counting Naja Holten. And now he had vanished with the little girl.

She closed her eyes and leaned back against the headrest.

※

The light was distant, almost out of reach, when Naja Holten opened her eyes.

Everything was silent. Sleep beckoned and she succumbed, drifting heavily away, but then it was there again.

The voice, calling out to her.

She tried again, struggling to open her cumbersome eyelids, clinging to the voice of the man who repeated her name.

"She's coming back," a woman said farther away.

Naja wanted to shake her head. She wanted the woman to be quiet so she could hear the man at her side. She sensed him come closer, felt his breath on her cheek.

"Sweetheart, wake up."

Jesper. She had been dreaming about him. Or at least she thought she had, but now she was no longer sure. Nothing seemed certain anymore. She was so tired.

"Wake up," he said again.

The light was dazzling when finally she opened her eyes fully. His face: She recognized the lines of his face, his hazel eyes moist and glassy.

He smoothed her cheek and wiped his eyes quickly with the backs of his hands so as not to cry on her.

More faces came and peered, unfamiliar faces. A stethoscope was put to her chest, her blood pressure measured.

"Squeeze my hand if you can hear me," said Jesper.

She wanted to smile at him, but her face felt oddly stiff, so she simply squeezed as instructed.

"You're in the Rigshospitalet," he said. "You were in a car accident."

Naja tried to shake her head again, but was unable to. She remembered the cloth pressed hard against her mouth, how it took away all her breath, how she had struggled with death as the night descended.

It was no car accident. But she had no idea how to tell them. Again she felt the cloth against her face. A flood of nausea flushed through her, compelling her to reach out so that she might pull herself upright.

"She's moving her arm," a woman's voice said.

Immediately she felt Jesper's hand against her back and glimpsed the vomit bowl he held up to her mouth.

And then it came. Her whole body trembled with cold, and still it came.

"It's the antidote," a deep voice commented, and she registered a man in a white coat who had appeared at the bedside. "It's working nicely."

She vomited again, a deluge, and Jesper held up a new bowl.

Naja closed her eyes and slumped back into her pillow, still freezing cold. But now her body relaxed. She tried to gain control of her mouth. It had opened for her to throw up. It could open again.

"Jesper," she breathed, and found her lips now obeyed the command.

"I'm here," he answered, close again.

"What do you mean, accident?"

"Nothing, it's all right," he replied quickly.

"He tried to kill me. It was no accident."

"I know. But he didn't succeed."

She remembered it all, recalling how it had felt to be in the very clutches of death. The darkness and fear. She would remember it for as long as she lived. Always she would be able to recall the terror, she told herself, and was suddenly lucid.

There was a knock on the door and she looked across to see a man with a neatly trimmed beard peering in.

"We'd like to speak to Naja," he said, introducing himself as Rønholt from the Search Department of the National Police. "Can I come in?"

She saw Jesper rise to his feet and felt a ripple of unease.

"Don't go."

"No, absolutely not," her partner replied swiftly, taking her hand in his again. "I'll stay right here with you. But you must talk to the police."

43

Four service pistols were aimed straight at him. The other officers stood with their hands already at their shoulder holsters.

He understood their wordless communication perfectly, the body language, the steely-eyed vigilance. He locked the car and raised his hands obligingly in the air to signal that it was okay for them to lower their weapons, which predictably they did not.

Then, before he knew it, his arm was twisted up his back and his jaw slammed painfully against the Mercedes's hood. He felt the heat of its metal on his skin.

He tried to lift his head, but a viselike hand forced him into immediate submission.

"Miklos Wedersøe," a voice rattled off in buoyant South Jutlandic. "You are now under arrest and will be charged with murder, interference with a human corpse, and the abduction of Isabella Sachs-Smith."

None of it came as any surprise to him, though it was odd that the officer had failed to mention the Angel of Death, he thought to himself as handcuffs snapped tightly around his wrists.

"Who are you reporting to?" he asked, once he was permitted to stand upright. "The negotiation unit or Roskilde Police?"

"Never mind that," replied the policeman, who was gripping his right arm at the elbow. "You just come with us."

The young man's hair was fair and curly, buffeted by gusts of wind. He looked like a farm boy, his cheeks blotched ruddy by sheer agitation and excitement, his nerves an uncertain flutter beneath the textbook exterior.

Miklos glanced at the other officers. They were alert and at the ready, their eyes attentive and keen. The gravity of the case was plain, he thought. But if only they knew. This was a mere diversion, and any minute now they would be forced to release him again and allow him to drive on.

Only then did he become aware of the stillness. There was no longer any traffic on the opposite roadway. The constant noise was gone. They had closed down the entire highway, he realized, and felt satisfied by the delay it would entail before normal traffic could be resumed, allowing him a clear start to his continued journey south.

An elderly man strode forward, glaring at him through eyes narrowed to slits of disdain.

"Where is she?" he demanded, his gaze fixed on the attorney, seemingly oblivious to the police officer at his side.

There was something about his tone that annoyed him. The man was insolent and rude, and Wedersøe took particular offense at the way he stared, like some windbag sheriff who thought he could banish the bad guys from town with a warning shot fired into the air.

He had anticipated a more civilized exchange, courteous communication between decent individuals, but now his own arrogance came to the fore and his eyes took in the man dismissively, looking him up and down as if to ridicule his every visible weakness.

"Might I inquire who is in charge here?" he said, making it clear he certainly did not consider the local pencil-licker worthy enough to have been handed such an important matter as a kidnapping. The man was obviously little more than a cattle driver.

But instead of replying to Wedersøe's question, he responded with one of his own instead.

"Do you want us to call witnesses before we search the vehicle?"

"No," Wedersøe replied with a shake of his head. "But save yourselves the effort. She's not there."

He looked at the three officers who stood peering into the Mercedes.

"We need the trunk opened," one of them said.

"If you're interested in saving the girl's life, you'll have to let me speak to Nymand," Wedersøe said. "I assume Roskilde is still in charge of the investigation."

Shifting the onus onto the police themselves was a deliberate move. Now it was up to them to make the right decision.

The man stuck his hands in his pockets and looked nonplussed.

"Are you going to hand over the key, or do we have to break the lock?" he said after a moment.

Wedersøe had been expecting to negotiate his way out before they began to search the vehicle. Now he felt the sweat seep from his pores once more. There was nothing to see through the windows. The icon was in the trunk.

"You're going to be needing a good lawyer," the local inspector or whatever he was mumbled as Wedersøe reluctantly handed him the key.

"I think I'm quite capable of representing myself, don't you?" he replied, wondering how the man could be so unaware of his practice in criminal law.

The lights flashed twice as the officers pressed the remote key and stepped up to the rear of the vehicle.

He watched as they opened the trunk. One of them leaned inside and lifted the quilt in which the icon was wrapped, only to step back and direct a shake of his head at his superior as he clunked the trunk shut and locked the vehicle after him again.

Obviously they were so desperate to find the girl that they were oblivious to all else.

"I wish to speak to Nymand or to the head of the negotiation unit," Wedersøe declared, sensing his composure return to him. "The girl has only a few hours at most. If you want to help her, I think we should be getting a move on."

He saw how the man's expression changed slightly, as if he were considering whether Wedersøe might be bluffing.

"I can prove she's still alive if you allow me to speak to whoever is in charge."

The other officers had closed in around them, but nobody spoke. Everyone stood still in anticipation.

"Right," said the man finally, turning toward one of the patrol cars and ordering the officer who still had a firm hold of Wedersøe's arm to put him in the back.

"No, you don't." Wedersøe reacted immediately. "I'm staying here."

He needed to be near the car. Near the icon.

The policeman gave him a look of appraisal in return.

"Just make the call," Wedersøe repeated without moving.

He watched the elderly man as he leaned back against the patrol car and took out his phone.

Obviously he didn't want the conversation broadcast over the police radio, Wedersøe realized with a rising feeling of having taken the upper hand. It was going to work. It had to.

He was unable to hear what was said but noted that the man began to speak, and after a few seconds he stepped toward him with the phone still in his hand, clearly holding the line. With a nod he ordered the officers restraining him to release the handcuffs, before handing Wedersøe the phone.

"Miklos Wedersøe speaking," he began after Nymand had presented himself. "I've got the girl. Let me go and you get her back. Providing, of course, that you agree to follow my instructions."

"We don't do deals," Nymand replied icily into his ear, prompting Wedersøe to smirk. The fat plod thought he could bluff.

"Oh, but you do," he answered calmly. "You have no choice. I am your only hope, the only person who can lead you to the girl."

They would never let the girl die. Human life took absolute precedence. Especially a child's, and especially an heiress to the Sachs-Smith fortune. Did they really think he was that stupid?

The silence that ensued was so protracted he began nevertheless to fear that Nymand had hung up.

"Tell me your demands," the chief superintendent said eventually.

"Once your colleague here is satisfied that the girl was alive this morning, you let me go. Two hours later, I call and tell you where to find her. But," he quickly added, "if at any time I suspect I am being followed or in any other way tracked or held under surveillance, that message will not, and I repeat not, be forthcoming."

"And what if you don't call us back?"

"In that case I'd be fair game and you would know I had no leverage by which to force any negotiation once apprehended. But trust me. I'll make the call."

He paused for effect before repeating the sentence that had been fixed in his mind all the way across the country.

"Nymand," he began, "it's up to you whether Walther Sachs-Smith's grandchild lives or dies. But time is of the essence."

He dipped his free hand into his trouser pocket and took out a small cassette tape, handing it to the policeman in charge along with the phone.

"Now, if this gentleman would care to let go of me for a moment, I'll get the camcorder out of the car."

The elderly inspector's eyes were no longer as narrow after Nymand's entry into the proceedings. He nodded for two officers to accompany the attorney to the Mercedes while conferring briefly with the Roskilde team over the phone.

Wedersøe held his hand out for the key, then opened the car door, slowing his movements demonstratively to show he had no intention of making a run for it.

There was no chance he could, so the gesture was mere theatrics.

The camcorder was in the side pocket on the driver's side. He picked it up and slammed the door shut, locking the car once more with the remote key.

❧

They watched the tape several times through, glancing up at him each time after the girl had spoken. His method had been the classic one, the girl holding the day's newspaper up in front of her so they could see the footage had been shot that same morning.

The policeman in charge had called Nymand again, his face twisted with displeasure. The girl had clearly been under duress and was apparently being held in a space so confined, no adult would possibly be able to sit upright in it.

Of course, it helped that she had whimpered and cried for her mother.

It was a very good recording indeed.

He noted the vicious look sent to him by the young officer who had earlier slammed him against the hood of the car, yet his condemnation didn't matter. Should he be judged by a simple farm boy? The idea was laughable.

"Difficult decisions take time," said the inspector, trotting out the well-worn cliché of any negotiation. "As I'm sure you understand."

Bullshit, Wedersøe thought to himself, amused that this bumpkin should underestimate him so.

He shook his head. "Now you let me go. If not, she dies," he reiterated, without waiting for the man to finish what he was saying. "You've got everything to win. She doesn't have long."

His eyes scanned the empty highway while he waited for the police to confer. He knew the local man and Nymand were hooked up to a decision-making unit invested with responsibility for the operation. The go-ahead had to come from there before he could be allowed to go free.

A pair of peasants like them would be sorely unable to make decisions of life and death, he thought, nodding in acknowledgment when it seemed the man in charge had finally been authorized to proceed.

"Two hours," Wedersøe repeated, confident no one had installed a tracking device in the car. For one thing, they wouldn't have had time even to requisition the necessary equipment before being deployed to the highway. Nevertheless, he impressed the point upon them just to make sure. "Don't try and track me. We need to be quite clear about this."

The inspector said nothing, but nodded. Old-school and obstinate. He had written something down on a notepad he had taken from his inside pocket.

"Call this number when you're ready to tell us where Isabella Sachs-Smith is being held," he said, instructing his men to move a couple of the patrol cars and allow him through.

"I want all traffic held back for five minutes after I've gone. And remember, the slightest suspicion I'm being followed or tracked and you lose your chance to find the girl," Wedersøe said again and stepped toward the Mercedes, relishing the feeling of once more having the upper hand.

44

It was pouring rain. All visitors to Roskilde Cathedral had been bundled outside and the head of the Special Intervention Unit already had his team in place. Clusters of inquisitive onlookers stood huddled beneath umbrellas as Nymand and his people cordoned off the church and went in.

The call had come exactly two hours after the police in South Jutland had been forced to let Miklos Wedersøe go.

"You'll find her in the cathedral," had been his brief message, shortly afterward traced to Hamburg. A search had now been instigated via Interpol, and police were on the lookout throughout Germany.

Four officers had been deployed to scour the church interior but they were still waiting for the dog handler to arrive from outlying Lejre with his German shepherd. An ambulance was parked at the entrance, and three constables manned the cordon.

Louise was on her way home after her visit to Gerd and Mona in Svogerslev when Thiesen rang and told her they had received word from Wedersøe. It had been Thiesen himself as head of the negotiation unit who had advised Nymand to let the attorney go: It was their only chance of finding the girl alive.

"Rather we lose him than her," he had said when Louise asked if he was sure they were doing the right thing.

"What if she's already dead?"

"We'd still like to find her, wouldn't we?" he replied, and Louise had to acknowledge he was right. Without question, they would.

"Okay, we're going into the crypts," Nymand commanded, striding from Christian I's chapel.

Louise had brought the chief superintendent up to date as to Wedersøe's seat on the parish council and that he might be expected to be rather familiar with the church building and all its nooks and hiding places. She herself had been there only once, on a school trip, so long ago now that all she remembered was the vast interior and the long aisle leading to the altar.

A constable had been dispatched to the house on Frederiksborgvej, charged with bringing back Isabella's pink nightdress. The dog handler had arrived, Louise noticed, and before long the dog had the scent of the garment and sat whining with obvious impatience. The verger had been instructed to open all rooms normally closed to the public, and once the search began he scuttled anxiously along on the heels of the police with worry etched all over his face.

In a corner over by the Trolle family's chapel, the iron gate stood open and Louise could hear the dog handler already at work somewhere down the steps. The verger buried his hands nervously in his pockets as he talked about how there were some two thousand people buried in the cathedral.

"Seven hundred and five of them are in the floor," he said with a nod at the great stone slabs that lay bricked into the floor at intervals.

Louise shuddered and instinctively stepped aside, away from the graves most immediately underfoot.

"It wasn't that unusual when the church was still Catholic," he went on, though she wasn't really listening. Voices were ringing from the crypts, and a moment later the dog emerged, only to sit down facing the steps to wait for its owner, who then came into view shaking his head and instructing the verger to lock the gate again; there was nothing there.

As the dog handler moved on to the southern tower's chapel, Louise stepped up toward the altar. Beneath the chancel in whose column Harald Bluetooth was said to be interred, she crouched down and peered into the crypt below. The aged caskets were covered in thick layers of dust, and several were raised above the floor on low stone platforms.

She closed her eyes and listened. The four officers had gone upstairs and were now investigating the museum area normally only accessible during the daily guided tours.

The crypt was silent. She stood up and went on to the next grate, the room inside once more housing a number of caskets and at the rear a chandelier yet to be unpacked.

She called out, "Isabella! Isabella!"

The dog approached busily. They were in Frederik V's chapel now. Louise jumped when the verger suddenly spoke behind her.

"The royal children's crypt," he said, nodding downward. "The young who died too soon, they're all down there."

Louise straightened up and followed him as he stepped toward the gate and unlocked the crypt.

"It's bigger than the others," he said, about to go down the steps.

"Stay here," Louise ordered him at once, stopping him with a hand against his shoulder. The dust lay thick on the small, black coffins. Matted by time, they stood side by side. "The dog first."

The verger stepped back apologetically.

"Normally, admittance is for church staff only," he said, plunging his hands into his pockets again.

The officers came down the stairs from above.

"She's not in the tower, either," one of them said, pausing to watch as the dog handler went down into the crypt. It was the last place they still had to look.

Louise had withdrawn slightly and leaned up against the rough brick wall, hoping with all her heart they would find the girl before it was too late.

There was nowhere left to look. The verger had shown them every room, even informing them there had once been talk of constructing a tunnel leading over to Queen Ingrid and Frederik IX's burial site outside the church, but that the plans had been shelved. There were no hidden passages or secret rooms anywhere in the cathedral.

"Nothing, I'm afraid," the dog handler said, rewarding the German shepherd and thereby clearly concluding his work. "She's not here."

Louise closed her eyes and leaned her head back against the wall. Hope of finding Isabella alive was dwindling rapidly, and only now did she realize how certain she had felt that they would find the girl in the church as they had been told.

Nymand had been calling Wedersøe's cell phone every five minutes, though without contact. Now he buried his face in his hands. His bulky body swayed slightly on his feet, his shoulders drooped. "The bastard!" he spat despairingly as he looked up again.

45

Miklos Wedersøe pulled into the inside lane and turned off the Autobahn toward Wedel, a small town due west of Hamburg. He glanced at the clock and saw he had plenty of time.

Before calling the police in Denmark he had dumped his black Mercedes. It had been heart-wrenching to walk away from the 4.5-million-kroner car in the knowledge that before long it would be picked up by a truck and taken away as evidence in the case against him. He had left it with the keys inside a couple of streets behind the railway station, carrying the icon around the corner to the car Carl Emil had insisted should be parked ready to transport them onward. The red Opel had no navigation system, so he had been forced to buy an old-fashioned road map, which was now spread out on the passenger seat next to him.

Having made the call he switched off the phone, wary of being traced. Still, he was confident he had thought things through, and finding him would not be easy. Once the money had been transferred he would continue on through Germany before leaving the car and taking the train the last part of the way to Trier. From there he would enter Luxembourg.

They would be on his trail, of that he was in no doubt. Most likely they already were, and the hunt would be intensified when they failed to find the girl.

But she was where he had told them she was. It wouldn't be his fault if they still couldn't find her.

❦

It was dark as he drove through the town. His instructions were to pass through and continue for one kilometer before turning off to the left and continuing toward an iron gateway at the end of a tree-lined driveway.

The deal was to be completed at a manor house on the outskirts of the town. He had still not been in touch with the buyer in person, but his contact in New York had revealed to him that the purchaser was of a German family, though no longer resident in the country.

He flicked the lights to high beam and slowed down, his eyes darting to the trip counter. *One kilometer.*

It was with mixed feelings he prepared himself to bid the Angel of Death farewell. He was not nervous, not by any means; the slight tension he felt was more anticipation, he told himself, tempered by the relief of finally having gotten so far. And yet he could not deny that he was immensely saddened by the thought of giving up the icon. His desire to own it had been so powerful it had dulled almost every other emotion, like a hunger that could not be satisfied. Only the thought of the money, the entire undivided sum, was able to divert his mind from notions of defeat: Unexpectedly his dream of owning his own private island had come closer to fruition, and every opportunity would be his.

The sudden sight of the driveway, lined with its tall, leafless trees, filled him with a warm sense of expectation. There was no sign to indicate this was the place, but he felt certain it was. He braked and turned without signaling. There had not been a single car since he left the town.

The gravel track was level and wide, the main house as yet tucked from view. He crossed a small bridge and came to the gate.

A moat, he thought to himself, and felt impressed.

He stepped out of the car and went up to the gate. He leaned his weight into it and shoved hard. When it began to open, lights came on all the way up the drive to a castle-like building of stone with an imposing entrance.

He went back to the car and got in. There were lights on in two windows to the right of the steps. He pulled up, and a man emerged from the side of the house.

Miklos was unsurprised by his appearance: an elderly gentleman with white hair and a stick, stepping forward to meet him. The features of his face were hidden by the dim light, but he walked slowly, as if his legs were uncertain.

"Welcome," he said in English, without any trace of German.

Miklos accepted the man's outstretched hand and nodded as he explained that he could pull forward to the side of the building, from where it would be easier to carry the icon inside.

A dark wooden door stood open in the end wall. Light shone from inside, and a broad staircase led down into the basement.

"If you would be so kind as to carry it for me," the man requested, indicating the way. "As I'm sure you understand, I have been most anxious to finally behold the divine object. For years, no one really knew if she even existed anymore."

Miklos lifted the icon from the trunk and followed the man down the stairs into a large, illuminated room with white walls and heavy wooden beams in the ceiling. Thick metal bars lined the windows, and he was struck for a moment by the sense of having stepped inside a medieval castle. But what caught his attention most were the banknotes stacked up on the table.

Euros, neatly bundled.

He smiled at the man as he placed the Angel with great care on the cloth that had been spread out over the other end of the table.

The man stood for some time, gazing at the artifact in front of him, now and then reaching out to pass a hand over the rough metal of the frame and caress the glass.

"Do you know how I can be sure that what you have brought me is genuine?"

Miklos shook his head.

"Come here," the man said.

Miklos stepped forward as the old man leaned over the glass.

"Can you feel the tiny mark in the bottom left-hand corner of each pane?"

Miklos leaned closer to see.

"Oh, they can't be seen. Only felt. Gently, with your fingertips."

It was true: the smallest of nicks, exactly where the man had said.

"Proof of authenticity. It's what they did in those days."

"Interesting." Miklos nodded, already impatient to complete the exchange and be on his way.

"Let me show you something," the man went on, picking up his stick and beckoning him to follow.

Used notes, exactly as agreed, Miklos noted, indulging the man as instructed, albeit with a measure of annoyance.

"This will interest you, I'm sure," said the man, revealing that he owned another icon from the same period.

Miklos stepped into the corridor and walked with the man to a small recess at the end.

"Wait here, let me switch on the light."

The man doddered back to the staircase.

The clamor that ensued was deafening, like a thousand iron bars clattering to the stone floor at once. Miklos jumped in fright, striking his shoulder against the wall, his heart pounding in alarm as the lights went out and the cellar was plunged into darkness. Enraged, he rattled the bars of the portcullis that had descended to trap him.

He glanced around and could make out that the castle's dungeons consisted of several rooms. He was now confined to the first.

The man's shuffling footsteps came closer.

"How could you people bring it upon yourselves to even contemplate selling one of the world's most celebrated cultural treasures?" he demanded with disgust, a hint of German accent now traceable in his trembling voice. "My entire active life has been spent searching for the Angel of Death. Every single day for sixty years the icon has in some way occupied my thoughts. You would never dream of how close I have come. But the Sachs-Smith family has always denied that it was in their possession, so what does a person do?" he said inquiringly.

Miklos roared and thrashed at the bars.

"He waits," the old man went on, unabashed. "And in the end, people such as yourself unwittingly come to our aid. Greedy for money and willing to sacrifice even history's most precious artifacts to line your pockets."

He snorted and paused. As if his fierce passion was finally finding an outlet.

"You listen to me," Miklos said. "I'm going to call our contact and you two are going to have to sort this problem out. He's already transferring your money into my account, so you've got nothing to gain by holding me back like this. And the Angel of Death is yours."

"Go ahead and call," the man replied calmly. "Money, that's the only thing you can think about. Do you know how many years the Angel of Death hung in the Hagia Sophia before it went missing?"

No, he didn't, and he didn't care! But he had switched on his cell phone, its display lighting up the dark with the number of his contact in New York. He pressed the number and turned away with his back to the old man, seething with rage, when a phone suddenly began to ring.

It rang several times before Miklos realized that the phone he was trying to reach was ringing right behind him.

He wheeled around and saw that the man had stepped up to the bars and stood with the cell phone in his hand. Miklos stared in disbelief as the German took the call in faultless American.

"We got a problem," he said, his voice suddenly so familiar, adding that the bank transfer had most regrettably fallen through.

Miklos hurled his phone to the floor and leaped forward, clinging to the trellis.

"Bastard!" he screamed, realizing the contact he had so trusted had cheated him.

"And you are a cheap and common thief," the old man retorted.

"Tomorrow the icon will be transported to Istanbul, and by the summer I hope it will be restored once more to its rightful place in the Hagia Sophia."

And with that, he turned and left.

46

Louise drew her legs up underneath her on the church pew. The dizziness had come on as fatigue suddenly overpowered her. She closed her eyes and thought it was probably because everyone had felt so sure they were going to find the girl in the cathedral; now, with all hope seemingly extinguished, it hit doubly hard. They had nothing to go on. Nothing whatsoever. Apart from the fact that Isabella was in the hands of a madman.

An arch, Mona Jepsen had said. Roskilde Cathedral was full of them, but the girl was nowhere to be found. So much for clairvoyance. She got to her feet and went outside as the dog handler slammed the tailgate of his vehicle shut, the German shepherd panting inside. He had left the girl's nightdress on the shelf next to the tourist brochures, and Louise had promised to take it with her when she went.

Rain-soaked onlookers continued to stand and stare even though it was plain to anyone that the operation was over. Louise ducked under the cordon and zipped up her coat. Hands in pockets, she walked over to the enclosure where Queen Ingrid and King Frederik IX lay buried.

She had to get away, if only for a few moments, she told herself, walking on to the rear of the cathedral and following a low brick wall that ended in what looked like a small construction site where the earth had been dug up and broken-up church stones lay in heaps.

The derelict appearance matched the desolation she felt inside. For a moment she felt some small relief in the rain that lashed against her skin, alleviating any need for tears, she thought, and paused to turn her face to the sky. As she did so, she saw the arch.

Absalon's Gate, the archway joining the cathedral to the Roskilde Palace. For the first time she found herself desperately wanting to believe in clairvoyance.

She ran up and stood underneath the gateway's gray arch, looking straight ahead as Mona Jepsen had described to her, but seeing nothing other than the yellow-washed wall that closed the area off from the Stændertorvet square. Annoyed at herself for her momentary lapse, she sighed and turned to go back.

A woman left the cathedral's administrative offices with a bag slung over her shoulder. The Konventhuset from which she had emerged was an old diocesan meetinghouse next to the dean's residence. Absently, Louise watched the woman as she began to walk away. And then she saw it. Suddenly she found herself staring at a bricked-up window situated just above the cobbles. The recess in which it sat was shaped like a church window ending in a point at the top.

She gasped and ran up. A brass plate on the wall informed her that besides the cathedral's administrative unit the building also housed the office of the Roskilde Cathedral Parish Council.

✿

A Bobcat mini excavator drove past with a load full of gravel as Louise dashed back to the red-brick Konventhuset with a still-confused Nymand following behind in the rain.

"What's all this about?" he shouted after her, already out of breath, his face wet with rain as his four officers followed on his heels.

"The cathedral parish council has its office here and Wedersøe's got a key," she explained, holding the door for him as he caught up. "We need to get into the basement."

The desks where the administrative staff sat were empty. The woman she had seen must have been the last to go home.

Louise looked around.

"There's a stair over here," one of the constables shouted, and Louise hurried out into the passage where he was standing.

She found him holding open a low wooden door leading down into a stone cellar. The steps were narrow and steep.

"There's no light," he said.

Louise called Isabella's name, but no sound came from the darkness below.

Nymand joined her.

"Go on," he said, and she nodded. It was too narrow for him and she could hardly hold herself back.

Cautiously she began to climb down, feeling her way with her feet. The cellar wall was cold and damp, the air stale and fusty.

"Here's a flashlight for you," Nymand called to her, bending forward and handing her a Maglite.

The beam illuminated the black stone walls as she reached the bottom. Slowly she proceeded, calling Isabella's name as she went, her voice echoing back through a series of empty spaces. She concentrated on maintaining some sense of direction, inching her way forward to where she thought the bricked-up window would be, yet finding it difficult to orient herself. In several places the floor rose and she had to bend down so as not to hit her head on the ceiling.

Almost on all fours, she was moving toward the far wall when the beam of her flashlight picked out a trapdoor in the floor: a rectangular wooden hatch over in the far corner.

She scrabbled toward it and knelt down to pull the iron bolt aside, but it seemed to be stuck. Desperately, she swept the light around the room. Here and there, loose bricks lay scattered, dislodged at some point from the old brickwork. She picked one up and sat down before striking the bolt hard with it, following up with a pair of swift kicks with her heel until eventually it gave way.

She called out to Nymand and told him she was going farther down.

"Do you need any help?" he shouted back.

She got to her feet, took a firm hold of the hatch, and lifted it upward. It was heavy, but offered no other resistance.

"Isabella?" she called out, kneeling down again and using her arm and shoulder to bring the hinged hatch upright, then tipping it over out of the way. "Isabella?"

For a brief second she felt stupid. There was no sound forthcoming at all to indicate that anyone might be there. The only thing she could hear as she held her breath to listen was silence.

Louise shone the flashlight in. The space was little more than a crawl space. Utterly dark and cramped, only two steps leading down, and she realized quickly there was no room for her to descend.

"Is the dog still here?" she shouted up at Nymand, and lay down flat on her stomach to peer inside.

⧔

The girl was on her side up against the wall, her face turned away from the hatch and the steps that led up. Her hands and feet were bound with strips of cloth.

"Isabella?" Louise called out gently, but there was no reaction.

"She's here!" she yelled back toward Nymand, scrabbling to her feet and hurrying back to the bottom of the stair. "Get an ambulance over here. I can't tell if she's alive."

She returned to the hatch and got down on her stomach again to wriggle her way down into the space, placing the flashlight on the steps for light. She shuffled forward on her elbows toward the still-motionless girl, breathing her name with apprehension.

Cautiously she turned her onto her back. The little girl's clothes were damp and filthy. Louise saw the crumpled chamois leather next to her mouth, and the vomit, and wondered if the child had suffocated. She saw the congealed blood on her face and placed her hand against her chest, her ear to her mouth, and yet was unable to tell if she was breathing.

She heard sounds behind her. The rescue unit was on its way with a stretcher. Louise would have to climb out to give them room.

"We're with you now," she whispered, not knowing if the girl could hear her or not. "You've been found."

She pulled herself back through the trapdoor as the paramedics arrived, watching as they transferred her onto the stretcher and secured her frail body so they could bring her to safety. Slowly they slid her up the two steps, and once she was lying flat on the stone slabs of the cellar floor, they commenced the resuscitation procedure.

"We've got a pulse," one of them said after a few moments and asked for an IV to be prepared.

"It's the cold," the youngest of the two men explained as they crouched over the unconscious child. "And maybe a concussion, too. It looks like she was struck a few times."

"Is she going to be all right?" Louise asked, holding her breath.

"Too early to say."

They passed the stretcher up the narrow cellar stair, then promptly inserted the IV catheter before wrapping Isabella up warmly in layers of blankets.

Louise glanced around for Nymand.

"He's gone outside to phone the girl's mother so they can meet up at the hospital," one of the young officers said, watching as the stretcher was rolled inside the ambulance.

47

I just got back from the chapel in Roskilde," Rønholt began as Louise sat down in front of him in his office. "Grete Milling wanted to see her daughter."

Louise herself had just returned from the memorial service for Willumsen at Police HQ. It had been hard not to cry, especially because his wife had been there with a black silk scarf around her hairless head. Not everyone in the department was aware that she had resumed her chemotherapy, and it was obvious that a lot of people hadn't quite known how to approach her, as if their reluctance were compounded by her tragedy having doubled.

Louise had been on her way home when Suhr called her into the office.

"It was tough, I'll tell you," Rønholt said, wrenching her from her thoughts. Her mind had not been still since the homicide chief had closed the door after they got back from the service and begun by telling her he wanted her to be the first to know that he had already picked out Willumsen's replacement. The person in question was, as he put it, someone Louise was used to working with closely.

Immediately, she had thought of Henny Heilmann, her first team leader in the department, who had since moved on to radio communications. To be reunited with her would be brilliant.

"We'd tried to prepare her and had covered up her daughter's naked body," Rønholt went on. "But how do you prepare someone for something as grotesque and yet as lifelike as that?"

He shook his head bleakly and smoothed his neat beard.

"She had to have something to calm her down afterward. A good thing she had her new friend with her."

Louise knew Melvin had been there. She had asked him to be there when Jonas came home from school, and he had been most apologetic in having to decline on account of having promised his help elsewhere.

"I'd like to have been there and drunk a toast to Willumsen," said Rønholt, looking at her. "Only I didn't feel I could until the two of us had a little chat."

She raised an eyebrow, struggling to understand what he meant. After her meeting with Suhr, fatigue had been almost getting the better of her. The day had begun with her stopping to see Nymand. After a night in the hospital Isabella had regained consciousness. She had been suffering from hypothermia but was now in the clear, and the consultant in the children's section had assured the family that there would be no long-term physical effects from her ordeal.

Rønholt folded his hands in front of him, his eyes still fixed on

Louise's. He looked serious in a way she couldn't quite gauge, and she shifted uneasily on her chair.

"I've been extremely happy to have had your help," he said. "By the looks of it, we can expect Miklos Wedersøe to be transferred into Danish detention within the week. The old art historian who duped him has all their phone calls on tape and can fully document how the deal was set up. Apparently, he's been looking for the Angel of Death most of his life. With his network he's basically had human search engines running all over the world, so the minute something new cropped up about the icon he would know straightaway. That's how he got wind of Carl Emil Sachs-Smith putting feelers out in the collectors' circles. He put himself forward as a potential buyer and contact."

Louise nodded. She already knew the story from Walther Sachs-Smith, who for his part had been relieved to learn it was the art historian he had been striving to keep at bay for years who had stepped up when his son had decided to sell. She knew from Nymand that Walther had hired an army of lawyers to compile evidence in a case against Wedersøe.

"I've been particularly struck by your dedication in the matter of Jeanette Milling's disappearance, a case in which we had been floundering, to say the least," Rønholt went on.

Louise crossed her legs and kept her gaze on his, perplexed as to where he might be heading.

"Since our department was reorganized, or massacred as we prefer to say, we no longer have resources available to devote to cold cases," he explained. "Not even when we feel confident a crime may have been committed."

Louise knew that something like five out of the total of sixteen to seventeen hundred missing person reports that came in every year could be accounted to crime—probably more, given that Rønholt and his team lacked the means to devote themselves to each case fully.

The Search Department spent most of its time entering personal details into a nationwide register and then assisting in identifying persons found dead. Moreover, there was a certain amount of collaboration with Interpol concerning foreign citizens found in Denmark and Danes found abroad.

Rønholt paused and looked at her again.

"How do you feel about Michael Stig as new team leader after Willumsen?" he asked, changing track all of a sudden.

He offered her a peppermint and put the packet down on the desk as he studied her.

"To be honest, not good," she answered frankly. "I hadn't seen it coming. But he's the only one of us with a management qualification, so if we're not going to pull someone in from outside I suppose it has to be him."

"Now that we've solved this cold case, I've been given the go-ahead to set up a little unit," said Rønholt, picking up his thread from before. "An investigator and a specialist advisory officer in charge."

Louise leaned forward.

"We're conceiving it as a special inquiry service to investigate cold cases," he explained. "Missing persons."

"Who's going to be leading it?" Louise asked, reaching for another peppermint. All of a sudden her mouth felt dry.

"You are," Rønholt replied, fixing his eyes on her. "If we can drag you away from Homicide, that is."

They could. Especially now. She knew just looking at Suhr that he was aware she would not be happy with Michael Stig. And yet the decision had been made. He could have advertised the position and involved the rest of the team in the process. But it was already done, which led Louise to suspect that her colleague had already been ushered into the wings a long time ago, ready to take over from Willumsen when the time came. And that time was now.

"Who would the other person be?" she asked, sensing the butterflies in her stomach. She was flattered, of course, but at the same time hesitant and unsure of herself.

A whole new department under her responsibility. Staying with Department A meant keeping a much-coveted and presumably rather secure position as homicide investigator. But then there was Jonas. She couldn't go on working like this, never being home at the right time when he needed her.

"Who you choose would be your decision entirely," Rønholt answered. "And you'd be bringing your present salary with you, plus all the add-ons that go with heading up a unit."

She said nothing, but simply sat there staring into space, her thoughts churning in her mind. Specialist advisory officer. Rønholt had clearly thought the matter through. With that title she got her own department without needing the management qualifications.

"Think about it until Monday," he said. "But I'll need an answer by then."

Louise nodded slowly and got to her feet.

"So we'd just be two in this department?"

Ragner Rønholt nodded. "Yes," he said, a more serious look appearing on his face. "With a six-month probation period."

"Meaning?"

He shrugged apologetically. "Meaning you'd have six months to prove the unit's worth."

"And after that?"

"After that we see if there's a basis for continuation."

"And if there isn't, would I still have my job in Homicide?"

He shook his head. "I'm afraid I can't promise you that."

Louise picked up her coat and thought of Jonas. It would be a lot easier for her to spend time with him in the new job.

"When were you thinking I'd start?" she asked, wriggling into her coat.

"Whenever you want, as long as we get set up before the admin boys change their mind."

She stood for a moment, looking at the tidy orchids in his windowsill.

"I'll take it," she said, turning her head toward him again. "If I can start Monday and kick off with a week's vacation."

Her new boss frowned in surprise.

"I need a week off to be with a boy I've neglected," she explained.

"I'm sure it can be arranged," he nodded, politely stepping forward to open the door for her. "I'll make sure the offices are ready."

He jabbed a thumb down the corridor. "You'll be in the Rathole."

Louise stopped in her tracks.

"Sounds worse than it is," he reassured her. "It comes with its own kitchen area just downstairs. No one's used the place for ages, but names do have a habit of sticking, don't they?"

Right now she didn't mind where he put her as long as it was nowhere near Michael Stig.

She was already on her way along the corridor when Rønholt called her back.

"Actually, we could just as well do the formalities now, if you've nothing against it?"

He held up two sheets of paper, both of which he handed to her. She took them with a smile, skimming their contents quickly.

SEARCH DEPARTMENT, SPECIAL SEARCH AGENCY. SPECIALIST ADVISORY OFFICER LOUISE RICK it said at the top.

"You already had these done, didn't you?" she exclaimed with a look of surprise. "Have you spoken to Suhr as well?"

"I took the liberty of preparing matters in advance," he admitted with a shrug. "Just so that we could get started if you happened to say yes."

Louise dropped the job description into her bag and accepted the hand he extended toward her, sealing their agreement.

"You knew all along I would," she laughed, and shook her head at his presumption.

ACKNOWLEDGMENTS

A big thank-you to everyone who so kindly gave up their time to help me research this book.

The Stolen Angel is fiction and stems wholly from my imagination. Its characters are in no way based on existing persons. However, most of what I have written about the Hagia Sophia in Istanbul is correct, although as far as I know there was never a glass icon of the archangel Gabriel in the side aisle.

In this book, as in my previous ones, it has been crucial for me to do thorough research in order to make my story appear trustworthy and realistic. Thanks to my friends at Copenhagen's Police Headquarters, without whose help the framework around Louise Rick wouldn't hold. And a completely, unbelievably huge, thanks to Tom Christensen, Flying Squad, who has been with me from before the first line was written, and generously contributed with talk and details as the book was in progress. Tremendous thanks for your time and your empathy in the story.

Heartfelt thanks, yet again, go, as always, to my friend, forensic expert, Steen Holger Hansen, who is there to help out when a plot needs to be spun together. Without you there would be no book.

Great thanks also go to the journalist Lotte Thorsen, who is amazingly skilled with words.

A million thanks to my savvy, tireless, and wonderful American editor, Lindsey Rose, and to the spectacular team at Grand Central. It is a thrill, an honor, and an enormous joy to work with you all. I appreciate every single effort you've made on my behalf, and being part of this esteemed family. I'm very happy to be with you.

Thank you so very much to my supremely visionary American agent, Victoria Sanders, who has moved heaven and Earth for me, and to your fabulous and super-smart associates, the lovely and talented Bernadette Baker-Baughman and Jessica Spivey, whose great work, all around the world, leaves me filled with gratitude and aware of just how fortunate I am.

Thank you to the brilliant Benee Knauer, who knows what I am thinking and what I mean, and how to capture it perfectly. It means so much to know you are there; to have you behind and beside me.

I want to express my heartfelt appreciation to the American crime-writing community, and to my dear American readers. I cannot sufficiently convey how much your warm welcome has continued to mean to me; you have made my dream come true. I love this country so much that I have made a new home here. I'm loving it!

My warmest thanks must go to my son, Adam, whom I love with all my heart, and who has traveled every step of the way with me on this indescribable journey.

—*Sara Blaedel*

INTRODUCING...
THE UNDERTAKER'S DAUGHTER

If you enjoy Sara Blaedel's Louise Rick suspense novels,
you'll love her new series.

An unexpected inheritance from a father she hasn't seen since childhood
pulls a portrait photographer from her quiet life into a web of dark secrets
and murder in a small Midwestern town...

Please see the next page for an excerpt from
THE UNDERTAKER'S DAUGHTER,
coming in 2018.

1

What do you mean you shouldn't have told me? You should have told me thirty-three years ago."

"What difference would it have made anyway?" Ilka's mother demanded. "You were seven years old. You wouldn't have understood about a liar and a cheat running away with all his winnings; running out on his responsibilities, on his wife and little daughter. He hit the jackpot, Ilka, and then he hit the road. And left me—no, he left *us* with a funeral home too deep in the red to get rid of. And an enormous amount of debt. That he betrayed me is one thing, but abandoning his child?"

Ilka stood at the window, her back to the comfy living room, which was overflowing with books and baskets of yarn. She looked out over the trees in the park across the way. For a moment, the treetops seemed like dizzying black storm waves.

Her mother sat in the glossy Børge Mogensen easy chair in the corner, though now she was worked up from her rant, and her knitting needles clattered twice as fast. Ilka turned to her. "Okay," she said, trying not to sound shrill. "Maybe you're right. Maybe I wouldn't have understood about all that. But you didn't think I was too young to understand that my father was a coward, the way he suddenly left us, and that he didn't love us anymore. That he was an incredible asshole you'd never take back if he ever showed up on our doorstep, begging for forgiveness. As I recall, you had no trouble talking about that, over and over and over."

"Stop it." Her mother had been a grade school teacher for twenty-six years, and now she sounded like one. "But does it make any difference? Think of all the letters you've written him over the years. How often have you reached out to him, asked to see him? Or at least have some form of contact." She sat up and laid her knitting on the small table beside the chair. "He never answered you; he never tried to see you. How long did you save your confirmation money so you could fly over and visit him?"

Ilka knew better than her mother how many letters she had written over the years. What her mother wasn't aware of was that she had kept writing to him, even as an adult. Not as often, but at least a Christmas card and a note on his birthday. Every single year. Which had felt like sending letters into outer space. Yet she'd never stopped.

"You should have told me about the money," Ilka said, unwilling to let it go, even though her mother had a point. Would it really have made a difference? "Why are you telling me now? After all these years. And right when I'm about to leave."

Her mother had called just before eight. Ilka had still been in bed, reading the morning paper on her iPad. "Come over, right now," she'd said. There was something they had to talk about.

Now her mother leaned forward and folded her hands in her lap, her face showing the betrayal and desperation she'd endured. She'd kept her wounds under wraps for half her life, but it was obvious they had never fully healed. "It scares me, you going over there. Your father was a gambler. He bet more money than he had, and the racetrack was a part of our lives for the entire time he lived here. For better and worse. I knew about his habit when we fell in love, but then it got out of control. And almost ruined us several times. In the end, it did ruin us."

"And then he won almost a million kroner and just disappeared." Ilka lifted an eyebrow.

"Well, we do know he went to America." Her mother nodded. "Presumably, he continued gambling over there. And we never heard from him again. That is, until now, of course."

Ilka shook her head. "Right, now that he's dead."

"What I'm trying to say is that we don't know what he's left behind. He could be up to his neck in debt. You're a school photographer, not a millionaire. If you go over there, they might hold you responsible for his debts. And who knows? Maybe they wouldn't allow you to come home. Your father had a dark side he couldn't control. I'll rip his dead body limb from limb if he pulls you down with him, all these years after turning his back on us."

With that, her mother stood and walked down the long hall into the kitchen. Ilka heard muffled voices, and then Hanne appeared in the doorway. "Would you like us to drive you to the airport?" Hanne leaned against the doorframe as Ilka's mother reappeared with a tray of bakery rolls, which she set down on the coffee table.

"No, that's okay," Ilka said.

"How long do you plan on staying?" Hanne asked, moving to the sofa. Ilka's mother curled up in the corner of the sofa, covered herself with a blanket, and put her stockinged feet up on Hanne's lap.

When her mother began living with Hanne fourteen years ago, the last trace of her bitterness finally seemed to evaporate. Now, though, Ilka realized it had only gone into hibernation.

For the first four years after Ilka's father left, her mother had been stuck with Paul Jensen's Funeral Home and its two employees, who cheated her whenever they could get away with it. Throughout Ilka's childhood, her mother had complained constantly about the burden he had dumped on her. Ilka hadn't known until now that her father had also left a sizable gambling debt behind. Apparently, her mother had wanted to spare her, at least to some degree. And, of course, her mother was right. Her father *was* a coward and a selfish jerk. Yet Ilka had never completely accepted his abandonment of her. He had left behind a short letter saying he would come back for them as soon as everything was taken care of, and that an opportunity had come up. In Chicago.

Several years later, after complete silence on his part, he wanted a divorce. And that was the last they'd heard from him. When Ilka was a teenager, she found his address—or at least, an address where he had once lived. She'd kept it all these years in a small red treasure chest in her room.

"Surely it won't take more than a few days," Ilka said. "I'm planning to be back by the weekend. I'm booked up at work, but I found someone to fill in for me the first two days. It would be a great help if you two could keep trying to get hold of Niels from North Sealand Photography. He's in Stockholm, but he's supposed to be back tomorrow. I'm hoping he can cover for me the rest of the week. All the shoots are in and around Copenhagen."

"What exactly are you hoping to accomplish over there?" Hanne asked.

"Well, they say I'm in his will and that I have to be there in person to prove I'm Paul Jensen's daughter."

"I just don't understand why this can't be done by email or fax," her mother said. "You can send them your birth certificate and your passport, or whatever it is they need."

"It seems that copies aren't good enough. If I don't go over there, I'd have to go to an American tax office in Europe, and I think the nearest one is in London. But this way, they'll let me go through his personal things and take what I want. Artie Sorvino from Jensen Funeral Home in Racine has offered to cover my travel expenses if I go now, so they can get started with closing his estate."

Ilka stood in the middle of the living room, too anxious and restless to sit down.

"Racine?" Hanne asked. "Where's that?" She picked up her steaming cup and blew on it.

"A bit north of Chicago. In Wisconsin. I'll be picked up at the airport, and it doesn't look like it'll take long to drive there. Racine is supposedly the city in the United States with the largest community of Danish descendants. A lot of Danes immigrated to the region, so it makes sense that's where he settled."

"He has a hell of a lot of nerve." Her mother's lips barely moved. "He doesn't write so much as a birthday card to you all these years, and now suddenly you have to fly over there and clean up another one of his messes."

"Karin," Hanne said, her voice gentle. "Of course Ilka should go over and sort through her father's things. If you get the opportunity for closure on such an important part of your life's story, you should grab it."

Her mother shook her head. Without looking at Ilka, she said, "I have a bad feeling about this. Isn't it odd that he stayed in the undertaker business even though he managed to ruin his first shot at it?"

Ilka walked out into the hall and let the two women bicker about the unfairness of it all. How Paul's daughter had tried to reach out to her father all her life, and it was only now that he was gone that he was finally reaching out to her.

2

The first thing Ilka noticed was his Hawaiian shirt and longish brown hair, which was combed back and held in place by sunglasses that would look at home on a surfer. He stood out among the other drivers at Arrivals in O'Hare International Airport who were holding name cards and facing the scattered clumps of exhausted people pulling suitcases out of Customs.

Written on his card was "Ilka Nichols Jensen." Somehow, she managed to walk all the way up to him and stop before he realized she'd found him.

They looked each other over for a moment. He was in his early forties, maybe, she thought. So, her father, who had turned seventy-two in early January, had a younger partner.

She couldn't read his face, but it might have surprised him that the undertaker's daughter was a beanpole: six feet tall without a hint of a feminine form. He scanned her up and down, gaze settling on her hair, which had never been an attention-getter. Straight, flat, and mousy.

He smiled warmly and held out his hand. "Nice to meet you. Welcome to Chicago."

It's going to be a hell of a long trip, Ilka thought, before shaking his hand and saying hello. "Thank you. Nice to meet you, too."

He offered to carry her suitcase. It was small, a carry-on, but she gladly handed it over to him. Then he offered her a bottle of water. The car was close by, he said, only a short walk.

Although she was used to being taller than most people, she always felt a bit shy when male strangers had to look up to make eye contact. She was nearly a head taller than Artie Sorvino, but he seemed almost impressed as he grinned up at her while they walked.

Her body ached; she hadn't slept much during the long flight. Since she'd left her apartment in Copenhagen, her nerves had been tingling with excitement. And worry, too. Things had almost gone wrong right off the bat at the Copenhagen airport, because she hadn't taken into account the long line at Passport Control. There had still been two people in front of her when she'd been called to her waiting flight. Then the arrival in the US, a hell that the chatty man next to her on the plane had prepared her for. He had missed God knew how many connecting flights at O'Hare because the immigration line had taken several hours to go through. It turned out to be not quite as bad as all that. She had been guided to a machine that requested her fingerprints, passport, and picture. All this information was scanned and saved. Then Ilka had been sent on to the next line, where a surly passport official wanted to know what her business was in the country. She began to sweat but then

330

pulled herself together and explained that she was simply visiting family, which in a way was true. He stamped her passport, and moments later she was standing beside the man wearing the colorful, festive shirt.

"Is this your first trip to the US?" Artie asked now, as they approached the enormous parking lot.

She smiled. "No, I've traveled here a few times. To Miami and New York."

Why had she said that? She'd never been in this part of the world before, but what the hell. It didn't matter. Unless he kept up the conversation. And Miami. Where had that come from?

"Really?" Artie told her he had lived in Key West for many years. Then his father got sick, and Artie, the only other surviving member of the family, moved back to Racine to take care of him. "I hope you made it down to the Keys while you were in Florida."

Ilka shook her head and explained that she unfortunately hadn't had time.

"I had a gallery down there," Artie said. He'd gone to the California School of the Arts in San Francisco and had made his living as an artist.

Ilka listened politely and nodded. In the parking lot, she caught sight of a gigantic black Cadillac with closed white curtains in back, which stood first in the row of parked cars. He'd driven there in the hearse.

"Hope you don't mind." He nodded at the hearse as he opened the rear door and placed her suitcase on the casket table used for rolling coffins in and out of the vehicle.

"No, it's fine." She walked around to the front passenger door. Fine, as long as she wasn't the one being rolled into the back. She felt slightly dizzy, as if she were still up in the air, but was buoyed by the nervous excitement of traveling and the anticipation of what awaited her.

The thought that her father was at the end of her journey bothered her, yet it was something she'd fantasized about nearly her entire life. But would she be able to piece together the life he'd lived without her? And was she even interested in knowing about it? What if she didn't like what she learned?

She shook her head for a moment. These thoughts had been swirling in her head since Artie's first phone call. Her mother thought she shouldn't get involved. At all. But Ilka disagreed. If her father had left anything behind, she wanted to see it. She wanted to uncover whatever she could find, to see if any of it made sense.

"How did he die?" she asked as Artie maneuvered the long hearse out of the parking lot and in between two orange signs warning about roadwork and a detour.

"Just a sec," he muttered, and he swore at the sign before deciding to skirt the roadwork and get back to the road heading north.

For a while they drove in silence; then he explained that one morning her father had simply not woken up. "He was supposed to drive a corpse to Iowa, one of our neighboring states, but he didn't show up. He just died in his sleep. Totally peacefully. He might not even have known it was over."

Ilka watched the Chicago suburbs drifting by along the long, straight bypass, the rows of anonymous stores and cheap restaurants. It seemed so overwhelming, so strange, so different. Most buildings were painted in shades of beige and brown, and enormous billboards stood everywhere, screaming messages about everything from missing children to ultracheap fast food and vanilla coffee for less than a dollar at Dunkin' Donuts.

She turned to Artie. "Was he sick?" The bump on Artie's nose—had it been broken?—made it appear too big for the rest of his face: high cheekbones, slightly squinty eyes, beard stubble definitely due to a relaxed attitude toward shaving, rather than wanting to be in style.

"Not that I know of, no. But there could have been things Paul didn't tell me about, for sure."

His tone told her it wouldn't have been the first secret Paul had kept from him.

"The doctor said his heart just stopped," he continued. "Nothing dramatic happened."

"Did he have a family?" She looked out the side window. The old hearse rode well. Heavy, huge, swaying lightly. A tall pickup drove up beside them; a man with a full beard looked down and nodded at her. She looked away quickly. She didn't care for any sympathetic looks, though he, of course, couldn't know the curtained-off back of the hearse was empty.

"He was married, you know," Artie said. Immediately Ilka sensed he didn't like being the one to fill her in on her father's private affairs. She nodded to herself; of course he didn't. What did she expect?

"And he had two daughters. That was it, apart from Mary Ann's family, but I don't know them. How much do you know about them?"

He knew very well that Ilka hadn't had any contact with her father since he'd left Denmark. Or at least she assumed he knew. "Why has the family not signed what should be signed, so you can finish with his…estate?" She set the empty water bottle on the floor.

"They did sign their part of it. But that's not enough, because you're in the will, too. First the IRS—that's our tax agency—must determine if he owes the government, and you must give them permission to investigate. If you don't sign, they'll freeze all the assets in the estate until everything is cleared up."

Ilka's shoulders slumped at the word "assets." One thing that had kept her awake during the flight was her mother's concern about her being stuck with a debt she could never pay. Maybe she would be detained; maybe she would even be thrown in jail.

"What are his daughters like?" she asked after they had driven for a while in silence.

For a few moments, he kept his eyes on the road; then he glanced at her and shrugged. "They're nice enough, but I don't really know them. It's been a long time since I've seen them. Truth is, I don't think either of them was thrilled about your father's business."

After another silence, Ilka said, "You should have called me when he died. I wish I had been at his funeral."

Was that really true? Did she truly wish that? The last funeral she'd been to was her husband's. He had collapsed from heart failure three years ago, at the age of fifty-two. She didn't like death, didn't like loss. But she'd already lost her father many years ago, so what difference would it have made watching him being lowered into the ground?

"At that time, I didn't know about you," Artie said. "Your name first came up when your father's lawyer mentioned you."

"Where is he buried?"

He stared straight ahead. Again, it was obvious he didn't enjoy talking about her father's private life. Finally, he said, "Mary Ann decided to keep the urn with his ashes at home. A private ceremony was held in the living room when the crematorium delivered the urn, and now it's on the shelf above the fireplace."

After a pause, he said, "You speak English well. Funny accent."

Ilka explained distractedly that she had traveled in Australia for a year after high school.

The billboards along the freeway here advertised hotels, motels, and drive-ins for the most part. She wondered how there could be enough people to keep all these businesses going, given the countless offers from the clusters of signs on both sides of the road. "What about his new family? Surely they knew he had a daughter in Denmark?" She turned back to him.

"Nope!" He shook his head as he flipped the turn signal.

"He never told them he left his wife and seven-year-old daughter?" She wasn't all that surprised.

Artie didn't answer. *Okay*, Ilka thought. *That takes care of that.*

"I wonder what they think about me coming here."

He shrugged. "I don't really know, but they're not going to lose anything. His wife has an inheritance from her wealthy parents, so she's taken care of. The same goes for the daughters. And none of them have ever shown any interest in the funeral home."

And what about their father? Ilka thought. *Were they uninterested in him, too?* But that was none of her business. She didn't know them, knew nothing about their relationships with one another. And for that matter, she knew nothing about her father. Maybe his new family had asked about his life in Denmark, and maybe he'd given them a line of bullshit. But what the hell, he was thirty-nine when he left. Anyone could figure out he'd had a life before packing his weekend bag and emigrating.

Both sides of the freeway were green now. The landscape was starting to remind her of late summer in Denmark, with its green fields, patches of forest, flat land, large barns with the characteristic bowed roofs, and livestock. With a few exceptions, she felt like she could have been driving down the E45, the road between Copenhagen and Ålborg.

"Do you mind if I turn on the radio?" Artie asked.

She shook her head; it was a relief to have the awkward silence between them broken. And yet, before his hand reached the radio, she blurted out, "What was he like?"

He dropped his hand and smiled at her. "Your father was a decent guy, a really decent guy. In a lot of ways," he added, disarmingly, "he was someone you could count on, and in other ways he was very much his own man. I always enjoyed working with him, but he was also my friend. People liked him; he was interested in their lives. That's also why he was so good at talking to those who had just lost someone. He was empathetic. It feels empty, him not being around any longer."

Ilka had to concentrate to follow along. Despite her year in Australia, it was difficult when people spoke English rapidly. "Was he also a good father?"

Artie turned thoughtfully and looked out his side window. "I really can't say. I didn't know him when the girls were small." He kept glancing at the four lanes to their left. "But if you're asking me if your father was a family man, my answer is, yes and no. He was very much in touch with his family, but he probably put more of himself into Jensen Funeral Home."

"How long did you know him?"

She watched him calculate. "I moved back in 1998. We ran into each other at a local saloon, this place called Oh Dennis!, and we started talking. The victim of a traffic accident had just come in to the funeral home. The family wanted to put the young woman in an open coffin, but nobody would have wanted to see her face. So I offered to help. It's the kind of stuff I'm good at. Creating, shaping. Your father did the embalming, but I reconstructed her face. Her mother supplied us with a photo, and I did a sculpture. And I managed to make the woman look like herself, even though there wasn't much to work with. Later your father offered me a job, and I grabbed the chance. There's not much work for an artist in Racine, so reconstructions of the deceased was as good as anything."

He turned off the freeway. "Later I got a degree, because you have to have a license to work in the undertaker business."

❧

They reached Racine Street and waited to make a left turn. They had driven the last several miles in silence. The streets were deserted, the shops closed. It was getting dark, and Ilka realized she was at the point where exhaustion and jet lag trumped the hunger gnawing inside her. They drove by an empty square and a nearly deserted saloon. Oh Dennis! The place where Artie had met her father. She spotted the lake at the end of the broad streets to the right, and that was it. The town was dead. Abandoned, closed. She was surprised there were no people or life.

"We've booked a room for you at the Harbourwalk Hotel. Tomorrow we can sit down and go through your father's papers. Then you can start looking through his things."

Ilka nodded. All she wanted right now was a warm bath and a bed.

❧

"Sorry, we have no reservations for Miss Jensen. And none for the Jensen Funeral Home, either. We don't have a single room available."

The receptionist drawled apology after apology. It sounded to Ilka as if she had too much saliva in her mouth.

Ilka sat in a plush armchair in the lobby as Artie asked if the room was reserved in his name. "Or try Sister Eileen O'Connor," he suggested.

The receptionist apologized again as her long fingernails danced over the computer keyboard. The sound was unnaturally loud, a bit like Ilka's mother's knitting needles tapping against each other.

Ilka shut down. She could sit there and sleep; it made absolutely no difference to her. Back in Denmark, it was five in the morning, and she hadn't slept in twenty-two hours.

"I'm sorry," Artie said. "You're more than welcome to stay at my place. I can sleep on the sofa. Or we can fix up a place for you to sleep at the office, and we'll find another hotel in the morning."

Ilka sat up in the armchair. "What's that sound?"

Artie looked bewildered. "What do you mean?"

"It's like a phone ringing in the next room."

He listened for a moment before shrugging. "I can't hear anything."

The sound came every ten seconds. It was as if something were hidden behind the reception desk or farther down the hotel foyer. Ilka shook her head and looked at him. "You don't need to sleep on the sofa. I can sleep somewhere at the office."

She needed to be alone, and the thought of a strange man's bedroom didn't appeal to her.

"That's fine." He grabbed her small suitcase. "It's only five minutes away, and I know we can find some food for you, too."

❧

The black hearse was parked just outside the main entrance of the hotel, but that clearly wasn't bothering anyone. Though the hotel was apparently fully booked, Ilka hadn't seen a single person since they'd arrived.

Night had fallen, and her eyelids closed as soon as she settled into the car. She jumped when Artie opened the door and poked her with his finger. She hadn't even realized they had arrived. They were parked in a large, empty lot. The white building was an enormous box with several attic windows reflecting the moonlight back into the thick darkness. Tall trees with enormous crowns hovered over Ilka when she got out of the car.

They reached the door, beside which was a sign: JENSEN FUNERAL HOME. WELCOME. Pillars stood all the way across the broad porch, with well-tended flower beds in front of it, but the darkness covered everything else.

Artie led her inside the high-ceilinged hallway and turned the light on. He pointed to a stairway at the other end. Ilka's feet sank deep in the carpet; it smelled dusty, with a hint of plastic and instant coffee.

"Would you like something to drink? Are you hungry? I can make a sandwich."

"No, thank you." She just wanted him to leave.

He led her up the stairs, and when they reached a small landing, he pointed at a door. "Your father had a room in there, and I think we can find some sheets. We have a cot we can fold out and make up for you."

Ilka held her hand up. "If there is a bed in my father's room, I can just sleep in it." She nodded when he asked if she was sure. "What time do you want to meet tomorrow?"

"How about eight thirty? We can have breakfast together."

She had no idea what time it was, but as long as she got some sleep, she guessed she'd be fine. She nodded.

Ilka stayed outside on the landing while Artie opened the door to her father's room and turned on the light. She watched him walk over to a dresser and pull out the bottom drawer. He grabbed some sheets and a towel and tossed them on the bed; then he waved her in.

The room's walls were slanted. An old white bureau stood at the end of the room, and under the window, which must have been one of those she'd noticed from the parking lot, was a desk with drawers on both sides. The bed was just inside the room and to the left. There was also a small coffee table and, at the end of the bed, a narrow built-in closet.

A dark jacket and a tie lay draped over the back of the desk chair. The desk was covered with piles of paper; a briefcase leaned against the closet. But there was nothing but sheets on the bed.

"I'll find a comforter and a pillow," Artie said, accidentally grazing her as he walked by.

Ilka stepped into the room. A room lived in, yet abandoned. A feeling suddenly stirred inside her, and she froze. He was here. The smell. A heavy yet pleasant odor she recognized from somewhere deep inside. She'd had no idea this memory existed. She closed her eyes and let her mind drift back to when she was very young, the feeling of being held. Tobacco. Sundays in the car, driving out to Bellevue. Feeling secure, knowing someone close was taking care of her. Lifting her up on a lap. Making her laugh. The sound of hooves pounding the ground, horses at a racetrack. Her father's concentration as he chain-smoked, captivated by the race. His laughter.

She sat down on the bed, not hearing what Artie said when he laid the comforter and pillow beside her, then walked out and closed the door.

Her father had been tall; at least that's how she remembered him. She could see to the end of the world when she sat on his shoulders. They did fun things together. He took her to an amusement park and bought her ice cream while he tried out the slot machines, to see if they were any good. Her mother didn't always know when they went there. He also took her out to a centuries-old amusement park in the forest north of Copenhagen. They stopped at Peter Liep's, and she drank soda while he drank beer. They sat outside and watched the riders pass by, smelling horseshit and sweat when the thirsty riders dismounted and draped the reins over the hitching post. He had loved horses. On the other hand, she couldn't remember the times—the many times, according to her mother—when he didn't come home early enough to stick his head in her room and say good night. Not having enough money for food because he had gambled his wages away at the track was something else she didn't recall—but her mother did.

Ilka opened her eyes. Her exhaustion was gone, but she still felt dizzy. She walked over to the desk and reached for a photo in a wide mahogany frame. A trotter, its mane flying out to both sides at the finishing line. In another photo, a trotter covered by a red victory blanket stood beside a sulky driver holding a trophy high above his head, smiling for the camera. There were several more horse photos, and a ticket to Lunden hung from a window hasp. She grabbed it. Paul Jensen. Charlottenlund Derby 1982. The year he left them.

Ilka didn't realize at the time that he had left. All she knew was that one morning he wasn't there, and her mother was crying but wouldn't tell her why. When she arrived home from school that afternoon, her mother was still crying. And as she remembered it, her mother didn't stop crying for a long time.

She had been with her father at that derby in 1982. She picked up a photo leaning against the windowsill, then sat down on the bed. "Ilka and Peter Kjærsgaard" was written on the back of the photo. Ilka had been five years old when her father took her to the derby for the first time. Back then, her mother had gone along. She vaguely remembered going to the track and meeting the famous jockey, but suddenly the odors and sounds were crystal clear. She closed her eyes.

✣

"You can give them one if you want," the man had said as he handed her a bucket filled with carrots, many more than her mother had in bags back in their kitchen. The bucket was heavy, but Ilka wanted to show them how big she was, so she hooked the handle with her arm and walked over to one of the stalls.

She smiled proudly at a red-shirted sulky driver passing by as he was fastening his helmet. The track was crowded, but during the races, few people were allowed in the barn. They were, though. She and her father.

She pulled her hand back, frightened, when the horse in the stall whinnied and pulled against the chain. It snorted and pounded its hoof on the floor. The horse was so tall. Carefully she held the carrot out in the palm of her hand, as her father had taught her to do. The horse snatched the sweet treat, gently tickling her.

Her father stood with a group of men at the end of the row of stalls. They laughed loudly, slapping one another's shoulders. A few of them drank beer from bottles. Ilka sat down on a bale of hay. Her father had promised her a horse when she was a bit older. One of the grooms came over and asked if she would like a ride behind the barn; he was going to walk one of the horses to warm it up. She wanted to, if her father would let her. He did.

"Look at me, Daddy!" Ilka cried. "Look at me." The horse had stopped, clearly preferring to eat grass rather than walk. She kicked gently to get it going, but her legs were too short to do any good.

Her father pulled himself away from the other men and stood at the barn entrance. He waved, and Ilka sat up proudly. The groom asked if he should let go of the reins so she could ride by herself, and though she didn't really love the idea, she nodded. But when he dropped the reins and she turned around to show her father how brave she was, he was back inside with the others.

Ilka stood up and put the photo back. She could almost smell the tar used by the racetrack farrier on horse hooves. She used to sit behind a pane of glass with her mother and follow the races, while her father stood over at the finish line. But then her mother stopped going along.

She picked up another photo from the windowsill. She was standing on a bale of hay, toasting with a sulky driver. Fragments of memories flooded back as she studied herself in the photo. Her father speaking excitedly with the driver, his expression as the horses were hitched to the sulkies. And the way he said, "We-e-e-ell, shall we . . . ?" right before a race. Then he would hold his hand out, and they would walk down to the track.

She wondered why she could remember these things, when she had forgotten most of what had happened back then.

There was also a photo of two small girls on the desk. She knew these were her younger half sisters, who were smiling broadly at the photographer. Suddenly, deep inside her chest, she felt a sharp twinge—but why? After setting the photo back down, she realized it wasn't from never having met her half sisters. No. It was pure jealousy. They had grown up with her father, while she had been abandoned.

Ilka threw herself down on the bed and pulled the comforter over her, without even bothering to put the sheets on. She lay curled up, staring into space.

3

At some point, Ilka must have fallen asleep, because she gave a start when someone knocked on the door. She recognized Artie's voice.

"Morning in there. Are you awake?"

She sat up, confused. She had been up once in the night to look for a bathroom. The building seemed strangely hushed, as if it were packed in cotton. She'd opened a few doors and finally found a bathroom with shiny tiles and a low bathtub. The toilet had a soft cover on its seat, like the one in her grandmother's flat in Bagsværd. On her way back, she had grabbed her father's jacket, carried it to the bed, and buried her nose in it. Now it lay halfway on the floor.

"Give me half an hour," she said. She hugged the jacket, savoring the odor that had brought her childhood memories to the surface from the moment she'd walked into the room.

Now that it was light outside, the room seemed bigger. Last night she hadn't noticed the storage boxes lining the wall behind both sides of the desk. Clean shirts in clear plastic sacks hung from the hook behind the door.

"Okay, but have a look at these IRS forms," he said, sliding a folder under the door. "And sign on the last page when you've read them. We'll take off whenever you're ready."

Ilka didn't answer. She pulled her knees up to her chest and lay curled up. Without moving. Being shut up inside a room with her father's belongings was enough to make her feel she'd reunited with a part of herself. The big black hole inside her, the one that had appeared every time she sent a letter despite knowing she'd get no answer, was slowly filling up with something she'd failed to find herself.

She had lived about a sixth of her life with her father. *When do we become truly conscious of the people around us?* she wondered. She had just turned forty, and he had deserted them when she was seven. This room here was filled with everything he had left behind, all her memories of him. All the odors and sensations that had made her miss him.

❧

Artie knocked on the door again. She had no idea how long she'd been lying on the bed.

"Ready?" he called out.

"No," she yelled back. She couldn't. She needed to just stay and take in everything here, so it wouldn't disappear again.

"Have you read it?"

"I signed it!"

"Would you rather stay here? Do you want me to go alone?"

"Yes, please."

Silence. She couldn't tell if he was still outside.

"Okay," he finally said. "I'll come back after breakfast." He sounded annoyed. "I'll leave the phone here with you."

Ilka listened to him walk down the stairs. After she'd walked over to the door and signed her name, she hadn't moved a muscle. She hadn't opened any drawers or closets.

She'd brought along a bag of chips, but they were all gone. And she didn't feel like going downstairs for something to drink. Instead, she gave way to exhaustion. The stream of thoughts, the fragments of memories in her head, had slowly settled into a tempo she could follow.

Her father had written her into his will. He had declared her to be his biological daughter. But evidently, he'd never mentioned her to his new family, or to the people closest to him in his new life. Of course, he hadn't been obligated to mention her, she thought. But if her name hadn't come up in his will, they could have liquidated his business without anyone knowing about an adult daughter in Denmark.

The telephone outside the door rang, but she ignored it. What had this Artie guy imagined she should do if the telephone rang? Did he think she would answer it? And say what?

At first, she'd wondered why her father had named her in his will. But after having spent the last twelve hours enveloped in memories of him, she had realized that no matter what had happened in his life, a part of him had still been her father.

She cried, then felt herself dozing off.

Someone knocked on the door. "Not today," she yelled, before Artie could even speak a word. She turned her back to the room, her face to the wall. She closed her eyes until the footsteps disappeared down the stairs.

The telephone rang again, but she didn't react.

Slowly it had all come back. After her father had disappeared, her mother had two jobs: the funeral home business and her teaching. It wasn't long after summer vacation, and school had just begun. Ilka thought he had left in September. A month before she turned eight. Her mother taught Danish and arts and crafts to students in several grades. When she wasn't at school, she was at the funeral home on Brønshøj Square. Also on weekends, picking up flowers and ordering coffins. Working in the office, keeping the books when she wasn't filling out forms.

Ilka had gone along with her to various embassies whenever a mortuary passport was needed to bring a corpse home from outside the country, or when a person died in Denmark and was to be buried elsewhere. It had been fascinating, though frightening. But she had never fully understood how hard her mother worked. Finally, when Ilka was twelve, her mother managed to sell the business and get back her life.

After her father left, they were unable to afford the single-story house Ilka had been born in. They moved into a small apartment on Frederikssundsvej in Copenhagen. Her mother had never been shy about blaming her father for their economic woes, but she'd always said they would be okay. After she sold the funeral home, their situation had improved; Ilka saw it mostly from the color in her mother's cheeks, a more relaxed expression on her face. Also, she was more likely to let Ilka invite friends home for dinner. When she started eighth grade, they moved to Østerbro, a better district in the city, but she stayed in her school in Brønshøj and took the bus.

"You *were* an asshole," she muttered, her face still to the wall. "What you did was just completely inexcusable."

The telephone outside the door finally gave up. She heard soft steps out on the stairs. She sighed. They had paid her airfare; there were limits to what she could get away with. But today was out of the question. And that telephone was their business.

Someone knocked again at the door. This time it sounded different. They knocked again. "Hello." A female voice. The woman called her name and knocked one more time, gently but insistently.

Ilka rose from the bed. She shook her hair and slipped it behind her ears and smoothed her T-shirt. She walked over and opened the door. She couldn't hide her startled expression at the sight of a woman dressed in gray, her hair covered by a veil of the same color. Her broad, demure skirt reached below the knees. Her eyes seemed far too big for her small face and delicate features.

"Who are you?"

"My name is Sister Eileen O'Connor, and you have a meeting in ten minutes."

The woman was already about to turn and walk back down the steps, when Ilka finally got hold of herself. "I have a meeting?"

"Yes, the business is yours now." Ilka heard patience as well as suppressed annoyance in the nun's voice. "Artie has left for the day and has informed me that you have taken over."

"*My* business?" Ilka ran her hand through her hair. A bad habit of hers, when she didn't know what to do with her hands.

"You did read the papers Artie left for you? It's my understanding that you signed them, so you're surely aware of what you have inherited."

"I signed to say I'm his daughter," Ilka said. More than anything, she just wanted to close the door and make everything go away.

"If you had read what was written," the sister said, a bit sharply, "you would know that your father has left the business to you. And by your signature, you have acknowledged your identity and therefore your inheritance."

Ilka was speechless. While she gawked, the sister added, "The Norton family lost their grandmother last night. It wasn't unexpected, but several of them are taking it hard. I've made coffee for four." She stared at Ilka's T-shirt and bare legs. "And it's our custom to receive relatives in attire that is a bit more respectful."

A tiny smile played on her narrow lips, so fleeting that Ilka was in doubt as to whether it had actually appeared. "I can't talk to a family that just lost someone," she protested. "I don't know what to say. I've never—I'm sorry, you have to talk to them."

Sister Eileen stood for a moment before speaking. "Unfortunately, I can't. I don't have the authority to perform such duties. I do the office work, open mail, and laminate the photos of the deceased onto death notices for relatives to use as bookmarks. But you will do fine. Your father was always good at such conversations. All you have to do is allow the family to talk. Listen and find out what's important to them; that's the most vital thing for people who come to us. And these people have a contract for a prepaid ceremony. The contract explains everything they have paid for. Mrs. Norton has been making funeral payments her whole life, so everything should be smooth sailing."

The nun walked soundlessly down the stairs. Ilka stood in the doorway, staring at where she had vanished. Had she seriously inherited a funeral home? In the US? How had her life taken such an unexpected turn? What the hell had her father been thinking?

She pulled herself together. She had seven minutes before the Nortons arrived. "Respectful" attire, the sister had said. Did she even have something like that in her suitcase? She hadn't opened it yet.

But she couldn't do this. They couldn't make her talk to total strangers who had just lost a relative. Then she remembered she hadn't known the undertaker who helped her when Erik died either. But he had been a salvation to her. A person who had taken care of everything in a professional manner and arranged things precisely as she believed her husband would have wanted. The funeral home, the flowers—yellow tulips. The hymns. It was also the undertaker who had said she would regret it if she didn't hire an organist to play during the funeral. Because even though it might seem odd, the mere sound of it helped relieve the somber atmosphere. She had chosen the cheapest coffin, as the undertaker had suggested, seeing that Erik had wanted to be cremated. Many minor decisions had been made for her; that had been an enormous relief. And the funeral had gone exactly the way she'd wanted. Plus, the undertaker had helped reserve a room at the restaurant where they gathered after the ceremony. But those types of details were apparently already taken care of here. It seemed all she had to do was meet with them. She walked over to her suitcase.

Ilka dumped everything out onto the bed and pulled a light blouse and dark pants out of the pile. Along with her toiletry bag and underwear. Halfway down the stairs, she remembered she needed shoes. She went back up again. All she had was sneakers.

ABOUT THE AUTHOR

Sara Blaedel's suspense novels have enjoyed incredible success around the world: fantastic acclaim, multiple awards, and runaway number one bestselling success internationally. In her native Denmark, Sara was voted most popular novelist for the fourth time in 2014. She is also a recipient of the Golden Laurel, Denmark's most prestigious literary award. Her books are published in thirty-seven countries. Her series featuring police detective Louise Rick is adored the world over, and Sara is excited for the launch of her new Undertaker's Daughter suspense series in the United States next year.

Sara Blaedel's interest in story writing, and especially crime fiction, was nurtured from a young age. The daughter of a renowned Danish journalist and an actress whose career included roles in theater, radio, TV, and movies, Sara grew up surrounded by a constant flow of professional writers and performers visiting the Blaedel home. Despite a struggle with dyslexia, Sara found in books a world in which to escape when her introverted nature demanded an exit from the hustle and bustle of life.

She tried a number of careers, from a restaurant apprenticeship to graphic design, before she started a publishing company called Sara B, where she published Danish translations of American crime fiction.

Publishing ultimately led Sara to journalism, and she covered a wide range of stories, from criminal trials to the premiere of *Star Wars: Episode I*. It was during this time—and while skiing in Norway—that Sara started brewing the ideas for her first novel. In 2004 Louise and Camilla were introduced in *Grønt Støv* (*Green Dust*), and Sara won the Danish Academy for Crime Fiction's debut prize.

Today Sara lives in New York City, and when she isn't busy committing brutal murders on the page, she is an ambassador with Save the Children and serves on the jury of a documentary film competition.